THE STILETTO

James J. Sullivan

ORIGINAL WRITING

© 2011 James J O'Sullivan

All rights reserved. No part of this publication may be reproduced
in any form or by any means—graphic, electronic or mechanical,
including photocopying, recording, taping or information storage and
retrieval systems—without the prior written permission of the author.

978-1-908477-00-2

A CIP catalogue for this book is available from the National Library.

Published by ORIGINAL WRITING LTD., Dublin, 2011.

Printed by CLONDALKIN GROUP, Clonshaugh, Dublin 17

CO-EDITED BY

MICHAEL J MCCANN AND ANNE HOLLAND

To all I met in transit

INTRODUCTION

Judge James (Jim) O'Sullivan (now retired), completed a novel when he was a young solicitor; however, he knew nothing about the world of publishing nor did he have any friend who was familiar with the printing of literature, with the exception of his drinking friend, the late great Brendan Behan.

Behan answered the call as the young solicitor knew he would, his mother being a Kearney from just outside Portarlington. They agreed to meet at Brendan's uncle's cottage. Lest the young solicitor be short of money, Brendan arrived with a bottle of whiskey and, lest Brendan were short, Jim O'Sullivan brought two bottles of whiskey. It was in the maelstrom age of alcoholic drinking.

They sat before a blazing fire, Behan in the middle, between the uncle and the young solicitor, a bucket of spring water between them and the bottles of whiskey. Each of the three drinkers was supplied with a good-sized jug, in the region of a pint and a half. Filling the jug to about three quarters with whiskey, each would dip the jug into the bucket of water with great care.

Jim O'Sullivan gave Behan a loose-leafed book who began to read it aloud.

After some considerable time, Behan stopped reading, stood up and took the young solicitor's hand; shaking it, he said, "You've written a best seller." Then he wrote on the first sheet—"*I wish I had written this book*"—and he dated and signed it.

What with the heat of the fire and the whiskey, all three fell asleep and when they woke up, it was discovered that the loose-leafed book had slipped off Behan's knee and into the fire whilst he slept and it was burnt to a cinder.

One of the young solicitor's greatest talents in life was his capacity to consume intoxicating liquor. On a few occasions, there used be drinking competitions and the young solicitor was so far ahead of the field that he was usually handicapped.

The liquor was always whiskey, except after a certain time on the bar-room clock, the young solicitor would, instead of whiskey, be handicapped insofar as whilst the other competitors got their glasses of whiskey, he would be given a very special concoction, a pint glass half-filled with cheap Spanish brandy and cheaper champagne, roughly half and half, to fill the pint glass, which he would then drink without taking the glass from his lips. Sometime later, he would be further handicapped by drinking a full pint glass of red wine, again without taking the glass from his lips until the glass was empty, and then continue to join the other competitors with equal measures of whiskey. The young solicitor would always be the last man standing.

That was more than 40 years ago, and no alcoholic drink of any kind has been tasted by Jim O'Sullivan in over four decades. He was a non-drinker when appointed to the Bench and made up his mind to be the best judge in the land, which is to say after Oliver McGuinness, who was probably the best, and Pat McCarton.

Now a judge, Jim O'Sullivan set up the first successful Alcoholic Rehabilitation Court, outside the United States of America, in the centre of Dublin, with Sister Marie Joseph, Sister Caoimhín and Dr 'Stevo' Stevenson. These two nuns were the most spiritually-minded ladies he had ever come across, never either seeking or allowing publicity for the wonderful work they achieved. Apart from her academic achievements, Sister Caoimhín was at that time an authority in the field of drugs and drug-related literature.

The Alcoholic Court, alas, has disappeared and nothing of substance has replaced it, yet alcohol continues to play a major role as a primary cause of prosecuted crime in general and family disputes in particular.

On retirement, the once-apprentice solicitor, former young solicitor, sober lawyer and now retired judge then sat down to write *The Stiletto*.

CONTENTS

Comhairle Contae
Átha Cliath Theas
South Dublin County Council

CHAPTER 1

Donal Moran leaned against the field gate and gazed pensively across the fertile meadows which stretched before him.

It had been thirty years ago, on the evening after he had bought the land, that he had come and had stood in triumph with his mother, Rosie, at the same gate and stared in awe and wonderment at their purchase. Now, though she had long since departed this life, he could hear her voice in his head as clearly, as if she was still standing beside him.

"Money! Money is one of the most important things in this life! It is particularly important for someone like you, Donal Moran, who, being born out of wedlock, came into the world without a father. Of course, that's not your fault. More than likely, it was mine. However, it is you who will have to live with its implications. Moreover, blaming me or anyone else won't cause the name of a father to be inscribed in the blank space on your birth certificate, no less advance your station in life. Money, I'm telling you, is all-important! It's important to everyone, but it's especially important for an orphan boy to accumulate money. People the world over respect money. Even where we live here in a rural area outside Baileix, whatever they might like you to believe, money is all-important to them, too. At the end of the day, money counts with them same as everyone else.

Everyone respects money, even the Church. Don't ever forget the Church when it comes to money. It's bishops, priests and nuns – oh, yes! – especially the nuns respect those who have accumulated money."

Rosie would always put special emphasis on nuns when talking about money. Her experience of nuns at the time of his birth had left her with a deep-seated distrust and dislike of every woman who wore a habit whatever her order or vocation.

"Wealth", she would say, "brings power and independence. People with money can purchase what they fancy. They can buy things which are excluded to ordinary folks, such as stylish cars and gracious homes. Certainly, Donal, and don't you ever forget it. Those people who have acquired wealth can live much more comfortably than those who have not."

Because of his respect and love for her, he listened with rapt attention to all she had to say and though uneducated, she was an interesting and compelling raconteur and possessed a fine, intelligent mind. Because she believed with such conviction the message she was imparting, she influenced him on the need to follow her advice and make a success of his life.

He had inherited from her his quickness of movement and sharpness of wit. But whilst she was waspish and angular of appearance, he was broad shouldered, muscular and stood over six feet in height. At fifty three years of age, his hair was still in a dark cluster of curls about his head with just a hint of grey around the temples. Every morning of his life, he carefully selected a well-tailored suit with matching tie and handkerchief – and he always wore gold cufflinks.

The impact of his powerful shoulders and strong hands had to be paternal characteristics, but there again, he could not tell for certain since he had never met any of his father's people. It didn't even seem odd to him. In the Ireland of the 1950s, that was the way it was for those who were born out of wedlock. As it was in the beginning, is now and ever shall be, world without end, forever and ever, *per omnia secula seculorum. Amen.*

The custom was that the father shared neither his name nor moral responsibilities with such a child. That fell exclusively to the mother who shared also the stigma of the birth with her infant. It was as though Catholicism placed a mantle of protection around the father and, by that very action, placed itself and the father outside the temple of the Holy Ghost, or so Rosie believed. Praise be to God, she would add, in His angels and in His saints! These were her very words. As a child when she spoke that ominous phrase, he used to imagine the Holy Ghost as a dove that flew protectively around mothers and their babies whilst outside the circle of the bird's flight, outside the warmth of the temple, old and disgruntled prelates lived in cold and dampness.

Sometimes, he wished he had shared her optimism and cheerful spirit, her easy manner in company even with strangers. By nature shy and introverted, he was inclined to be taciturn and in the matter of human relationships, lamentably obdurate.

"You must always remember your humble origins, Donal, and how I saved you from being adopted by others when you were but a few days old. You were born in the summer of 1948 in the orphanage run by the Sisters of Mercy outside Roscrea town."

Thirty years had passed since the evening they had leaned at the gate where he now stood, and marvelled at becoming landowners. Twenty acres wasn't a large tract of land by any standards, but it was land and it was a beginning and besides, he wasn't much more than twenty years of age at the time. The purchase had been made possible by virtue of their hard work, scrimping and saving on both their parts. Down all the years, he could recall that first euphoric flush of pride in cash, surrounded by solicitors, agents and those locals who had come to pry and see what they could see.

By dint of dedication, acumen and hard work, Donal Moran became a success in the world of business, and now standing there reminiscing, acknowledged he was at that moment a man of substance and influence, of wealth and property. He didn't consider there was anything meritorious in his spectacular achievements. Rather, he looked upon his accomplishments as having been brought about by his good fortune. For all his success, he was a simple man rather than a proud one.

Oh, yes! Now, he was a man of substance and influence all right, and ... and ... It sometimes bothered him that he couldn't get his tongue around the last word. The word he wanted to add was respect, and though it was a simple word, to him it was one of the most important in his vocabulary. Yet when he added it on, it just didn't sound right. There was a ring of uncertainty to it as if the very characteristic he so dearly yearned was missing from his makeup. Too goddamn well, he knew that it was because of his origins that the word tripped awkwardly off his tongue. But not only that, it was also what his unfortunate wife had done to him and more especially the shame brought about by his son, Joe.

When compared to his business achievements, his personal life had been a disaster – one of pain and humiliation. Over the years, he had learned that sometimes pain can be overcome and there are times, too, when it can be cured. Humiliation is intense in its application. Seemingly, there is no let up in its persistence. It has to be endured.

Joe, his second son, and there were only the two boys, had hardened his father's heart and the shame he had brought on the family would only die with Donal Moran in his sins. Yet for all the pain he had suffered because of his unfortunate wife, unlike his Joe, he bore her little or no ill will. She seldom crossed his mind since they had parted company all of fifteen years ago. However, when it did, he still shivered inwardly as he thought back on their disastrous marriage.

All too soon, there had been no relationship of any kind between them, neither sexual, spiritual nor social. They had shared nothing in common. It was just one complete, unmitigated mess.

Like so many inexperienced and uneducated men before him, he had believed marriage to a woman of upper-class background would have been a decided advantage. Besides, he had been in love with her after a fashion. Certainly, he had desired her physically during their courtship and she had appeared keen enough during the engagement. All too late, he learned the noblest accomplishments either a man or woman can bring to marriage are kindness, consideration and character.

Instead, his unfortunate wife brought with her the most horrific of psychosexual problems. Masochism dominated the marriage bed and their lives.

At first, he didn't know how to react to her pleadings to beat her, to strike her. She had to show him how it was done.

"With your open hand, your open hand, I said. Why can't you do it properly? No, not that way, this way! Look, let me show you again! Like this! Look!"

She used to implore him to beat her across the face, buttocks and thighs. "Hard, hard," she would implore him."Oh, harder! Harder! Harder still! Much harder! Oh, yes! Yes! Now mount me!"

As he would strike harder and faster, so she would begin to writhe in agony. Lying on her back beside him she would roll and twist in a sweet agony of pain, occasionally shrieking out aloud and screaming at him to take her.

At first, through lack of knowledge, he wondered if other couples lived in that same way. If perhaps, it was the natural way of making love that a man just struck a woman a couple of blows and then, in her words, mounted the woman. An act of aggression, of violence, of agony and submission. Or was it just that she was a sick person? Perhaps there was something wrong with himself. After all, did a man not denote strength, aggression and supremacy? So maybe, as she so often accused him, he was just too faint-hearted to act out his proper role of manliness.

There again, was he right in thinking it was unnatural, bizarre behaviour on her part? That she was sick, suffering from some frenetic disorder or other. Eventually he came down on the side of his being normal. It had to be she who was sick.

On the second night of their honeymoon, with a good deal of impatience towards him, she acknowledged her broad experience in lovemaking despite her deception on that issue prior to the marriage. Her admission offended him, not that he was in anyway prudish, but because she had deliberately set out to deceive him lest he would have rejected her because of her promiscuity. Now that she was married, it appeared she didn't give a tinker's curse for his sensitivities.

Lying sideways to him, she had placed her lips close to his ear and then, as if imparting some casual confidence, whispered shamelessly, "My sweet, but you'll have to try harder if you are to win my complete love. I know more about lovemaking than you do, my pet. You see I've had many a man in my time – the

5

last one in the Savoy Hotel. You understand, pet, it was by accident. I met him by chance. We spent the whole night, love. The whole night. He knew where to strike me and when. Then pet, he had a terrific erection. Do you know how old he was? He was sixty. That's right, sixty years of age. He could hold an erection for hours and strike me. I'd do anything for him. I would for you too, love, but you'll have to strike me. You've got to beat me. You won't hurt me when you learn to do it properly."

Oh, God, but it was ugly. Ugly. Ugly.

In the end, it was just too much as by nature he was inclined to be gentle and caring towards women and children. This kind of association revolted him. He turned completely against her and rejected her outright after five years of hell.

Therefore, when he found her in bed with a red-headed drunken priest with whom he had more than a casual acquaintance, it didn't have the slightest affect on his emotions. He knew she was up to something devious that day. He just walked into the bedroom unannounced and looked at her, unashamedly beside the curate, naked except for some bedclothes thrown partially across them. Then, he looked to the priest who uttered a nondescript grunt. It might have been of embarrassment or could have been of drunken mirth.

What really mattered in that moment was that he felt nothing towards her, neither anger nor pity. There were no feelings, no emotions. He simply stood inside the door looking at them in a detached manner. Of course, there was no sentimentality or empathy on her part either. There never had been. From the very outset, he had meant nothing to her. His role in her scheme of things in the marriage had been nothing more than a reliable meal ticket. There had been no warmth or love, just animal-like wants and desires that he considered inhuman.

In that moment standing by the door, looking impassively towards her, he realised with relief that the hideous years of trying to live with her were at an end. Now it would be easier to get her out of his life, get her out of his house and sight. It didn't matter what the cost. It was necessary for his sanity and peace of mind.

CHAPTER 2

Nothing about her ever surprised him and yet, he was somewhat taken aback by the ease with which she departed, smiling and expensively dressed as she confronted him for the last time. It might have been different. She could have launched a verbal or even physical attack. Once she had taken a serrated meat knife to him. As a result, he counted himself lucky to have rid himself of her so easily.

He had been standing talking to some workmen in the utility room when she breezed in, heavily perfumed, coiffured and extravagantly dressed in a lemon suit, the skirt of which was far too short for a woman of her years and proportions. Despite the fashionable clothes, she appeared vulgar to him. Then, there was nothing unusual about that. For all her talk about upbringing and background, she simply lacked feminine dignity.

"I'm off now," she had said."I'm not one for goodbyes, as you know. Besides, I'm in a hurry, love. I've a date."

She was smiling all the while through her white teeth, a smile he surmised which indicated she was on medication. Then lifting her hand, she waved towards him even though only a few feet divided them at the time. A dramatic departure appeared important to her.

"*Au revoir.*"

At the same time, her eyes sought out one of the younger men present with a sly, crafty smile. She could never be accused of subtlety.

That was all. She just walked out with a smile and a wave of her hand, leaving him with the children, walking away without another word or gesture.

She bore him two sons. Nowadays Richard, the eldest, and his wife were living at home with him in Clooney Abbey. The girl he had married, Priscilla, was every bit as dull as Richard was and likewise lacked inspiration and originality. It surprised neither himself or herself nor anyone else that they were childless. Perhaps the effort wasn't worth it. He smiled inwardly at the thought.

The other son was Joe. He had loved Joe – but Joe had broken his heart. Having wasted his own time and his father's money at the prestigious Clongowes Wood college, he left home at eighteen years of age. He returned home occasionally from his indolent lifestyle, always drunk, something which Donal could neither understand nor tolerate. Even now, all these years later thinking back, it still annoyed him, grieved him. It maddened him. That's right, he told himself, as he looked out across the fields. It maddened him even now thinking back on his behaviour.

Nor did he, the father, even obliquely consider he might have failed his son Joe. There was no failure on his part. Look at the very considerable sums of money that he had spent on Joe's education. How much more, he wondered, would have been spent had the boy not decided to abandon his academic pursuits and depart.

It was all of six years now since he had last seen him.

Joe had left the house after an altercation with his father, his brother Richard and Richard's innocuous wife, Priscilla. In his drunken state, he had managed to draw even poor Priscilla into the bitter domestic quarrel. Next morning, Joe had left for London. After a short sojourn in England's capital, a city that Donal considered one of the most generous, Joe returned to Dublin. Just two days later, he was charged with armed bank robbery. He was subsequently convicted and sentenced to nine years' imprisonment.

The first Donal Moran had heard about it was when he had read it in the newspapers and it nearly took his senses away. His heart almost stopped. Then, it was on all the airways: "Son of prominent business tycoon."

Immediately on reading, it he had rushed down the hallway to demand of Richard and Priscilla why they had not informed him. Listening to their shocked responses, it was clear that neither they knew and had only that moment learned of it. That didn't surprise him. It would be just like that pair to be deaf when no doubt the whole countryside was shouting the incident aloud to the four corners of the world.

In that moment, he decided he would never have anything to do with Joe again.

He moved back from the gate with a start, suddenly remembering the phone call he had had earlier that morning. It was from some wretched girl on behalf of Joe announcing that she was coming to see him. The goddamn cheek of her! Obviously, she wanted money. He banished the thought and returned to the gate, leaning on the top rung. He looked out across the fields without actually seeing them.

The voice of his mother, as if she were there talking to him, then sounded in her ears again.

"Others who gave birth to children in that hideous place had no say in what happened to their babies once they were delivered of them. Some of the children were boarded out, as adoption was called in those days, immediately they were born, whilst others remained on with their mothers for anything up to a year and longer. Imagine the agony and hysteria of parting from a child of a year old, or even two years old, from its mother forever. The reason it was possible for the nuns to treat those poor girls thus was because they were led to understand they were amongst the least of all God's creatures, instead of His most precious, for hadn't they brought not only new life into the world, but also hadn't they fashioned a soul as well. A soul, mind you, Donal, that's immortal.

Aye, Donal, isn't it a great thing a woman can do. Isn't it a great miracle peculiar to womankind that she can bring not only life into the world but also an immortal soul?"

At this point in the narration, she would fall silent and, with head slightly raised and eyes looking into the distance, add, "It was the only place where a poor demented girl could go in them days in Ireland. Is it little wonder God never blessed us with prosperity in this auld country of ours, always begging and borrowing off our neighbours and exporting our children? It's the will of God I tell you, the will of God."

After saying this, she would stand for a moment in reflective silence, her lips moving imperceptibly offering up a prayer for those poor innocent girls, as she was wont to call them, and a prayer too for those who tormented, ill-treated and entrapped them.

"On the night I arrived at the orphanage to have you, a girl had objected to her baby being taken. The nuns physically and forcibly wrenched the child from her. Afterwards the girl ranted and screamed in a bewitched state, beside herself at the loss of her baby, the one and only thing she'd ever owned and treasured – a beautiful boy that had been given to her by the Creator of all things. It was all she had. All she had ever wanted was her beautiful baby boy.

"And I can tell you, Donal, the child was by any standard a beautiful baby, there was no doubting that. That girl never thought she could be responsible for anything as perfect as her infant, especially as she had such a low image of herself. Oh, it was a sin! A sin, I'm telling you, to have taken that baby from her. Not only did they take her child but also as a punishment, they locked the creature into a room on her own to demonstrate to the others how the convent's strict discipline operated and to ensure that no one would be tempted to break any of its rules.

"Even her friend at the orphanage who sought permission to visit the poor *crayture* was herself punished for her pains. Eventually, the girl was rehabilitated back into the life of the convent. To be fully redeemed, she had to spend the next six months almost entirely on her knees on the corridors polishing and shining, awaiting the restoration of her privileges.

"One afternoon the Reverend Mother, accompanied by the local parish priest, was passing along a corridor where the girl was scrubbing; and then, in front of a good many other women, she drew the priest's attention to the errant girl.

"Do you see that bold strap of a girl there, Father? Well, she came to us to have her baby, like all the other girls who come into our little holy family here in the convent. She's a bold girl and after I went to the trouble of getting a very nice family to adopt her baby with the help of prayers to the Mother of God, she objected. That's right, Father, she who could never rear a child herself, objected. She, whom we have to look after, she, who cannot fend even for herself, saw no wrong whatever in depriving the child of a proper upbringing.

"The parish priest declared it would be necessary to re-church the girl, as was the custom in those days for women who brought a soul into God's Kingdom. The Catholic Church seemingly believed that once divine intervention created a soul through conception, and the birth of an infant, then that miracle placed women outside the jurisdiction of the Church.

"Did you know that, Donal?

"It would also be necessary for her to go to confession, he ordered. His manner implied she was being punished by her participation in the act of worship, rather than fulfilled by sharing in the spiritual experience of the Sacrament."

It was a salutary lesson for the other guests of the orphanage, who didn't wish to suffer the same fate, she told him. Being fearful for themselves, they readily gave the requisite assurances that their babies could be taken from them without hysterics.

They were particularly shocked that the poor girl was reprimanded in the august presence of the Parish Priest. For a considerable time afterwards, the girl was treated as some pariah of the establishment, and some of the others avoided all contact with her lest their friendship be interpreted as sharing in her attitudes.

However, Donal's mother was determined. Her mind was made up. Let it be a boy or a girl, in sickness or in health, but she would keep her baby. Moreover, when her mind was made up, she would be no pushover. She reckoned she was a match for the Reverend Mother any day. Not that she underestimated that very important person or any of her nuns for that matter. Rather, with an appreciation and understanding of their methods, she could apply herself to a greater study of their traits and behaviour patterns, trusting none and determined to succeed. The Reverend Mother was a small tough woman with a flat oriental kind of face, who called on the Mother of God to aid her every twist and turn of the day, a practice which offended rather than impressed his mother particularly.

The impression she got was that the nun's repetitive entreaties in the name of the Mother of God were more in keeping with a careless indifference to faith generally rather than a sign of any genuine piety or supplication. A highly intelligent woman with a brilliant talent for administration, but devious and dangerous, a hypocrite of the first order, was his mother's assessment of the Reverend Mother.

"I knew, Donal", she would often say, "that I would nurture and rear you as good as any parent or any two for that matter."

It was in the nature of things that the sisterhood would keep a strict and watchful eye on all their charges. Certain girls, however, could be depended on to fit in with the rules and regulations and with the generally accepted scheme of things. These girls were granted generous privileges denied those who had failed to gain favour. Once a girl had gained that exalted position in the convent's pecking order, seemingly from that moment on, she would be trusted implicitly.

Stories abounded of girls being arrested out on the roads by the Gardaí and being brought back with their infants. As time progressed her greatest fear, apart from that of failure, was the actual manner of her being spotted, challenged and finally trapped, either by a Garda officer out on the road, or worse still, within the bounds of the convent with her child wrapped up for the journey. These and the will to succeed were the thoughts that concentrated her mind from one day to the next as she carefully laid her plans for escape.

At an early stage of her sojourn, she learned there were two criteria upon which a girl would be assessed and deemed trustworthy. First and foremost, there was her willingness to work, and whilst there were good and willing workers amongst those girls, few would excel as his mother in that regard.

Secondly, there was what an old nun, Sister Agnes, with whom she had deliberately established a rapport, referred to as a girl's attitude of mind – how she comported herself and adapted to the life of the convent. Would she cause problems for the nuns, especially as the time approached for her infant to be boarded out?

Against her nature, she adopted an obsequious and fawning attitude towards the sisters and especially, towards Sister Agnes, who carried every little tittle-tattle tale back to the Reverend Mother.

Late one evening, Sister Agnes called her and, smiling sweetly, placed a key in her hand. It was the most cherished possession any girl could have in the convent. It was the ultimate reward for a girl deemed trustworthy. All doors and corridors were under lock and key, but those chosen few who possessed a key could enter and exit as they pleased.

Donal's mother waited patiently for the right moment. There was an in-between time in the daily routine, between evening and night when the time allotted for work had finished but before bedtime. It was a period of informality at the end of the day and this was when she chose to make good her escape.

Each evening at that very hour, after her baby had been born she headed out with him, ostensibly to work in the yard and occasionally, further afield. She remained out for an hour or two to allay their suspicious of her real intentions which were to establish a pattern of her absence each evening at this time.

About the third evening, she spotted old Sister Agnes coming down the avenue. The old crone was still spying and checking on her! It was to be expected. What was important now was to decide how best to deal with her and, my God, but that was important. Pretend not to have seen her and continue working with greater endeavour. There must not be the slightest suggestion that the nun was intruding. On the contrary greet her warmly, extend to her the hand of friendship.

"What are you doing down here on your own, Rosie?" asked Sister Agnes.

"Oh, Sister, how lovely to see you. I'll tell you what I'm doing. I'm gathering sticks, Sister. I'm going to clear out that shed by the kitchen and stack them in there. Nothing better than dry faggots to light the fires in those big cold rooms of the convent in wintertime. Come over here by the trees and you'll see the bundles I've gathered."

"Well, aren't you the great girl."

Then a lengthy pause, her suspicions as yet not fully allayed.

"And I see you've brought your little man along with you."

Careful! Careful! Now that was the moment of truth. Don't show the slightest sign of motherhood, of love or of belonging.

"I wanted to talk to you about that, Sister. Remember that you promised me you'd have a farmer's place to board him out. He's becoming a kind of a burden on me."

"I see. I see. What would you do yourself then?"

"To tell you the truth, Sister, I'm happy here, and I was wondering would it be at all possible for me to spend a few months working here. All I'd want is me bed and board. I like it here in the convent, Sister."

"The old nun said not a word, Donal, but about turned and leaning on her stick bent her steps eagerly in the direction of the convent and the Reverend Mother."

Her ploy had worked. Then, she suffered a sharp and instant shock as she realised this would have to be her last night at the convent. The time of escape was upon her. Suddenly, she became fearful and frightened.

Her last night was one of trepidation, for no matter how often or how determinedly she banished the dread thoughts of her pending escape they would persist in coming flooding back, telling her of all that would go wrong on the morrow.

All next day as the time of the flight drew nigh, so too did her fears increase. Then the hour was upon her. It rang out from the church bell as it tolled the Angelus, proclaiming the time of six o'clock prayers. Little groups began gathering to recite the Angelus as the bell's sound reverberated throughout the building. Though it wasn't especially a public pietism at that time of day, nonetheless women and nuns gathered in little groups to intone quietly the canticle and its responses.

Just for an instant, she had been almost overcome with fear. For one moment of anguish, it was as though her legs and brain had become paralysed – as though she could not face up to the mission that was now upon her. This was the most important assignment of her life and failure must not be entertained. After all the careful planning of every single move these past few tortuous weeks, there could be no turning back now. With fists clenched tightly by her sides and eyes closed, she made a resolution that it was to be now or never. She told herself to get up and go.

With the key given to her in trust, she let herself out through a side door into the backyard. Incredibly, there was no one in the cowshed as she sped between the tails of the cows ranged back-to-back along its length. Leaving the cowshed, the next obstacle was the lofted cart shed. Likewise, it was empty. Next was the small yard.

"Careful, now! I had to be very careful there, Donal. This would be the one place where there was bound to be someone. There was always someone coming or going, mixing or cutting something or other in the small yard. And would you believe it, but there was no one."

She was running now by a well-thought out escape route onto the back laneway which led to a country road. For the first time, she became aware of the chill of the evening air. So concerned had she been with the escape plan and the child's welfare on the journey that she had completely forgotten to guard herself against the freshness of the oncoming night.

Two hours she had spent out at this time each evening without anyone becoming alarmed as to her whereabouts. That meant she had two hours now to put a distance between herself and the convent.

The country road would be dangerous because cyclists could come upon her unexpectedly, swiftly and silently. Neighbours of nuns in the 1940s were all powerful. By cycling up to the convent and reporting to the nuns that they had seen a girl with a baby heading for the Dublin road, they could ingratiate themselves and gain some favour or other with their powerful religious order neighbours.

It was essential therefore to keep careful vigil as she fled along this country road with its high hedges of hawthorn, ash and hazel trees, making its many twists and turns perilous to negotiate in safety. She had chosen the Dublin road, prepared to take her chances with some urban stranger who might pass along its route. For the city dweller might show more compassion than the convent's rural neighbours.

Before long, it did not matter that her arms were beginning to ache from the weight of the child, for up ahead she spotted the Dublin road.

"Nineteen forty, I can tell you Donal, was a bad time to hitch a lift, for it was a time of petrol rationing. Few motorists travelled the roads except those under special licence, such as the Army and Gardaí, judges and the clergy and, of course, certain civil servants. There were always a few moonlighters. Those who despite the horrific penalties were prepared to take risks. Anything that could propel a car was used, such as paraffin, or a concoction of paraffin, diesel and petrol.

"Many a moonshiner experimented with fermenting potatoes and brought grateful smiles of relief to the faces of stranded travellers. Cars enveloped in smoke chugged forward on all kinds of alcohol products."

Inwardly, she hoped it would be one of the risktaking voyagers who would accommodate her in her flight, for the likelihood of being reported by one of those adventurers would be remote.

Two hours before anyone would be alerted to the escape. Two hours before the Gardaí would be informed and the usual sordid hue and cry organised in pursuit.

"Another girl has run away from the convent," the Guards would be told."Maybe some o' you men would help bring her back, the ungrateful girl, and a grand family waiting to adopt the poor little baby. Ah sure, what else would you expect from the likes of them girls!"

"Ah yer right there, Sister. Sure, it's too good to them girls ye are entirely. Ah, too good to them, Sister, too good to them entirely."

"Not one of them," Donal's mother said, "neither him nor her, ever said 'but it's our mother, our sister, our daughter that you're talking about.' We. Us. That's whom you're talking about. You're talking about us.

"Stranger still that ne'er a word was ever spoken or finger pointed at them as bucked them girls, them mothers, sisters and daughters of ours. Incest by a father, raped by a brother or son. As if it would have been unethical to point the finger of recrimination and association at our father, brother or son!

"Praise to be God, Donal, in His angels and in His saints! Ah sure, as the head Sister used to say, the Mother of God is good. She'll look after us. T'auld hypocrite!"

Often she recalled how she turned right in the direction of Dublin, away from Roscrea and the convent. Ahead of her lay a straight stretch of roadway with a dip half-way along its length. Except for the high ditches on either side, it afforded very little cover. Clearly, she was going to be totally exposed as she walked. At the sound of a car coming behind her she threw herself and the baby headlong into the ditch and peered nervously after the car as it sped past.

Now that was a stupid thing to have done, for how else was she to put a safe distance between herself and the convent if not by motor car? If she were to make good her escape, it would have to be by car. So eventually, she would have to take a chance on some complete stranger. Hope and pray that a Good Samaritan would pass the road and show her compassion. The alternative was unthinkable, not to be entertained. As soon as her escape was discovered, she would be picked up almost immediately by the Gardaí, for she would be exposed the length of this roadway.

Oh, the humiliation and the loss she would suffer. What of her baby? At the thought of the dire consequences facing her, she breastfed him, shielded by the bushes, then crawled bravely up out of the ditch, and faced towards a small black car which was approaching at that very moment from the Roscrea side.

She held her position well out on the roadway as the car slowed down. A terrible fear seized her as it drew to a halt. For there, seated behind the wheel was an elderly priest. Her heart beat furiously as she stared in open-mouthed incredulity at her fate.

Before she could assess her position or put a question to him or conjure up some feasible excuse to explain what she was doing out on the road at that hour of evening with a child wrapped in a hessian sack, he looked at her sympathetically and smiled.

"Are you running away, my dear?"

They were the kindest words she was ever to hear, she often recounted afterwards.

What made them special was the way in which they were spoken and the benign expression on his face as he spoke.

"I wouldn't blame you for getting out of that place."

Then as if addressing the countryside, the whole world or perhaps no one in particular, he added in an undertone, "Ah, but there are queer things being done in the name of the Church, that sometimes I despair. There are a lot of queer people in this old world of ours and the Church certainly had its share of them."

He fell silent for a moment.

"Where are you heading for?"

"To tell you the truth, Father, I don't know."

Again, he fell silent and whistling a merry tune tapped out the melody on the steering wheel as they drove along. Sometimes, too, he would break off and hum the tune in a surprisingly lyrical voice.

She noted how well dressed he was. His suit was one of the finest black materials. His shoes were brightly polished and his silken white hair neatly groomed.

"You know I might have a place for you – a place where you could rear your child in relative comfort for a few years."

She knew then the Good Samaritan had truly crossed her path and, at last, she was able to relax knowing she was safe in his keeping.

"I'll speak with the local parish priest and the Sergeant as well and tell them you're under my care. You'll have nothing to fear as long as you're a good girl which I'm sure you are."

CHAPTER 3

Father Whelan, for that was his name, brought her to the borders of what he referred to as the King's and the Queen's County, now known as the Laois-Offaly borders. Its earlier regal name was given to it by Queen Mary, the Tudor woman, and the principal town was called after her. They were the first areas to be planted in Ireland by the British Militia under the Catholic Queen, Mary Tudor and her Spanish husband, Philip of Spain, in 1556 with the support of no less a personage than His Holiness the Pope of Rome. It was little wonder, then, that years later the same Vatican was to support and encourage William of Orange's victory at Aughrim and the subsequent brutal suppression of a defenceless people throughout the length and breadth of the country.

It was in that gentle land that Fr Whelan placed her under the care of an elderly couple who were giving up on the management of their fifty-five acre farm. Their only child, a son, was a permanent resident in St Fintan's Psychiatric Hospital, Portlaoise, the same town that up to recent times was called Maryborough.

When parting with her at the end of the evening, leaving her in the couple's care, Fr Whelan handed her the then princely sum of five pounds.

Mick and Hannah Hogan were self respecting people with generous natures, so it was a happy atmosphere in which Donal Moran spent his formative years. His mother always took time out to instruct him in the important issues of life. Those who respected God and their elders, she would impress on him, would find the vicissitudes of life easier to bear. She especially insisted on enlightening him on the role money played in people's lives. She encouraged him to be ambitious, determined and to seek out success, wherever it could be found.

Fr Whelan proved to be a wonderful friend, and he spoke in an easy familiar way about religion and God. Donal's friendship with him was such that he eagerly looked forward to the priest's letters and even more to his visits.

"Always pray directly to Jesus," he would say."Ask Jesus for little things. Get into the habit of asking Him for small favours. Talk to Jesus and ask Him to look after you. Jesus will always listen to little children. If ever you are in trouble and you pray hard enough and believe in the prayers you say, then your wish will be granted."

Sometimes Donal thought that if Fr Whelan had lived a while longer he might have influenced his life to a greater extent, and that as a result Donal might have been a better Christian. Occasionally, it bothered him that he wasn't.

Donal's mother, Rosie, was responsible for running the household and, by her industry and integrity, she gradually took over the running of the farm and its finances as well. Soon, the elderly pair relied on her implicitly.

In an extraordinary coincidence, Mick and Hannah not only died on the same day but also on Donal's tenth birthday. The farm was duly sold in accordance with their wishes and the proceeds held in trust for the upkeep of the son who was languishing in the local Mental hospital and, by all accounts, would eek out the rest of his days there.

Donal's mother was chuffed nevertheless to discover she was held in such high esteem that she was included in the troika of trustees appointed to administer the will and the estate, and that she was provided with a cottage for her and Donal to live in.

Even as he advanced in years, Fr Whelan continued to call at regular intervals, invariably bearing presents of exotic boxes of chocolates, cheeses and the like. He also brought many interesting books. Though looking well when he celebrated the funeral Mass for Mick and Hannah, he was to follow on after them within six months, on Good Friday in the year 1951.

Rosie cried all that day.

"He was one holy man for sure. Oh my God, but I adored him," she sobbed. "I loved him, Donal. He's in heaven as sure as there is a sky above us."

Donal felt a sadness creep over him as he stood at the field gate these thirty years on. He thought back over those happy, blissful, carefree days of childhood, and all those beautiful people, now dead and gone. They were the best days he would ever know and the happiest. He often dwelt on them, and on those who had guardedly influenced his early years.

He didn't have anything like that happiness today, even though he had acquired many priceless possessions and great wealth. He was now the owner of Clooney Abbey and its five hundred acres of rolling pastures, meadows and precious timber. As he thought of it, he looked back over his shoulder and admired its clusters of oak and beech trees which were visible on the landscape a half-mile distant from where he stood. The unusual Palladian-style house and its extensive stables and outbuildings were hidden behind the foliage. Was the girlfriend's impending visit an attempt by his jailbird son to lay his grubby hands on his father's fortune, he wondered?

The river flowed sluggishly between the Abbey mearings and those of John and Mary Boyle. He allowed his thoughts to dwell on the couple for the briefest of moments before the river caught his attention again. He traced its slow meanderings to the point where it entered the Abbey lands and then it, too, was hidden from view by the abundance of greenwood before it passed beneath the beautiful old treble-arched stone bridge which had been built some two hundred years before.

He swept his gaze back towards his left, beyond the black bog with its polythene covered heaps of harvested turf mull snaking in straight lines across the landscape until they disappeared from view. Few and fewer were the men who collected at the site of the old bagger sheds to draw their wages on Friday evenings. They were almost totally gone, as the lark and all the other songbirds had gone before them and the yellow furze bushes and the bracken were no longer there either, to crackle and shimmer on warm summer evenings. For those, too, like the men, the songbirds and even the great bogs themselves, had become spent forces.

Still turning to his left, he was looking almost straight ahead once more, but upwards and beyond the foothills of the Slieve Bloom, beyond the village of Rosenallis, and further still to the steep fields of Cappard. His eyes rested for a moment on the smooth curve of the mountaintop before dropping down to where Portlaoise, the county town, lay on the flat plain surrounded by bogland, grassland and mountain.

Just off the southern route, off the main Dublin to Cork highway, the little village of Emo nestles amidst the beech and conifers of the flat surrounding countryside. It lies about half-way between the town of Portlaoise and the spot where Donal stood. The circle of his gaze was almost complete.

The thought of Emo reminded him of a local story which had almost become folklore. At the insistence of the local peasantry and in defiance of her husband Lord Portarlington and the British militia, Aline, Countess of Portarlington, was laid to rest on the fifteenth day of January 1874 in the village cemetery at Emo. A great gathering came to demonstrate and mourn her passing even though an arctic-like blizzard blew in across the land on that morning.

It had been handed down from one generation to the next that she was the daughter of London bankers, the Jewish Dawson-Damer clan who married her off to Lord Portarlington of Emo Court when she was a mere child. She brought to the marriage the means and the money to redeem the accounts due on the estate because of his profligate living. She also brought maidenly grace.

The village and its surrounds have been noted for the number of attractive girls who hail from that part of the world. Yet it is said, not one could ever compare with the striking beauty of that young girl, Aline, Countess of Portarlington.

Portarlington himself had the reputation of being a drunkard and a scoundrel. Stories abounded of his perverse, deviant sexual habits. The youthful Aline, frequently whipped with a riding crop, often remained in her room, reluctant to let the servants see her injuries. It was said Portarlington sometimes travelled from London with carriages of prostitutes and English noblemen. The tenantry would have to light his route with lanterns whilst the beautiful Aline was expected to stand with the servants at the entrance hall to welcome this motley company. Frequently, she was forced to be an observer at the ensuing unseemly orgies.

It had been darkly whispered of her profligate husband that he had an insatiable appetite for wine and women and that, in the handsomely carpeted rooms of Emo Court, he would lie throughout the night with these girls, all of them drunk and naked with huge log fires to keep them warm, and he lurching from one girl to the next and from one room to another, his appetite for sex and booze unquenchable.

Aline found common ground with the tenantry. Their poverty and causes became her concern. She went on hunger strikes to assuage the sufferings inflicted on them by her husband and the militia.

One week, while Portarlington was in London gathering about him the usual riff-raff to transport back to Emo Court, Aline assembled some locals and servants beneath the magnificent dome of the great hall. They gathered there the leftover wallpaper of previous generations, which they had located throughout the house. They began cutting and shaping it into designs and then fixing the strips to the dome with paste and brass tacks. It was to demonstrate their poverty and destitution, as well as Aline's. As they stared at the finished work, it became clear they had accomplished a creation of exceptional mathematical exactitude, a work of surreal splendour.

After Aline passed away, it was said of weariness at the age of fifty one, the local people claimed her as one of their own. Defying all and sundry, they demanded that her body be buried in their cemetery with their own people with whom she had shared her life. A great tumult ensued and, fearing a disturbance which might not be easily contained, the militia yielded to their demands. She was interred with much love in a place of honour amongst the people whom she loved in the cemetery at Emo village.

Though it was but a few years after the great famine of forty five, the poor put together their ha'pennies and farthings and engaged a reputable sculptor to shape her image in white marble. It represented her as the young bride they remembered when she first came to Emo, as pure and white as the driven snow.

Father O'Mahony, the Jesuit historian, believed the Virgin appeared to Aline to comfort and console her in her trials and tribulations. It was after the order taking up residence at Emo Court that they realised what they had inherited on the wallpapered domed ceiling. It was a tapestry of surreal beauty, a design of mathematical preciseness, a masterpiece of folk art which would remind future generations, irrespective of nationality or creed, how the oppressed can sometimes transcend fear, deprivation, oppression, and lewdness with creativity and dignity. To preserve this unique work, the Jesuits encapsulated the entire ceiling in heavy sheets of plastic.

Donal's eyes and thoughts returned from the village to the fields stretched out before him and to his mother once more. Her belief in faith was of a peculiar, mercurial kind. One moment Rosie would be over pious, involved in all kinds of novenas and retreats and, the next, near to denying the existence of a God.

Country funerals are noted for the large crowds which gather to pay their respects to the dead and offer condolences to the living. Donal had a clear recollection of her looking down into the freshly turned earth of a grave one afternoon, surrounded by other mourners.

"Once they put you under that ground there, then there you stay, that's the end of you. Surely someone of all the millions who have gone before us would have come back to speak of the glories of heaven. Surely just one, not an army now mind you, or yet a small crowd! Wouldn't you think just one would have come back to communicate with us? When you think of all those poor souls who have gone before us, would it be expecting too much that one of them with whom we were acquainted would come to tell us what it was like on the other side, so to speak to assure us in our faith and convictions. Wouldn't it lead you to believe there can be nothing on the other side?

"Maybe," she would add, looking from one to another of her listeners as they contemplated the newly covered grave and her words, "maybe there just isn't another side."

Then at other times, she would be moved by a great fervour and this would motivate her to spend hours praying in the local church, or journeying off to one of the many centres of pilgrimage scattered about the country. There again, on some of these excursions, she could be quite irreverent and unkind claiming that some of the women who had accompanied her did so out of an excuse to have a day's outing rather than that they were motivated by any spiritual aspirations. Never being allowed any form of relaxation on their own by their stern husbands, they could take advantage of the outing, as the husband couldn't rightly refuse the parish priest's request for the wife to join the annual parish pilgrimage.

On every Good Friday, she was a humble and contrite Christian. On this day each year, Donal accompanied her to tend Fr Whelan's grave and to offer up prayers at the graveside for the repose of his soul. She often stressed to Donal the good fortune which the priest had brought into their lives, the compassion he had shown to her when she was the least of things. She encouraged Donal, too, to pray to the priest and ask him for guidance for assuredly he was in heaven.

The custom grew with them that, on each Good Friday, they would spend three hours visiting the parish church and the grave, between twelve noon and three in the afternoon, the three holy hours traditionally accepted from one generation to the next as the period He had clung dying to the wooden cross on Calvary.

After his mother died, Donal continued the practice. It wasn't that he was beholden to her memory or had given any promise. It was for another reason. Fr Whelan had been a precious friend and was undoubtedly an upright Christian man. There was a stronger, more unique characteristic which obliged Donal to go on his own on this annual pilgrimage to the priest's grave – because Fr Whelan had been a holy man. Yes. That was it. Fr Whelan could best be described as a holy man and there weren't too many of those knocking around in this hard old station called life.

Amongst the ordinary clergy or hierarchy, there aren't too many holy men to be found, Donal thought. Politicians there are a-plenty and PRO men and showmen, scholars there are too, hypocrites three, but holy men, no. Now, there's where the real problem lies. Not too many of the genuine John XXIII or Archbishop Runcie sort, the original holy men, untouched by politics, showmanship, plane-hopping or pride. The holy men and the saints were few and far between. Are there any, he wondered? Most of them have already gained their reward in this world and that is why people are losing respect for them, especially amongst Catholics.

Ah yes, he thought. He can count himself lucky to have known such beautiful people. He was fortunate, too, to have been reared by a woman such as his mother. He had loved her dearly, and wondered sometimes if it was because of that special relationship that he was unable to find love with anyone else.

From the moment he had decided he would never again have anything further to do with his son, Joe, he even forbade mention of Joe's name in his presence. As far as Donal Moran was concerned, his son wasn't just dead. He had never been born. He ordered that all his belongings be removed from the house. There wasn't to be a trace of him left about the place.

What made him particularly irate was that Joe stood trial without making any attempt to contact himself, his own father, and then served out the sentence without communication. With time off for good behaviour, in remission, it must be almost served out by now. That must be why this girl was coming down to see him after all these years. That, Donal Moran well knew, was why this first contact was being made – looking for money, the soft touch. He had always known, sooner or later it would come to that. Now this girl had left a message that she wanted to meet Joe's father and she would call around six. After all those years, what a goddamn impertinence on their part!

He was becoming extremely angry and again stepped back sharply from the gate in a fit of pique and ill will towards this girl, and just as fitfully returned, resuming his leaning posture as before, but now shaking with rage. Why on earth was she coming to see him except for money? Money, that was it! Money for Joe! The goddamn cheek of them! The name left on the message, Sharon, meant that it must be the same girl Joe had been living with up to and including the trial. Not that Donal had ever met her or wanted to, for she had then betrayed him. The bitch married Joe's accomplice in the robbery, the same man Joe refused to name at the trial or during the Garda investigations. What class of an idiot was he? Did Joe take his father to be the like fool?

It was admitted at the trial that there were no previous convictions, and no money taken. The prosecution called for a lengthy sentence because of the accused refusing to name his accomplice. Now, that man's wife was coming down to him for money. He had no doubt about that.

Then a strange thought entered his mind. Was Joe still handsome and broad shouldered and did he still have a head of brown curls? Would he still have the gentle smile which he had inherited from his grandmother, Donal's mother Rosie? What sort of girl was this who was coming down to see him? He could imagine what she would look like – a lot of body and little else – all leg, tit and tail without a scrap of common sense.

What particularly incensed him was that she had not given him the opportunity or the courtesy of refusing her request to visit him, but conveniently left a message over the phone with Priscilla that she would call that very evening at six o'clock. She had just described herself as a friend of Joe's. It was now four o'clock and his aversion to the girl was growing by the minute. He felt convinced she was on the make, and was forcing herself into the privacy of his home.

My God! That dame had some cheek, some impertinence to leave a message –"I'll be calling this evening at six to have a word with Joe's father." There was nothing about the silence of the past six years – just the message over the phone – "I'll be calling this evening at six to have a word with Joe's father."

So at long last, Joe the brave, the obdurate, was succumbing to the temptation of easy money. Precisely what he had known all along would be the eventual outcome. If Joe had known anything about his father then he would not have tried to avoid a personal encounter by sending this girl to deputise.

Six years was a long time. It was a long time for his son. It was a long time, too, for him. For in truth, despite his determination to rid his mind entirely of the boy, he had agonised throughout the length of his sentence. At times of weakness, he had toyed with the idea of going to see Joe, for in spite of his resolve to expurgate the memory, now and then he was haunted by the spectre of his younger son languishing in Mountjoy Prison.

His friend, Mary Boyle, encouraged him to visit Joe, and if there was one person's advice which he valued above all others it was Mary's. She had put it to him this way, "If it was only to clench your fist and hit him a belt in the gob, and then say to him, now tell me why you did it. Now tell me, why you made a fool of yourself and of the family? At least you'd have that much satisfaction, and then you could shake hands with him afterwards, if you still had a mind to."

However, the deed of which Joe had been convicted was such that deep inside, Donal Moran could neither forget nor forgive. It was a heinous crime and Joe deserved every day of the nine years handed down by the trial judge.

There was another side to the story, one no doubt which had been overlooked in the bravado of the moment. What about the social stigma of going through life as an outcaste of society? What about the wife he would marry and the children he would father? Wouldn't they all be tarred with the conviction?

For one born out of wedlock, this episode was particularly galling. In Donal's early years, he had had to live out the ignominy and shame of its imputations in the Ireland of the fifties. He wasn't such a fool as not to guess what the neighbours were now saying –"And why wouldn't he, with the background that's in it" – "I've always had me suspicions on how that man made all his money" – "It's only now we're beginning to hear the real story."

He had no doubt all the stories of his success were suitably embellished by his neighbours when discussing the son and, particularly, in confidences to strangers. They would say to one another – "What else would you expect from the poor son" – "It's the poor son I'm sorry for" – "You'll find he knows more than he's saying" – "More than the rest of us know."

His son had taken away from him the years of building up a valued reputation of respect and success in the locality and throughout the length and breadth of the county beyond. Joe had brought him crashing down. Stripped him of his honour and respectability, and returned him naked to his humble origins, to the orphanage-like society of wagging tongues and spiteful, jealous conversations. It put him in a state of uncontrollable rage at this girl's intrusion. It was back to being tainted by the orphanage in one fell swoop of Joe's inexplicable, unforgivable greed and selfishness.

Looking furtively to his left and then right along the hedgerows, and having satisfied himself that he was quite alone on this deserted country road, he opened the fork of his trousers and pissed down hard onto the bottom rung of the gate. Facing slightly to his left, he became aware of a presence, a shadow, a figure over his shoulder.

CHAPTER 4

He swung around and found a woman staring at his penis. He was holding it while continuing to relieve himself. She remained staring at him her eyes fixed, appraising him in a way which left him not only embarrassed but also dominated by her close presence. In his haste to button up, he pissed down inside his trouser leg.

It was none other than BoBo Doorley, she who had spent a good deal of time lately in the Mental hospital in Portlaoise, and who had the reputation of being a wilful and mischievous girl. She was also said to be vicious at times. Both her mother and father, simple people in their own right, were regularly assaulted by her. On the last occasion, when Mary Boyle had called the Gardaí, it took the strength of three men to hold her down whilst waiting their arrival and that of the doctor. That was some months back. Perhaps, she had just been released and was making her way home.

She had periods, Donal knew well, when she could enjoy lucid good health and reasonable contentment. Some neighbours believed that it was during these times she was at her most dangerous and malevolent. The advice locally was that she was a girl to be avoided at any time. As soon as the attacks on her parents would start up again, she would have to be re-committed without delay to the psychiatric hospital.

Although she was pale and dressed unflatteringly, she possessed an unusual sexual attractiveness, one which could not be explained entirely by the sheer beauty of her youth and pubescence. She was an attractive girl though untidy and looked unclean.

She walked over to where he was standing reservedly after being spied on. Placing a hand on his shoulder, she asked him directly, "What were you doing there?"

She showed not the slightest surprise that she had been standing close behind him whilst he had been pissing, not the slightest awareness of the delicacy of his or even her own situation. It seemed she was not bothered at all by what she had just witnessed.

Donal hesitated, at a loss at how to answer best what he had been doing.

"Sure, you saw what I was doing."

"I did," she rejoined quite impassively. She was now standing so close to him that her presence made him feel uneasy. He didn't know what he should do or whether he should do or say anything.

"If you're going my way, I can give you a lift."

The moment he spoke the words he realised he had said the wrong thing. He was afraid she would interpret the invitation as something more than the mere offer of a lift in the car.

"Oh, that's nice of you. I'd say you're a nice man. Are you? Aren't you separated from your wife?"

"I am. Yes."

"Do you have a girl?"

It took him a while to reply, becoming cautious as to how he should respond.

"No. Not at the moment."

"Do you like girls? Do you like doing things to girls? You know what I mean."

She looked to him for an answer and when none was forthcoming, she pressed on.

"A male nurse tried to have it off with me. Said he'd do it to me whether I wanted it or not. What do you think of that? He's one of the Condrons from over there, the far side of Baileix. You know them. John Paul Condron. What do you think of that?"

Again, Donal was lost for words. He felt uptight. Other men in this position, he realised, would have engaged her in some appropriate, trite conversation and encouraged her. They would have seen an opportunity which could be turned to their advantage – but not Donal Moran. He lacked the self-confidence to begin let alone follow up. He felt unsure in the company of women – especially in a situation like this.

"Well, did he ...?"

He found himself pausing unable to get his tongue around the right words.

Did he have it off with you was what he wanted to say? He wasn't able to be that direct, so, tongue-tied, he put the question awkwardly to her.

"Well did he ... um ... carry out his threat?"

She threw her head back and laughed out loud.

"What do you mean by his threat? Do you mean did he pull the knickers off me? No, he didn't. He was auld talk. He got his chance. He wasn't fit to. He wasn't any good. Some men aren't any good when it comes to a girl. Did you know that? Did you know some men are afraid of a girl? I pulled a young lad once but he upped and bolted off down the road with the fright."

She was now staring unashamedly at him in a way he knew she was sizing him up, trying to gauge his worth as a man, trying to decide if he, too, like the young nurse would pass up the opportunity.

"Are you any good with a girl? Are you shy? There's no need to be. You see you're a nice looking man."

He felt an uncomfortable wetness inside his trouser leg where he had pissed into it minutes earlier, but he was too embarrassed to look down to inspect the offending area. Every so often, she sought out that very spot on his trousers and then would avert her gaze again to his face.

BoBo was about seventeen years old and Donal knew she might be highly dangerous, he told himself the best thing for him would be to disengage from her immediately.

He opened the passenger door and let her in. On walking around the back of the car, he surreptitiously pulled at the opened zip of his pants, and was amazed at the expanse of the watermark which was so clearly visible on his trousers front.

From the moment she sat into the car, she talked incessantly. It reminded him of his wife. Perhaps they were two of a kind. Certainly, this girl by reputation was sick, highly volatile and dangerous.

She leaned over beside him, her hand touching his thigh as she placed her arm along the seat beside him.

"I often come up this road at night."

She turned around and faced him as she added, "Late. When its dark."

His hand on the wheel began to tremble and he knew it was because he was unable to overcome his fear of accepting the sexual challenge being thrown down to him. Even his breathing was becoming a problem. To his relief, the small cottage where she lived appeared just a short distance up ahead.

As he pulled up outside the entrance, she placed her hand very deliberately on his arm and turning fully around as before looked directly into his eyes and put it to him again.

"Remember what I said. I'll be up this road tonight when it's dark. I love the dark. I'll be at the field gate where I saw you just now."

Suddenly, she put her hand across and flattened out her palm over the wet patch on his trouser leg. Holding it there for the briefest of moments, she pressed her hand firmly against his inner thigh and rubbed her flat palm along the wet watermark. Next, she turned away and fumbled around the instruments on the side panel endeavouring to open the door. As he leaned across and undid the catch, she put her hand up to her nostrils and then rubbed it along her lips, and flicked her tongue along her palm.

As he drove away, it surprised him he was shaking and he began to breathe in and exhale large mouthfuls of air slowly to try and relieve the tension. What was wrong with him? Why was he so disturbed? Was it because he was lacking in some way? Was it the fear of a challenge, a sexual challenge, and he was admitting to himself there was a hint of male inadequacy? Oh, sweet Jesus! He just didn't know. Maybe he didn't want to know. Didn't want to admit to himself that he had backed down. Definitely, she had propositioned him. That in itself should not have left him so tense and nervous.

He punched the steering wheel of his car with the soft heel of his fist and swore loudly. He scratched at a bead of sweat coursing down under his vest. Jesus. That girl had upset him more that he cared to admit. It was his inadequacy in handling the encounter even though it was totally unexpected, which had shattered him. There again, he had done the right thing. There again. There again what? There again, with hindsight, to admit he could have dallied with her for a while longer. Then he recalled another girl years before in somewhat similar circumstances. She had been standing or rather leaning against him at the far end of a dancehall car park. They had been only partly hidden from the throng emerging at the end of the dance when suddenly, with her back against the car standing facing him, she pulled up her skirts. He had stood in hesitation, with one eye on the people exiting from the dancehall. She just dropped her skirts and walked away, muttering something. What was it she had said? Oh, yes. He remembered now. She ridiculed him and said, "What's this now? Were you afraid it wouldn't stand up?" That's what she had said to him, "Were you afraid it wouldn't stand up?"

Then as now, for some reason which he just could not explain, the episode left him shaking like a leaf.

Suppose, though, with hindsight, the same opportunity presented itself again. Possibly, he would react in the same uncertain, frustrated way all over again and that was the reason he was shaking. No other reason. No other explanation.

That loathsome girl was coming at six, and it was now after five. For heaven's sake! Clear the mind! Rid it of the disturbing effects of that encounter with BoBo!

The moment he drove into the yard his elder son, Richard, appeared as if by chance.

"Don't forget that girl is coming to see you this evening at six."

Richard hadn't one feature or mannerism which resembled himself, his mother or Joe. That sometimes bothered him. Richard's hair, light yellow in colour, had none of the richness and fullness of his or Joe's tousled dark mops, rather he was going bald at an early age. His physique, too, was the opposite of his own, not exactly puny but nonetheless a kind of a weakling. They just had nothing whatever in common, and when he considered the tricks which devious woman who had spawned him might have been up to, then Richard sometimes bothered him, but he never allowed himself to dwell too long on the subject.

Richard's wife, Priscilla, was small and had sharp beady eyes, a pointed nose and mousey hair. Richard and Priscilla would have been waiting and watching to waylay him all evening in order to ascertain what his attitude would be towards Joe, and this girl. What was the reason for her visit? Would it in any way concern them?

"I hadn't forgotten." Donal ventured nothing further.

It wasn't the answer Richard had been expecting. So, he changed course and fell into step alongside. Donal noticed Richard raise his gaze momentarily towards the kitchen window. No doubt, Priscilla was ensconced behind the curtain watching their every movement.

"What do you expect she wants?"

"I haven't an idea, Richard. Not a clue."

He went in through the back door without further communication. Priscilla was crossing over the kitchen as he entered. She gave the appearance of someone busy doing nothing. She won't refer at all to Joe's intrusion, Donal thought, but she will dictate to her husband what questions he should ask. Of the two, Priscilla might just shade it on a test of ingenuity. There again, it could happen that when that button was pressed nothing might appear on either screen. The register measuring ingenuity and enterprise might well read zero.

As a couple, they delighted in one another's company, posting cards to each other at Christmas, Easter and the New Year. On birthdays, they sent one another parcels through the post. In summertime, they went cycling and camping every other weekend. One never went into town without the other. Everything was done in tandem. It would be unfair to say they lived dull, commonplace lives, for they were extremely contented and happy with their lot.

The moment he entered, she searched his face for some trace or sign which might tell her something she didn't already know – something which he was holding back from them. However, Donal's inscrutable weather-beaten features told her nothing.

"Have you eaten, Dad?"

"No. I didn't have time, Priscilla."

"Could I get you something? A snack, maybe? Or something more substantial if you like?"

"A snack would be fine. Could I have it in the drawing room?"

He always tried his best to appear interested in what Priscilla was saying, at least, to be seen to approve of what she was doing. It was important to her. God knows, but she could do with a bit of praise now and then.

Try as he did there was awkwardness between them which he simply couldn't breach, as though he had some reservations about her competence.

He turned on the television in the corner of the drawing room. A soccer match, a European game, was showing on Sky.

In a matter of minutes, Priscilla came into the room carrying some newspapers.

"There's an English one here as well."

"You're very kind."

Then as usual, they ran out of talk. She remained standing by the door looking directly at him, not saying anything, not intending to say anything. She just stood there looking at him with a vacant expression expecting him to do the talking. He searched his mind but there was nothing to say. What he really wanted was to be left alone so he could go over in his mind the possible attitudes he might adopt with this girl who would be along in a short while.

"I think I'll have a glass of wine."

He pulled himself out of the easy chair and then had to walk by her where she had remained standing in the doorway. The wine was in the dining room on the other side of the hall.

Priscilla went to the kitchen and, in a short time, she returned to serve up a tasty light meal of smoked salmon on a bed of lettuce with a sprinkling of scallions and some sliced tomatoes, the whole accompanied by freshly baked brown bread.

"Richard and I have to go out for a while. Um ... that girl Sharon. She should be here shortly. You'll be all right, won't you?"

"Oh, I'm fine. This couldn't be nicer."

He indicated the meal as he was speaking, but he was thinking along other lines. Sharon. Sharon. How did Priscilla know her name? Why were she and Richard going out at the same time as the girl was due to arrive? Both of them had shown an inordinate interest in her visit. Now they were leaving. It didn't make sense. How did she know the girl's name?

"Sharon."

He tried to make it sound as if he wasn't too concerned. It came awkwardly off his tongue.

"Sharon," he repeated. "How did you know that was her name?"

"That's the name she gave when she phoned this morning," she said. "Cheerio."

With that, she was gone.

He walked over to the bay windows and watched the progress of their car down the avenue. It turned left and was immediately lost behind the shrubs and trees which skirted the roadside lawns, except for occasional glimpses, as it passed open spaces above the white wooden paling.

Another car, a dull red Ford, turned into the driveway and approached the house.

CHAPTER 5

A female driver stepped out and swept her gaze over the impressive lawns, gardens, trees, and house before turning her attention to the entrance. Donal had to step back sharply from where he was standing by the window lest he would appear to be peeping.

The girl, apparently unabashed by the impressive surroundings, brazenly opened the front door without knocking or making any effort to announce her presence. So, she had little regard for ordinary courtesies or manner, Donal thought.

What galled him particularly was that the front door, normally locked, had been left open. The girl strolled nonchalantly through into the hallway. He heard her footsteps along the corridor which led down to the kitchen at the back of the house, and listened as she retraced them. He sat down just as the drawing room door opened slowly.

Unannounced, she thrust her head inside, overtly smiling as she peeped in at him.

"You must be Dad, then."

She appeared to be amused at what she had said, or it could be she was amused at him.

His rage was so great that his immediate reaction was to shout at her to leave his house immediately and never set foot in it again. However, there wouldn't be any satisfaction in disposing of her, without first teaching her a well-deserved lesson.

He remained seated and took a small sip of wine. Next, he sampled a piece of the salmon. He chewed on it slowly and deliberately in an effort to dissipate the anger boiling up inside, and to offend her. She could not be mistaken at being treated little better than an intruder, unless she was stupid, which he doubted. It was his turn to be rude.

Undaunted, she strolled into the room, leaving the door open behind her, and after a precursory glance about planked her bottom down on the arm of the best chair in the house, a delicate Chippendale of which he was justly proud.

Don't shout at her. Don't even attempt to scold her. Keep the head. Keep the cool. The better to triumph over her. Yes, triumph! Dance on her grave! Triumph over this obnoxious girl!

Seemingly, she was still amused at him, for she was looking directly at him with laughter in her eyes.

"But you are Dad, aren't you?"

He was beside himself with rage. Was there no end to this insufferable girl's effrontery?

"Yes, I am Joe's Dad."

As soon as he had replied, he knew he should have ignored the question. His response sounded weak, but then he had always lacked the cutting edge, the wit and self-confidence to be sarcastic. Whilst trying to conjure up something offensive to snap back at her she began talking.

"You're just as he described."

She was smiling again as if it still amused him.

"What do you want?" He spoke sternly and stressed the word you. He repeated the question.

She could hardly be so naïve as to ignore such an obvious rebuff, and yet her reply was calm and measured. Obviously, she had taken not the slightest umbrage for she continued, as before, "There is a very definite resemblance between you both."

There it was again, that same sweet smile he so resented and found decidedly impertinent. She next took to appraising his features, evidently taking in his height, appearance and everything about him. He glowered back, becoming increasingly tenser by the minute, staring rudely and searching about in his mind for something offensive to say that would wound her.

Money! That was it. She was bound to have come for money.

"I'll have to ask you again. What do you want from me?"

"It isn't so much what I want. It's what Joe's asked me to do that has brought me down here."

So, the fine lady won't come out and admit she's come down to him looking for money. She wishes to avoid being implicated. There must be no suggestion of participation on her part. No, that would never do. How canny to emphasise it was his son who needed the money! Well, he's spent far too many years at boardroom meetings to fall for that silly little twist on words, and decided there and then that there had been enough niceties. It was time for a few home truths.

"So you've come down here to look for money from me."

She laughed nervously and when he looked around, she was no longer smiling. Instead, she looked genuinely surprised by his uncivil attitude, disappointed even that he had introduced such a note of common grossness. There was even a hint of disdain in her bright eyes as she appraised him as if assessing him anew. However, she had lost none of her composure.

"Money," she repeated. "No. No. Joe didn't say anything about money. Not at all. Joe didn't send me here to talk about money. Money? Oh God, no! Nothing like that. To be honest with you, I don't believe Joe is interested in money anyway."

"Then why in hell's name did the fool try to rob a bank, and make such a botch of it when he was at it?"

"Do you not think I've asked myself that same question a thousand times? I can tell you one thing. It had nothing to do with money. Sometimes, I think he did it just for the craic, for the sheer enjoyment of it."

"Then what brings you down here? What do you want from me? You know I've disowned him."

"Oh, yes! I'm well aware of that. It's in relation to another matter that he wished me to talk to you. You see Joe and I have a child. A complication has arisen about her. She's a little girl."

Then for some reason she added in an almost apologetic undertone, "Julie."

He must be careful. Everything about this girl infuriated him from the very moment he had first seen her – before he had first seen her, in fact. But a child! Whatever about Joe and this girl, they had had their chances in life and apparently blown them. A child was different. A child was entitled to its opportunities.

Joe wasn't married. This girl was married to another. He would want to be careful, very careful. Then it struck him forcibly. The money angle. It made more sense now. Of course! It was needed ostensibly for the child. What else? The child was Joe's way to his father's chequebook. This child, like himself and his great friend Mary Boyle, had been born out of wedlock. If Joe was the father, then there was need for caution, extreme caution and a cool head.

"What proof have I that this child is Joe's. What proof have I that it's ..."

His voice trailed off as he hesitated, and looking forcefully at her continued in a faltering voice, "... that the child is my grandchild?"

"Only that it is Joe's child."

"But you didn't marry Joe. You chose instead to marry his accomplice, his partner in crime. The man Joe had protected by refusing to name at his trial. Consequently saving the blighter's neck."

"Joe had been sentenced when I discovered that I was pregnant, and he wanted a proper birthright for our child. It was Joe wanted me to marry Tommy Gavin. He insisted. It was he who wanted it that way. I was at all times totally opposed to the arrangement. I didn't want to. I've regretted it my whole life since. Tommy Gavin is a mean man and a violent man, and always nasty to Julie."

Donal kept reminding himself to tread warily, with extreme caution. Better to talk to someone like Mary Boyle first, before committing himself to any promise or outright rejection. This problem needed the wisdom and integrity of a woman's counsel.

"I still can't understand why you acted so irresponsibly."

"When you are young and facing a nine-year prison sentence, it seems the end of the world, and, remember, I was pregnant. In that state, you don't have too many friends to offer advice or in whom you can trust. It was Joe who was appalled at the prospect of his child coming into the world without a father, or worse still, the child of a convicted bank robber. It was under pressure from that kind of background that we panicked and Tommy Gavin, wanting to save his own neck, was then as nice a pie and only too pleased, of course, to take on the responsibility as he always called it. It was solely for the child we made the decision, sacrifice if you like. But, it was a terrible mistake."

"Why should Joe have been party to such a stupid and foolhardy plan? He was ever irresponsible. But a fool? He was not a fool. You don't surely expect me to believe that, do you?"

"I'm not in the slightest bit interested in what you choose to believe. Joe didn't ask me to do that for my benefit or for his own. There was no merit in it for either of us. Just disgust. It was to give Julie a name, a birthright. Joe didn't want her to be a convict's daughter. Oh, God, I know we were stupid. That's the way it was. Now, we've got to live with it. It's like a nightmare. In the beginning, it seemed the right thing to do."

For the first time since entering the room, she fixed him with a defiant stare while she spoke solemnly and determinedly.

"Was our child not entitled to a birthright? Surely, Mr. Moran, you accept that even in this day and age a child born out of wedlock to a criminal is a little stigmatised?"

"I still don't understand why you've come to see me."

"Tommy Gavin, who is her registered father, has filed for custody. There is also a fear that he may attempt to snatch Julie from where she resides in care in a Dublin convent."

"And why would he want to do that?"

"Because he's mad, sick, and probably, out of spite."

Then somewhat impatiently, she added dismissively, "Oh, it's a long story."

"But surely, as the mother your claim will supersede all others. Why haven't you got custody of the little girl? Why don't you report him to the Gardaí?"

"No, I don't have custody of her."

Donal Moran walked over to the bay window and looked out but without seeing anything. Just as quickly, he returned to his seat. Anger still dominated his attitude towards her. He wondered what role she expected him to play. Perhaps his best bet would be to remain as he had been for the past six years – detached. However, because of the child, the proper thing would be to hear her out first.

"And why the hell do you not have custody of the child?"

She paused for a moment and for the first time since she had come into his presence appeared offended by his dismissive comment on her motherhood.

Pensively, she drew the fingers of her right hand down along the side of her neat black skirt and her leg tucked under her; she spoke without looking up.

"Yes, I supposed I deserved that comment. There again, perhaps I don't. After Joe was sentenced and I married Tommy as we'd planned, things got very rough for me. We weren't supposed to be together. He started to come around and began bashing me about and he drank to excess both night and day."

"I thought you said it was only an arrangement, not a marriage."

"That's right. But then, you don't know Tommy Gavin. He'd just come around and move in. I was terrified of him. I don't know how Joe got mixed up with him. He's a complete psycho. I'd be terrified of him this minute if he came through that door there."

"What about the little girl all this time?"

"Whilst he never interfered with her in a physical way, he was as objectionable as he could be. She felt the rejection. Then I got into drink and neglected Julie. For some twisted reason Tommy hates Joe's guts. No one seems to know why. As I said, he's mad. His mind is deranged. He can be dangerous, even though Joe took the rap for them both. Anyway, he phoned the welfare officer and Julie was taken into the care of the local authority in Liverpool."

"And what about your own family, your mother and father? Do you have brothers and sisters?"

"I don't have family."

She barely glanced up as she spoke.

"Our problem is that Tommy Gavin is registered as the father of the girl. How will anyone ever believe Joe and me? Joe is a convicted criminal, and needless to say the welfare of the child does not bother Tommy Gavin in the slightest."

Donal Moran felt confused. At first, he couldn't think of anything to do or say. Besides, she had not yet stated why she had come to see him. What role did she expect him to play? More particularly, what did she want from him? The meeting was taking on a whole new dimension and his earlier resentments now seemed less important.

"What do you expect from me? Why come to me? Really, I don't know anything about this child, this little girl. I've never met you before and, as for Joe, why you well know I have long since cut him out of my life. What has all this got to do with me right now? What do you want from me?"

"It has nothing whatever to do with you. Nor am I down here to ask you to do anything on our behalf. However, we have it on good authority that Tommy Gavin intends calling you as a witness on his behalf. He wants the court to know that not only is Joe unreliable as a witness and a father, being a convicted criminal, but also, in addition, on your evidence that you rejected him as a son, even before the trial, as being an unfit person to have within the family. Turned down by his own father! How much more unsuited does that make him to be a proper father to Julie?"

Sharon stood up out of the chair and fixed him with a cold stare. Her voice became a trifle emotional as she adopted a challenging attitude.

"Joe said he would not ask or expect you to do anything whatever for himself or his child. He emphasised that he never found you to be any help to him whenever he needed you."

Donal had been sitting down when she had addressed him and, apart from the one foray to the bay window, he had deliberately remained seated throughout and acted discourteously towards her, to demonstrate his rejection of both herself and Joe. Now, the conversation was taking on a whole new, dark twist. He was becoming the accused and she the prosecutor. When she had entered the room, he hadn't bothered to stand up or extend any greeting to her.

Now he found himself standing up, but not out of courtesy; he was shouting.

"What did you say?"

His belligerent manner was overbearing, as if by frightening her he might prevent her from repeating the words which she had just spoken. It was as though his aggressiveness might compel her to withdraw the words or frighten her to the extent she would be afraid to repeat them.

"What did you say? What did you say?"

Quite unperturbed, she faced him and, with her head a little to the side, was unflinching in her response.

"Joe explained that you were never any good when he needed you. It doesn't really matter to me, one way or another, what you think of us. I love Joe and I love Julie. You don't mean a fig to me. Get one thing clear in your mind. No one is down here to ask you to do anything for them. It's not expected of you. It's not being asked of you. No one is begging you to help in any way. Joe felt you should know about us and the child as the other side are depending on you to strengthen their case by calling you to say in evidence that you had found your son unworthy to be a member of your family ... that you denied your own son. They believe this will influence the court against Joe's suitability and mine. No, we don't want anything from the likes of you. Why should we? Why, we don't even want you to soften your evidence one way or the other. What brought me down to see you was first, to tell you about Julie and secondly, that the other side intend to call on you to give evidence against your own son. And now that I've passed on the message, I'm not obligated to you further."

She spun around bringing the meeting to an unexpected end and without further ado or words of farewell went smartly in the direction of the door.

All seemed changed, utterly changed in a matter of minutes. Donal's conscience was pricked by a flicker of guilt. He couldn't concentrate on what he should be thinking about, or what he should be doing, only that she mustn't be allowed to leave the room. After all, the child was his grandchild.

"Come back here! Don't you go!"

Unintentionally, he was still barking at her. She paused by the door but didn't turn around.

"I don't have to, you know."

She was still in command of her quiet voice and still facing away from him.

He was much more conciliatory in his tone when he again addressed her.

"Please, I don't want you to go for a moment. Leave me to myself for a second or two. But please, do not leave the room."

He walked over to the French windows again and gazed outside towards the avenue and the trees.

Even though the season was late in coming, it was now a beautiful spring day. The branches of the evergreens near the window moved gently in the light breeze, and the sun was reflected off the still waters of the pond at the side of the rockery. Little green shoots were to be seen everywhere in the hawthorn bushes, and the rooks, working hard on their nest building, cawed busily in the beech trees beyond the flower gardens. Everywhere he looked, bunches of gold and yellow daffodils were proclaiming the miracle of spring.

In a subdued voice, totally changed from the arrogance and impatience he had adopted earlier, he remained looking out on the idyll stretched before him and whispered, "Tell me again what Joe said."

She emphasised, as before, that she had come to see him merely to pass on the information about the child and the court case, nothing more, and she did not feel in any way further obliged to him.

"Basically, what Joe said was that, as far as he was concerned, you were never any good to him as a father."

There seemed an interminable pause before she added, "At least, as far as he was concerned."

She talked on in the same easy dispassionate voice.

"Joe left here because he understood Richard was getting married and the place was intended for Richard and his wife. On the few occasions that he returned, the only communication between you and him was your criticism of all the failures in his life, especially on the subject of his drinking. He had no pluses, just all failures. Only during the time his grandmother was alive was he happy here. She was nice to him, and understanding. After her death, he felt quite alone, an imposter, certainly not a son of the house. He has no wish to return here, or to meet you ever again. He is adamant in that. The only reason I came here today is because of your kinship with Julie. When the other side summon you, as they are going to, at least you will know what it's all about. Joe also said you would refuse to see me if I phoned and asked you for an appointment on his behalf. At least, he was wrong insofar as you did see me."

She paused in a way he knew she was going to add more and its impact was not going to be pleasant. He remained by the window and waited apprehensively for her to continue.

She was a remarkably self-controlled young woman.

"What Joe said was – I clearly remember what he said – 'much as that man hates me'."

She paused again and looked across the room towards where he was standing sideways on to her. He didn't look up yet he felt the penetration of her gaze.

"Much as that man hates me," she repeated, "I hate him twice as much. Why that man would be more concerned with what the neighbours thought than with his own son's welfare."

Hatred – never there when he needed you – the neighbours would come first – strong words and phrases, and when taken together they were damning.

Where arrogance and self-righteousness had reigned a few minutes before, doubt now tinged with guilt began to intrude, increasing in intensity with the passing of each second. It so concentrated Donal's mind as to rule out the possibility of thinking or responding with any degree of effectiveness.

What was the point now in explaining to this girl that he would have paid for third-level education only Joe dropped out? Joe's drunken visits home now seemed irrelevant, trivial, not worth remembering compared with other hardships in life.

"No," he said, "I suppose when he needed me for the trial I wasn't there."

"It wasn't just the trial," she answered gently but firmly.

"He didn't ask to see me either. Throughout all that time, he never once asked to see me."

"That's right. He didn't expect that you'd bother with him and, of course, you didn't. He knew he didn't mean that much to you."

Standing facing the window, Donal Moran leaned against the sill. He buried his head in his hands and in the darkness of his shuttered eyes cast about in his mind for something to say. Seemingly, there was nothing. His mind was blank, and there was a throbbing in his head brought on by the word 'hatred' and a rising sense of guilt.

"I loved that boy," he said at last and in desperation.

"I don't think, Mr. Moran, you understand what love is. You seem to be a fair-weather lover – one who loves exclusively on his own terms when the weather is fine and to his liking. It's easy for the parent to love a child who is doing all that pleases the parent, but when something goes drastically wrong of which the parent disapproves, the parent is then needed by the child and the parent's love put to the test. How often in Ireland do we see the unmarried daughter being rejected and secreted away to a place of confinement, when the parents' love for their child is secondary to all other considerations? Love is about saying 'yes' to the wrongdoer who is in need. You never loved Joe, Mr. Moran."

Silence enveloped the room. She looked towards him. He was, as before, looking out of the window. When he did speak, his voice seemed unsure and she thought she detected the slightest trace of a tear. From where she was standing, she couldn't tell for certain.

"You can tell him from me that nobody – just nobody and I mean nobody – will take his child away from him. I will see to that."

Throughout his life, Donal Moran had been a practical man and that was part of the reason for his success in business. Often he quoted one of the first lessons which he had ever learned. He remembered it as he stood there, told to him by a labourer going about his daily work – 'never joust at windmills, or work in your own light, or try to drive water up a hill'.

Never, and certainly not now, was he going to try to drive water uphill.

What made it possible for him to apply these three principles throughout his working life was his inherent ability to overlook the part which guilt played in his transgressions. Others might agonise for weeks or months, or even years, over the culpability of their ways, but not Donal Moran. Instead, he would apply himself, his energy, his time to setting matters to right in a practical common sense way. He was able to forget his sinfulness in a way of which only the very successful seem capable.

Now, fate was playing an ironic twist in their lives. Here was his son and this girl, who had both undergone a painful sacrifice in the interests of their child. Now, they were embarking on a further traumatic struggle for her custody. Now, he was the grandfather, once a child who likewise had been saved from a similar fate because of the absolute love and determination of his mother. He was now being accused of having spurned his son and of contributing to his granddaughter being assigned to the very fate from which he had himself been rescued as a child.

There were tears in his eyes as he turned back towards her and an edge of remorse in his voice.

"So you don't think that he would meet me at this time, if I went to the prison?"

"No, that wouldn't be wise. Obviously, you don't fully understand his feelings. That would not be a wise thing to do at all. I only came here to caution you lest you are called by the other side. That's all. I didn't come bearing an olive branch."

"Yes. I suppose it's understandable."

Then he looked fully at her, appraising her as if for the first time, evaluating her worth as a person.

"Tell me, how did you meet Joe?"

"I was a typist in a solicitor's office and had just begun studying at university at night to become a solicitor."

"You were doing well for yourself."

"Yes, I suppose I was doing all right."

"And then, you threw it all away on my big stupid son."

She didn't take it for what it was intended, a light-hearted aside. Instead, she seemed peeved by the remark.

"I wouldn't exactly say that."

He was now smiling and she smiled back.

"I will be seeing the solicitor tomorrow and will try and fit you in for an appointment with him. That's the best I can do. Of course, you understand that I will have to speak to Joe first. I would never do anything without consulting him."

She walked towards the door, turned back and looked towards him.

"What else is there to say?"

Then, she was gone.

Donal resumed his stance by the window. This time, it didn't matter whether she saw him watching her or not. The cruel words she had spoken were ringing in his head. As she got into the car, his eyes followed her. She still looked to him to be a very ordinary girl. However, he knew now she wasn't. For there were quite extraordinary things about her, not least of which was her strong character and loyalty to Joe and their child.

A chill was creeping into the late evening air. He took up the glass of wine and finished it. Such a mistake not to have offered her a drink, a cup of tea, coffee or whatever, he thought, especially as she had come quite a journey. How very rude of him. Such a blockhead!

"Oh, Jesus – help me now."

Pausing for reflection, he added with conviction.

"And Joe, too." He paused again "... and his two lovely ladies."

The fire was set. A box of matches lay beside the table lamp. He lit a match and put it to the kindling of twigs and paper and soon bright flames began to dance in the grate. Before long, the aroma of hand-cut turf sods pervaded the air and the room began to warm up.

Across the hallway in the dining room was the drinks cupboard. As he groped through the bottles arranged along shelves, it occurred to him he how seldom he did this. A regimen of strict frugality in his daily life was normal. It was against his natural instincts to open a bottle of wine for himself just to drink a glass or two. Today however was different. It wasn't like any ordinary day. It had brought new and far-reaching changes to his life. There was nothing he could do about them now, this minute, at this late hour of the evening. Though not a drinking man, he poured the first of what he knew would be strong measures.

The alcohol would upset him. It always did, but he was going to drink this evening, whether or which.

What about a bottle of white for a change? Why not? Dulce. Why not again? The glass became important. He picked one with a roped stem and a large globular bowl. He held it up to the light as he poured a full beaker. It tasted good. He swallowed a drop more. It was pleasant on the palate, easy to take. There's not too much volume in a beaker of wine. He filled the large glass to the brim again and quickly drank it.

Next, he took a bottle of fine French brandy from the cupboard. It is said that brandy is best sipped from a special brandy glass, the better to appreciate its singular bouquet and texture.

Donal Moran poured a stiff measure into his wine glass. After all the shape of the glass, or the remnants of a drop of sweet white wine, could hardly change the taste of the liquor, let alone its scent and colour.

He swallowed. It wasn't as palatable as the sweet white wine. A drop of peppermint was what was needed. There's nothing like peppermint to give brandy a bit of a twang. He found it easier to sip. The peppermint made it effortless to swallow.

A gleaming bottle of Powers Gold Label caught his eye. Using the same glass, he half-filled it with the golden liquid. Now which was it to be, red lemonade or a drop of spring water?

He held the glass against his closed lips and, without sampling, it smelled its strong aroma with deep breaths, and held it there for a few seconds. A smile crossed his features and a pleasant wave of intoxication passed through him as he felt his spirits beginning to rise already.

"I'll drink a toast. To my granddaughter! By God, but I'll not see you wronged."

He downed the whisky in one gulp, and shook his head and made a wry grimace, and shouted aloud,

"Ye ha who!
Rise up a laddie and give us a trate,
and give us a bit of yer Christmas cake.
What about another drop of whisky
to keep a fellah company?
Fill her up, me fine fellah!
I'll run her up.
I'll run her down.
I'll run her into Clinnygowan.
I'll break her back.
I'll bind her knee
and I'll carry her home on a holly tree.
Ye ha who!"

He took the glass with him back to the drawing room. There was a football match on Sky. He couldn't tell if it was the same one as he had been looking at earlier.

He heard footsteps in the hallway. Richard and Priscilla had returned and now joined him before the fire. Immediately, they began putting questions to him about the girl.

There was no reason why he should give them any information, apart from saying she was a charming girl and that Joe was going to be released in the next few weeks, if not days. After all, she had come to him in confidence to let him know that he might be called by the other side to give evidence against his own son. That was the bit which was hard to swallow. It was unthinkable that his evidence might be instrumental in depriving his granddaughter of being reared and claimed by her own. A man couldn't live with that! Donal Moran couldn't anyway. After all, his granddaughter was an innocent little girl. It would be a breach of trust to relay the conversation which he had had in confidence about the child.

Priscilla was intent on staying put by the fire and foraging for information. Repeatedly, she reverted to Sharon's visit. She hadn't the slightest interest in the football match. Yet, she viewed the screen as if it was her only interest, while at the same time she saw nothing wrong in talking and distracting others who were interested. Donal mentally put her lack of awareness of others down to nothing short of backwardness.

He could never understand his son's infatuation for her, his total commitment to please her every whim. Whilst she stayed put before the fire, Richard would also remain there. She would not have to tell him to. He would know by her attitude that it was expected of him. She would not have to communicate with him either by sign or by covert gesture. It was as if there was an interaction of mental telepathy at work between them. They were nice people but, divine God! – there were times when they could drive a sane person around the twist, so persistent and ... and pathetic, that was the word, their attitudes. The atmosphere was becoming just about intolerable for Donal.

He stood up out of the easy chair and, tossing down the last of the whisky, made for the door.

"I'm going out for a while."

Richard offered to chauffeur him in to wherever he wanted to go, but Donal declined.

There was a slur in his speech and giddiness in his step as he made for the door. By heavens, he was in irrepressibly good humour, and was tempted to give vent to another "*Ye ha who!*"

CHAPTER 6

He drove down the short avenue beneath the tall beech trees leading to the road gate. Bright yellow heads of daffodils on either side of the avenue waved to and fro in the gentle breeze which nonetheless had a touch of ice to its sting. Overhead, chattering rooks made a loud cacophony as they built their nests in preparation for parenthood. What a great noise and fuss and racket they created as their nest building progressed!

Donal Moran realised his thoughts were not those of a sober man. He was losing control. For some bizarre reason, his mind was becoming obsessed with thoughts of the afterlife, especially with his own ghost. As he drove along, he wondered if his ghost came back, say in a hundred years time, would it remember the roads and side roads or the little familiar twists and turns of the journey. Would the fact of his having been dead all those years extinguish the memory? He had to be drunk. He had to be very drunk. Well, what the hell about it if he was?

Would that woman tending tulips in her front garden look up and recall having seen him before? Would she say, "Oh, Mr. Moran, it's nice to see you again. It's been a long time."

She might not be able to see him, perhaps, him being a spirit. Perhaps, she would just go on tending her tulips, pressing down the clay with trowel and strong fingers around each delicate and beautiful bulb. He began to wonder if in fact spirits were not all around and going the roads, and seeking out old haunts, and sitting in old chairs or walking under beech trees, or along the banks of rivers on days when the sun is high in the sky, and mayflies with legs dangling down would dip up and dip down into the sun pools of the lakes and rivers.

Would his spirit or ghost, or whatever it was, watch fish jumping along the length of the smooth river surface of fly-bobbing waters in the haze and sunshine of summer evenings?

He must be very drunk to be thinking so, for how could a woman of today remember him in a hundred years time? He must be very drunk. For didn't he know that no one ever came back? Only he was so gloriously drunk! How could he have forgotten?

How often did he hear his mother say, "Once they put you under that earth there, then there you remain, I'm afraid," adding, "That's the end of it, of you, of me, of all of us. God help us!"

Up ahead and to the right was Patsy's pub. On a Monday evening, there wouldn't be too many patrons in there. That was just as well for he didn't relish the thought of being seen in his present condition by too many people or of having to socialise either. Locally, he was reckoned to be a man of abstemious habits and he liked that reputation. It was important to him that people recognised his successes.

Having grown up amongst them from the humblest of beginnings, it was important that his standing in the community be recognised. After all, he was the owner of Clooney Abbey and is adjoining estates, as well as numerous other business ventures throughout the county and country, was he not?

Suddenly, his mind became directed to the daily and English papers on the passenger seat beside him. He remembered Priscilla giving them to him in the drawing room earlier in the evening, but he had no recollection of his bringing them out to the car. Yet there they were. Ah, what the hell! Someone put them there, and now he would put them to good use in the pub. Reading the papers would be easier than engaging someone or other in an unwanted conversation.

"You're very welcome, Mr. Moran." Patsy sounded genuine as he came down the counter with his hand outstretched in greeting.

"How are you, Patsy? I'm afraid I'm under the weather myself. But I'll try a glass."

"Whisky, if I remember rightly."

"Yes. Whisky, it will be."

"You're all right, Mr. Moran. You never did too much wrong in all the years I've known you. Why shouldn't you go a little under the weather now and again? Helps to clear out the auld system, I always say."

Patsy withdrew to where the glasses were suspended from the ceiling, selected one, and held it up towards the light to show it was polished and shining. After pouring the measure, he left down a jug of spring water and a bottle of red lemonade beside the drink and politely withdrew to continue with polishing more of his glasses.

There was a large lounge bar, dimly lit, but from where Donal Moran sat at the counter, he could make out that the few customers scattered about were locals. Some exchanged snippets of trite conversation with him and others nodded a reserved greeting. However, there was something amiss. Definitely, something was wrong. They were guarded in their attitudes towards him.

Slowly, he turned over the pages of the paper, aware he was being watched, as though expecting something to happen. The atmosphere was charged with expectancy and embarrassment.

He glanced over the headlines. They were the same as usual. A stabbing in Connemara and another in Athlone. An old woman living alone in County Mayo was robbed, raped and, of course, tortured. What the hell sort of a country had we? It had to do with the way we were being reared. It had to do with home life. That's where the fault really lay. Of course, you couldn't say that in Ireland. No one would ever acknowledge that. The holy Catholic Irish family! Such a load of codswallop! Such a shower of hypocrites! He was feeling cynical. Divine God, we must be terrible eejits, Donal thought, in a new, alcohol-induced clarity.

Still they were watching him, casting furtive glances in his direction as they talked in undertones. They were withdrawn and silent for the most part but watching, closely watching, yet pretending not to be watching.

Then suddenly, the secret was out. For there, staring at him out of the legal page was Joe's photograph. Over it, was the caption, "Convicted Bank Robber to Contest Paternity Suit".

At that moment, Patsy came down the counter and poured a large drink without the aid of the measure and bravely tried to break the terrible spell of embarrassment which had descended on the place. John Carthy approached and stood beside Donal Moran at the counter. John Carthy was a lean man who had spent a lifetime with Bórd na Mona on the bogs.

"You know something, Mr. Moran, I'll call you Donal. Do you remember you and I ran to school together in our little bare feet on days of spring, summer and autumn?"

Without waiting for a reply, he placed a bronzed muscular hand on the paper, and prodding Joe's photo with a finger, said spiritedly, "I had many's the pint with him. He's not as bad a lad as he's made out to be. No, Joe's not a bad lad. Meself and the missus was up visiting him in Mountjoy only two weeks gone."

It sounded like a reproof, a criticism to Donal Moran for John Carthy would know, and all the men present would know, that Donal Moran hadn't been to see his son since the arrest.

Then for no apparent reason, John Carthy began to laugh, a chuckling, nervous laugh, for the subject he had broached was a tricky one. "When I asked Joe what he'd do when he'd come out he said this, 'Remember,' says he, 'they never found the money'."

John Carthy went into peals of jittery laughter. Some of the men about the premises joined in, in encouragement. They were all like John Carthy, upright, honest-to-god kind of men.

A moment's awkward silence followed during which no one seemed able to offer anything to relieve the tension except the yellow wooden clock with swinging pendulum which loudly ticked away the moments of waiting; ticked away the moments of embarrassment. Tick. Tock. Tick. Tock.

As if in reparation lest he had offended the poor father, John Carthy added with the nodding approval of all the men present, "He wasn't that sort of a lad. He's not the sort of a lad who'd steal money. You know why he did it, Mr. Moran? He did it for the craic. That's right. He did it for the craic. As a dare."

Then silence, except for the sound of the yellow clock with its weights hanging down, swinging. Tick. Tock. Tick. Tock.

John Carthy was at a loss as to what he should do or say next. He muttered something incoherent and, turning away, sought out a seat at the other end of the room.

Tick. Tock. Tick. Tock. The yellow wooden clock with weights hanging down was loudly ticking their lives away.

Donal Moran picked up his tumbler of whisky and swallowed. He shook his head wryly. Patsy refilled and Donal Moran just as quickly gulped it down. With bottle in hand, Patsy looked apprehensively and disapprovingly towards him. Donal well knew that he had almost lost total self-control. Without further ado, he turned and walked out the door. In the car, he had difficulty in inserting the ignition key and couldn't remember whether he had paid for the drinks or not. He hadn't invited anyone to join him in a drink. Had he been rude to the proprietor or the customers? He couldn't remember. He couldn't remember where he was. He couldn't remember where he was going. He couldn't remember anything.

CHAPTER 7

A high wind sent the dark clouds scurrying across the
night sky, reeling across the heavens, obliterating the
moon at intervals. It was a warm wind and the rain
stayed away.

That was the kind of night that was in it, as BoBo set out
along the road. BoBo was up to no good as she hit the road
on this wild and dark and windy night. There was a faraway
look in her eyes. It was a look, too, of want, a look of longing.
She was out for divilment and her tail was up. Oh, yes! BoBo
was out for divilment and her tail was up as she hit the road.
Never before had she had a premonition as convincing as she
was experiencing on this night.

Even before she rounded the bend on the road, she knew.
Some inner feeling told BoBo that tonight was to be the night,
and then suddenly, even before she rounded the bend, the
unmistakable trace of cigarette smoke reached her. It floated
past her in the gale. She quickened her pace and headed towards
it, up there around the turn, in the blackness up ahead.

The night was as clear as the moon which now and then
lit up the land for a few seconds as its light broke through the
racing clouds. There, at the same gate as she had met with
Donal Moran earlier, look! Look up there! There it was again,
the bright glow of a cigarette being drawn on. It was going to
be on this night of high wind and darkness. Just for an instant,
she hesitated and slowed her pace, but only for the briefest
of seconds, for almost immediately, she bent her steps again
purposefully in the direction of the glowing spark up ahead
of her at the gate. Could it be that this person ahead knew of
her approach? Could it be the same Donal Moran she had met
earlier and left in no doubt what she was after? At the thought
of him, a wave of excitement welled up inside her.

As she moved towards the lighted cigarette, her heartbeat
quickened. From the position of the glow, she calculated the

man – she presumed it was a man – to be inside and partly hidden behind the thickest of blackthorn bushes which had been allowed to grow unhindered at the edge of the field as a windbreak for cattle.

One thing she knew for certain. It was a man who was up there. He would know she was coming towards him and he would wait, wait for BoBo. It was what she wanted. Everything told her, her mind, her body, and her aches and pains all told her that it was intended for her. It was to be this very night. She wasn't going to pass it up.

From a distance, she called out to him, but he didn't reply. She knew he would wait. She was being drawn to him like a magnet and, tonight, she knew it was going to be all right.

Eagerly, she approached him.

"You're out late like meself."

The clouds parted then just for a fleeting second and as the moon shone its auricular light down upon them, in that transitory moment, she could tell he was an enormously tall man, angular and lean. He wore a peaked cloth cap pulled down tightly over his forehead, face and large aquiline nose.

The gate was ajar and, without further invitation, she went through the gap and walked over to where he stood tall, lean, strong, and silent beneath the bushes close to the ditch.

She had never seen any man quite so tall and was dominated both by his silence as well as his great height. She had a desire to touch him. Raising her hand, she laid it on his shoulder. She had to stretch upwards because of his height, and was about to put a question to him when he audibly spat the cigarette butt out the side of his mouth and placed an enormous open hand on her face and patted her left cheek.

He didn't say anything, just put his open hand on her face and stroked her cheek. In that instant, she had an apprehension as his hand caressed her face and he look at her in silence – he might be a man of extreme mood swings, even of violence, if it should become necessary to assert his will.

Now with added firmness, the stranger tapped her cheek again with the flat of his hand, causing her to withdraw a step. Notwithstanding, he persisted in striking her a further number of light taps. They didn't exactly hurt her. She didn't feel soreness or pain, rather her cheek began to smart and she fitfully grabbed his hand and began kissing it.

Suddenly, he seized her about the waist, at the same time swinging her around and pulling her backwards into him, pinning her arms in front of her by the vice-like grip of one enormous hand. Still, he spoke not a syllable as he moved his other hand across her body and over her breasts, around her waist and down the length of her legs and back to her breasts again. All the while, he was pulling her backwards into him and rubbing his beard stubble against her face and neck. She thrilled to the power and warmth of his body leaning across her back and shoulders. Sometimes, his chin rested on her head but, all the while, he held her in a grip of frenzied control.

BoBo would take on anyone, for she was afraid of neither man nor beast. For a woman of such slight build, her physical strength was exceptional. Now, she was powerless in the hands of this compelling giant.

He forced his rough beard along the side of her face again and it hurt her. She averted her face but his stubble found it again. His weight increased causing her to yield. His hands were underneath her skirts and, suddenly, he struck her three or four raps with the flat of his hand along her thighs. His lips pressed hard against her ear which seemed to explode as his guttural voice spoke.

"I know what you like. First time, I saw you I could tell the way it was you wanted it. And I'm going to give it to you that way."

This enormous man could do as he please with her. She was a rag doll in his hands, and like a rag doll he now lifted her off the ground and planted her facing the gate, hidden to the right by the thicket of bushes. She wondered about the view to their left, should a passing motorist catch sight of them. BoBo didn't give a damn one way or another. He too glanced apprehensively to the left. BoBo noted that and wondered if it was significant.

He pushed her hands onto one of the lower rungs of the gate, forcing her to bend at the waist but keeping her legs upright and slightly apart, her back taking his weight.

"Don't you let go of there."

His voice came across to her as tense and commanding in a manner which brooked no argument.

She felt his hands explore freely beneath her skirts; he tore at her underwear and ripped off her pants. They fell down around her ankles. His teeth were gripping into her shoulder. There was an ache in her hands and legs from the weight pressing relentlessly down on top of her.

It was going to happen to her. For the first time in her life, it was going to happen to her there and then, standing by this wrought iron field gate.

His excitement and anticipation came through to her as he began opening his trousers. All that concerned her now was that, in her eagerness, she might do or fail to do something which needed to be properly executed, and if not might prevent him having his will with her.

If only she could relieve the ache in her hands and legs from the weight of him, to ease the pressure, an imperceptible shifting of the hands and the position.

"Stand quiet, yeh bitch." She wasn't afraid of him. "I told yeh to stand, yeh bitch." There was a dark threat behind the words. No doubt, this man would strike her if he had to, so she made no response.

"If yeh move again I'll kill yeh, yeh bitch."

Forcibly, he thrust her legs further apart.

His teeth were fixed to her shoulder again. His stubble of beard rubbed along her face. Without any regard for her maidenhood, inexperience or youth, he suddenly drove up into her from behind. She let out a scream of shock and alarm and agony as he violently sundered her virginity. His grip tightened and his weight bore further down on her as he thrust up into her with rapid strokes, the while he bucked and cursed and shouted like some mad dog wolf stripping its teeth for a death struggle.

"Yeh'll kill me," she screamed at him in agony,

"If yeh let go o' that gate, be Jasus but I'll kill yeh."

He shifted his position so that, now, it was as though he had mounted her and straddled her in a sitting position and yet held her up at the same time, but there was no let up from his demonic frenzy. She tried to move but found she couldn't because of the way he was now straddled across her. Now, she was being belted against the gate.

She screamed curses into the night air, as she found a strange feeling of passion begin to overwhelm her. Her grip broke and she fell beneath him. He threw himself on top of her and, wrapping himself around her, bucked and cursed her as she lay under him on the ground. Then slowly, slowly she was being transported and she screamed again louder as her head seemed to burst and she was overwhelmed with joy.

CHAPTER 8

Mary Boyle was standing before the long mirror in her bedroom admiring the firmness and shape of her body. She was wearing only a pair of jeans and was turning from side to side in front of the mirror the better to take in the full contour of her breasts. Suddenly, she was distracted by the sound of a car engine revving and seemingly shunting backwards and forwards. From the sound of it, it was in the yard immediately below where she stood, semi-naked. Behind her in the large bed lay her elderly husband, John, sleeping peacefully.

Why would anyone want to come to the house at this hour of night, and make such a commotion in the process? It was a good half past midnight. In her hurry and anxiety, the clothes which she had taken off only a few moments before were now inexplicably nowhere to be seen. So she pulled on John's pullover which flopped half-way down her thighs. Hurriedly, she turned on the arc light in the yard by the switch at the bedroom door and turned out the bedroom light. Through a chink in the curtains, she was able to peer down into the yard.

It was their neighbour and good friend Donal Moran. She flew down the stairs and out into the yard.

"Is everything alright?"

The window on the driver's side was fully down and he was looking through at her smiling stupidly in a dire state of inebriation. He began to back the car as if planning to drive out again.

Relieving him of the car keys became the uppermost thought in Mary's mind. How to get them without a struggle was the problem. He was so drunk he would possibly refuse to hand them over. He would have to be outwitted, not the easiest of propositions.

"Are you coming in?" she asked, at the same time as she opened the driver's door. He leered drunkenly and waved the back of his hand to her, which she interpreted as a refusal to leave the car.

The keys were in the dash and the engine was running.

The proper thing to do now would be to extricate them without provoking him into some kind of counter action.

"Come on in, Donal, and have a cup of tea."

In the manner of a drunk, he stared suspiciously at her but made no response or move to get out of the car. Immediately she added guardedly, "Come on in and have a drink. I'll join you in one myself."

In his cups, he stared drunkenly towards her, now smiling, now looking solemnly through glazed eyes so there were times when it seemed he might be unconscious. However, he made no move to get out of the car.

"Damn you," Mary muttered out of his earshot, "it's typical of you Donal Moran. Much as I respect you, admire you, love you albeit in an innocent kind of way, even under the influence of drink you're not able to let your guard down for a single moment."

She put her hand under his arm and made to help him out of the seat, but there was no budging him.

"Come on, Donal. Come on," she chucked at his arm.

There was no response. She decided there and then to become more reproachful in her manner.

"Come on, Donal. Come on now at once. Will you please get out of the car? Come on, Donal, and do what you're told. Will you please turn off that engine? Come on now, I'm getting cross with you."

She stretched out her hand positively but guardedly in the direction of the keys. Drunk and all as he was, he was on to her.

"No! No! No! No! Mary. No! No! No!"

He pushed her back forcefully and laughed. With the door of the car swinging outwards, he drove in a semi-circle across the yard, then turned and sped out of the gate on to the road. Fortune smiled on him as there was no traffic coming in either direction.

Should she drive after him? Or would that precipitate him into acting in a still more hostile, irresponsible and dangerous manner? She returned to the kitchen and touched the switch on the electric kettle, and turning off the yard light, she sat into a chair at the top of the table where she pulled the daily paper towards her.

Where on earth had he been? How did he get into that state? In all the years she had known him, she had never seen the man in such a state.

Joe's girl had called on Donal that day. Could it be that a small ray of light had shone through that stubborn mind? Yet for all his obduracy, Mary knew only too well, if the truth were told or admitted to, that in spite of himself, he worried about Joe. Though he wouldn't say or wouldn't admit it even to himself, he still loved Joe.

Apart from his marriage, Joe was the only other failure in Donal Moran's life. a life noted for its success and generosity. Mary guessed that he seldom thought about that marriage and was certain there was little or no blame attaching to him. He had just married the wrong girl.

It was different with Joe. He was his son and he would have to take some of the blame for the manner in which Joe's case had been mismanaged before the courts. Knowing him as she did, Mary had little doubt that he accepted his share of culpability, not openly in discussion with others, but the hard way in private, in the secrecy of his mind. Of course, he wouldn't pretend to anyone. Stupid, perhaps, but in many ways it was part of the man's makeup that he could accept responsibility for his errors. He wouldn't run crying to another to vindicate his guilt. That wasn't his way. He wouldn't share the problem with anyone. God knows, Mary had broached it often enough. He wasn't able to bring himself to discuss Joe's difficulties with anyone. He could not admit that well-meaning people, by their warmth and affection, might help him to move away the pall of loneliness and hurt. Mary knew he must suffer more because of his own reticence. He kept it bottled up in the confines of his own mind, doubtless brooding over it, twisting and turning it about in his thoughts so he developed a persecution complex on account of Joe.

Unless that girl … Mary suddenly remembered the girl's visit had been due earlier that evening. Maybe she had managed to direct a glimmer of light into the dark recesses of his mind. No, not a hope there either, Mary dismissed the thought. For hadn't he been planning to offend her even before he had met her? Mary realised then what she should have put to him, what might have caught his attention. If only she had thought of asking him how the meeting with the girl had gone, it might have precipitated some response, apprehended his suspicions and got him out of the car.

Now there was no point in trying to be constructive in what might have been, of trying to be categorical in a hypothetical situation. The fact of the matter was Donal Moran was out there somewhere on the roads in charge of a car and he was paralytic from drink. Donal Moran was a very special person, a sincere friend and Mary would never forgive herself if anything untoward happened to him. Yet, there was nothing she could do except wait and pray.

She made herself a cup of tea and added a light spoon of sugar. She lit a half corona and though she had to be out and about in the morning by six thirty, sleep had deserted her. She turned on the radio and drawing the paper towards her glanced at the date. Monday, Monday the twenty second. Good God! It would be her birthday tomorrow. No. Not tomorrow, but today. For it was now Tuesday, one thirty a.m. and she, Mary Boyle was forty two on this Tuesday morning.

Immediately the old thoughts and the old pangs came flooding back to haunt her. It shouldn't be so, life had been good to her, always had been. She had been a very lucky woman. So there shouldn't be regrets or sense of loss. She told herself these things and in addition, instead of chalking up her disappointment, she should be counting her blessings, thanking the Lord for what He had sent her. With her husband, she farmed one hundred acres of land as good as a crow ever flew over. Outside in the milking parlour were fifty milch cows and in the Bank and in Agricultural Credit Corporation as near as dammit to £150,000 between one deposit and another. All machinery on the farm was modern and maintained in good working order and condition.

Yes. Life had been good to her, she reflected as she sat puffing on the small cigar and drinking tea on this her forty-second birthday. As well as the comfort of life on a well-run farm, there were occasional holidays and those special trips to Dublin. She couldn't forget those. Mary adored those few days every year at the Spring and Horse Shows with John, staying at one of Dublin's top hotels, partaking of all that was on offer, and indulging themselves to the full.

There were many special things about those visits, from lingering over a leisurely breakfast in one of the city's many splendid hotels to morning coffee in the foyer amidst the throng and bustle, the regal colours of gold, pink and purple, hand-woven carpets and glass chandeliers. Or to stroll down Grafton Street to Bewleys for a cup of coffee, a cream cake and drag on the old half corona, with perhaps an unhurried read of the papers. Then, it would be time to head out to the RDS by taxi, leaving the car in the hotel parking lot lest they might partake too liberally of the refreshments on offer at the Show or in one of the many excellent lounge bars to be found in that part of genteel, little ole shabby Georgian Dublin.

Yes, life had been good to Mary and she acknowledged as much sitting there at the table, on this her forty-second birthday, whilst her husband, John, thirty years her senior, slept soundly in the room overhead.

Yet after all these years together, she still felt a loss by virtue of John's impotence. On the verge of middle age, she was still a virgin. Many times, she had told herself that there was no loss, that it was her own selfishness and wantonness which grieved her and that there would be no agony, if only she would – could – rid her mind of those recurring thoughts, forever wondering what it would be like to share lovemaking. However determined she was, the loss and the pain returned to haunt and torment her. Ever since the day it was explained to her, that her husband John, her beautiful John, the John whom she loved and respected, was impotent, unable to have an erection, her world had turned upside down.

CHAPTER 9

Yes, life had been good to Mary, she admitted to herself. She had lived a charmed existence since coming to this house forty two years ago as a babe in arms with her unmarried mother shortly after her birth in the old County Home in Kilderry. Unlike her good friend Donal Moran, Mary never regretted being fatherless. On the contrary, she acknowledged that she had been more privileged in her upbringing than most.

She had been nurtured in genteel surroundings by John and his sister Sarah, and her mother too. Her poor mother. Poor mother. She pronounced the words aloud without looking up from the paper opened out on the table before her. Turning over a page, she repeated the words. Poor mother. Mary could not remember a period when her mother had not been ill. John and Sarah, the essence of kindness, never complained.

Six months they were supposed to have stayed with John and Sarah, but when the time had elapsed and they were ready to depart, Sarah couldn't find it in her heart to send them away.

"John," Sarah had said to her brother, "It wouldn't be lucky or right to put a poor woman and her baby to the road."

The amenable John always left such decisions to his sister. She always consulted him but, as Mary was to learn years later, he would be supportive. A quiet, dignified man, he was a tower of strength. Mary literally did not know life without him and his noble appearance and gentle resonant voice.

It was Sarah who had reared Mary. Sarah had a heart of gold even when she pretending to be cross with her young charge. She liked to dress Mary in the prettiest of dresses and get her to turn about and pirouette on the kitchen floor for neighbours and strangers alike or whoever happened by.

"Look at her! Isn't she pretty? Isn't she the prettiest girl you've ever seen?"

Sarah would spend hours every week brushing Mary's golden tresses, tying ponytails and ringlets and affixing bobbins and ribbons. Whenever Mary neglected her studies or her personal cleanliness, then Sarah would be genuinely cross. She would become tight-lipped and taciturn, and an ominous silence would fall on the house. John, uncomfortable in the frigid atmosphere, would sometimes try to relieve the tension by passing some innocuous remark. Sarah would fix him with an icy stare. John knew better than to tempt providence twice in as many seconds. He would withdraw his peace offering and revert into silence. Nothing would break the charged atmosphere of the room except Mary's offer of unconditional apology, voicing her regrets, saying she was sorry. Then and only then, would Sarah relent and forgive.

Sarah, standing at the sink or by the stove, would spread out her arms and invite Mary to give her a big hug. Mary would leap into the outstretched arms and the incident would be forgotten.

Mary loved Sarah more than anyone else – even more than her mother – for undoubtedly she was one of the beautiful people. Even now, after all those years since her unexpected death, Mary still missed her and remembered her with fondness in her nightly prayers.

It had happened one afternoon when Mary cycled into the yard after school. Her heart missed a beat, for there drawn up close was an ambulance with both its rear doors opened out to the back door of the house. It had to be Mum. She dropped the bicycle instantly and raced into the kitchen.

The doctor and John were in deep discussion.

"What's happened? What's happened?"

John put a caring arm around Mary's shoulder. "It's Sarah, I'm sorry to say. Ah, maybe when she gets to hospital …" and his voice trailed off unable to tell Mary how bad it really was.

Bursting into tears Mary ran down to the bedroom where Sarah was being transferred onto a stretcher. Kneeling beside her, the tears streaming down her cheeks, she momentarily obstructed the passage of the stretcher bearers, in trying to get closer to Sarah. What frightened her more than anything else was Sarah's appearance. It was as though she was unaware of what was happening around her. John said afterwards that when Mary cried out in anguish at sight of Sarah, there was the flicker of recognition and the hint of a raised hand as Mary repeatedly kissed her. It was Sarah's last and only farewell for she died of a massive heart attack in the ambulance on her way to the hospital. She had been a very special person and Mary felt she would never again have a friend quite like her.

Her death had been a terrible shock – one it took Mary ages to get over. In the beginning she was inconsolable, shattered by the unexpected suddenness of the event. Even months later when talking to John or her mother, Sarah's image or memory would flash before her mind and she would have to run off on her own, unable to stem the flow of tears as thoughts of Sarah and her generosity came flooding into her mind. It happened a few times in class at school, too, and she would burst into a fit of uncontrollable crying. Sister Mary Joseph was most sympathetic and explained that it was understandable to cry for the loss of a true friend.

"Do not try to suppress your tears, my dear," Sister Mary Joseph had said, "Would it not be shallow of us in the extreme, if we were to forget someone we loved above all others, before the clay had settled on their grave?"

Sarah's sudden demise brought far-reaching changes to all their lives. Mary's mother's health continued to deteriorate and John could not be expected to wait on her as he was too busy out on the farm. Besides, it embarrassed her mother having John fuss about her. She had always seen herself as the pregnant servant girl, poor spiritless woman that she was, putting people about, embarrassing them by her one and only indiscretion. Mary did all she could but it was a strain, what with school attendance during the daytime and study in the evenings. It became too much for her. So at the end of one summer holiday, when it was time to go back to school, she decided to remain at home. As usual John did not become involved in the decision making, but was comforting in his support after Mary had made up her mind.

As for her mother, she was now in an advanced stage of illness, and yet she lingered on for a further two years. Then she began to lose her sight, and from that time on was reluctant to leave the bedroom. One evening she called Mary and said she would like to be taken out into the yard to drink a cup of spring water from the deep well at the bottom of the yard. Mary was surprised at how frail she had become. John ran to fetch the drink. She swallowed only the tiniest drop before asking to be brought back to her room. If anything, the little journey had weakened her and to Mary's disappointment brought no joy or uplifts to her spirits. That night, after the doctor had reported her situation as hopeless, she uncomplainingly passed away. John's old friend Donal Moran kept vigil with them throughout the night.

Mary loved everything about the farm work, the tractors, the milking, saving the crops, cutting and storing the silage. John let her do all the tractor work and they were very happy times for her.

She recalled now, as she sat at the table puffing on her half corona, how Donal Moran had come to sit with them one evening. He drew their attention to Mary's situation in the event of some chance event or incident, some fatal accident striking down John. Then what would be Mary's position? Not a man to mince his words, he spelled it out directly. He stressed Mary would have no rights whatever. He reminded them that relations, complete strangers, could come and take over. Mary would have no option but to leave the only home she had ever known and the farm she loved so much. These strangers would be within their rights in putting her out on the road.

Mary had never thought about it before and now after Donal had concluded she remained silent. She didn't think that it was her place to offer suggestions. However, she was quite frightened at the prospect as set out by him. She loved farming. She loved this place. She couldn't imagine herself in any other setting. It would break her heart if she had to leave. John listened attentively in silence and then said he would immediately have a word with a solicitor and the parish priest, Father Murphy whom he had found a good adviser in the past.

"After all," he said, "whatever I have here is going to be Mary's after my time."

The very next morning, he visited the bank manager and had Mary's name added to the account as joint owner. Mary was taken aback by the alacrity with which he set about settling his affairs and by his generosity. She now knew he cared a great deal about her.

She recalled the almost comical episode with the parish priest. He was 82 years old and had thick, wiry white hair above a square face. He looked gaunt and swung both his arms and feet out as he walked. On even the hottest day of summer Fr Murphy would wear a suit of clerical black, dog collar and a pair of heavy country boots laced up over his ankles. He was fond of a drop of whiskey and yet there were long periods of his life when he abstained totally. It was darkly whispered about that he fasted frequently and regularly did penance. He was a direct man and a holy man.

John had promised the priest a sum of money after Sarah's death and when he came out to the farm, he asked Mary how much money was in the envelope. She told him one thousand pounds. He declined to take it, saying he had come to advise John on the kind of assignment he should make to Mary, while at the same time, safeguarding John's own rights.

He would like a glass of whiskey and was partial to some seed cake, if Mary had any.

She did not, but she had a bottle of Scotch whisky.

"Is it a 12-year-old?"

Mary scurried off to the press where she found the mature liquid, and brought it in with some glasses.

Fr Murphy sank back into the easy chair, crossed his legs and swung one boot. He joined his hands as if about to offer up prayers. He pursed his lips and pressed the tips of his fingers against them. He was silent.

Mary could recall everything about that afternoon, including what was said and done. She poured the whisky."I'll leave now," she said, heading for the door.

"You'll do nothing of the kind," Fr Murphy said in his strong, rich voice."You'll stay right where you are. After all, this concerns you more than anyone else. You could put another drop into that glass and get me a few sweet biscuits."

Mary ran down to the kitchen and came back with a box of assorted biscuits which she opened and left beside the priest.

"Would you care for a drop of water or red lemonade in your drink, Father?" John asked.

"I'll have it the way it is, the way it was made, the way it was intended to be. If the men who distilled it wanted to make it watery, they'd have added the water themselves."

A further silence ensued. Mary sat down a little way behind the priest to his side from where she was facing John. John sat opposite the priest in anticipation of the advice he would give. In later years, Mary always burst out laughing whenever she told the story in John's presence. It was as if it was yesterday instead of 20 years ago.

"Well, father," John began hesitantly, "you have some idea of the problem we have here. I think Donal Moran was talking to you. Really, we want to know the best way to safeguard Mary's future interests in this place. What solicitor ...?"

"You'll be needing no solicitor, John Boyle," Fr Murphy cut across him."What age are you, John?"

Nonplussed, John stammered, "I'm 52, Father. That's right, Father, I'm 52."

"And Mary, what age are you?"

"I'm 22, Father."

"Well, I'll tell you now what I have in mind. You're both living under the same roof and farming and working together. And you know, but it isn't right. Do you know what people are saying, John? Do you know what they are saying? You can imagine, John, what they are saying."

Mary studied John's expression. He looked shocked.

"It's not right, John, that the two of you should be living under the one roof. That's the problem I have to address, and Mary's inheritance is the one you have to see to, John.

"You're fifty two and Mary's twenty two. You're still young enough, John, to have a family and when you're old and feeble, why Mary here will look after you, if you see what I'm getting at. And when her turn comes, why, the children will look after her. Now, what could be fairer than that? If anything happened to you, Mary here, your wife, would inherit everything."

With that he got up out of the chair, took hold of the whisky bottle, and stood over John where he was seated with the glass still untouched in his hand.

"Drink that, John Boyle."

There was a fair good measure in the glass. John looked at it apprehensively. He enjoyed a drink, but in moderation. He liked to sample it and spend a little time over it.

"It wasn't made for looking at." Fr Murphy was getting impatient."Will you drink it down?"

John put the glass to his lips and lowered the measure in one long gulp. Then, he shook his head wryly. Fr Murphy took the glass from him and proceeded to half-fill the long tumbler with a very large measure indeed. Then he turned and poured a liberal quantity into his own.

"Stand up, John Boyle. Stand up."

John got to his feet uncertainly. Fr Murphy faced him, glass in hand.

"Now. let's drink a toast to this wedding."

He clinked his glass against John's and stared at him in a daring manner.

"Bottoms up," he blurted and held John's stare. Raising his glass slowly, whilst still holding John's eyes, there was no way out for John. He gallantly lowered the drink without once taking the glass from his lips. Fr Murphy took him by the two hands.

"Congratulations, John. I know that it's the right thing to do.

"Mary," he walked over to her."You're a good girl and I know this is the right thing for you, too. As your parish priest, I wouldn't like you to disobey me. I know you won't. You'll be very happy here. You're that already."

CHAPTER 10

Mary never regretted it. She knew John didn't, either. Fr Murphy was a well-meaning man, affectionately known locally as one of the last of the old-style Irish parish priest, an endangered species.

And now, sitting at the table twenty years on, she acknowledged her strong affection for John. Affection. There was a false ring to the word. It didn't seem to meet the case – her feelings were much stronger than that. She loved him. She loved him despite the problem which had arisen, and which twenty years on she knew was insurmountable. From the start of the marriage, she had realised John had difficulties but, in her innocence, it never occurred to her, even obliquely, what the problem was. At first, it didn't concern her unduly, principally because she didn't understand precisely what was wrong.

When he had merely put his arm around her, on the first night of their honeymoon in the Gresham Hotel in Dublin, she was surprised more than disappointed. She had anticipated something more than an innocuous kiss, a mere peck on the forehead, when they were lying side by side in bed.

It never occurred to Mary that her husband, her noble John, was impotent. She knew nothing about such things. She had expected that John would turn towards her, would touch her, would want her. Perhaps, he was being reserved on this first night in deference to her maidenhood, her age, perhaps even the disparity in their years. She had anticipated a straightforward, uncomplicated, and beautiful act of love.

But after the second night, and every other unconsummated night thereafter, she lay in bemused and unrequited expectation, wanting him ... wanting him to want her. She prompted him as best she could in her innocence and shyness to no avail. Where now his turning towards her and touching her as she had dreamed? Where now his desiring her? Where now her dreams? Where now the first night of honeymoon with eager anticipation of him easing her out of her enticingly scented, specially selected frilly nightie? Of him touching her, of her bearing his weight and relaxing her legs slowly outwards and grasping him, and of them making love together?

After they arrived home from their ineffectual honeymoon, the pattern was the same. John still made no effort to make love to her, to seek her out amorously during the day, or to whisper sweet nothings in her ear. Was there something wrong with her, she wondered? She felt she had some idea of how it should be, and tried to coax John to respond to her approaches.

Just once in that first month, he turned towards her and put his hand on her nightdress. He pulled it up slightly and touched her leg with his fingertips. She held her breath and reciprocated by turning towards him, praying silently. Up along her thigh, his fingertips moved and she thrilled to his gentle touch. He sought out her arm and her shoulder, then suddenly pulled his hand away and turned over on his back, almost as if he was embarrassed.

More than anything, Mary wanted to give herself body and soul to her charming man, the man she loved and admired. The excitement drained from her as he turned away and she felt at a complete loss, utterly dejected.

Hard and embarrassing though it was for her to do so, she had the courage then to tackle John in as gentle a way as possible, for surely there had to be a problem with him. Or was it with her?

Perhaps, he didn't love her enough to desire her physically. Suppose he had married her simply so that their teamwork on the farm could continue without interruption, or worse still because he was sorry for her, or because he felt obliged to look after her.

She lay silently beside him, feeling inadequate. Her own experience was nil but she had seen enough of the farm animals – the bull, the ram, the stallion – to realise that John would have to have a firm penis to penetrate her.

She leant across and undid the centre button of his pyjama top and began exploring his upper body. She was shaking with pent-up emotion and experienced a twinge of excitement as her hand passed across and through the dense hair on his chest. Then downwards across his belly. Her fingers pulled open the string of his pyjama trousers. She moved her hand downwards, tentatively along his thigh. His body was hard and angular and stimulating to her touch, so different from the soft flabby texture of her own. Her hand crept upwards again and she made little circles with her index finger around his tummy button. Then down again, until her hand moved over and her fingers gingerly circled around his penis.

Dead as a maggot, it lay inert along the inside of his thighs.

She leaned across him and, cradling his head in her arms, told him she loved him and she always would. Bravely, she whispered that it didn't matter to her.

Now, all these years on, she recalled their conversation clearly.

"You know, it doesn't make any difference to me. You know that. It was just that I thought maybe you wanted to, and that you were waiting for me to give you the go-ahead."

She didn't believe that herself, but she wanted to continue the conversation now that it was started. Vaguely, she hoped they would come to some decision to resolve the problem with, perhaps, medical treatment, she didn't really know.

But all he answered was, "I'm sorry."

She detected a note of melancholy in his soft brown voice. "Who do you think we should talk to?" She tried to sound matter of fact, so the subject would not seem too secretive or shameful to John.

"Personally, I wouldn't like to talk to anyone." He spoke with uncharacteristic firmness.

"What would you say to Donal Moran, for instance?" Mary continued on gamely, pretending not to notice the rebuff.

"Oh, no! Definitely not Donal Moran."

"What about the parish priest then?"

Even before he replied, she felt the small advantage she had held for the briefest of moments was slipping from her grasp. She had overplayed her hand. She should have been gentler, more guarded in her approach.

"The parish priest!" He rejected her proposition out of hand, as if it were unworthy of discussion. It was most unlike John to be so resolute. Though a big man, and strong, he had always been courteous and amenable to her suggestions in the past, so obviously this subject pained him grievously.

"No, I wouldn't like to talk to the parish priest. In fact, I wouldn't like to talk to anyone about it, good, bad or indifferent. It would be much too embarrassing for me."

He had been lying on his back; now he turned sideways towards her and said, "And besides, as you say yourself, it doesn't matter that much to you. That being so, we'll leave things the way they are, in the name of God. We've been happy together up to now and I know we always will be."

Mary knew he was right. Unfortunately her longing for physical lovemaking became an obsession, more so after the doctor's prognosis regarding John. She comforted herself by thinking that older age would eventually dispel the longing and that with the passing of the years that the yearning would gradually abate. On this, her forty-second birthday, the desire was as strong as ever.

As if to reassure herself, she put her hand inside her blouse and felt the shape of her beautifully rounded breasts. They were still as they had been when she was a young woman, just as the juices secreted between her legs were, too. If anything the desire increased as the years passed. Frequently, she would go to the church to light a candle and kneel before the statue of the Virgin, and beseech the Virgin to take away this affliction. Then turning her head towards the tabernacle she would speak directly to God.

"Is it physical or mental, Jesus?"

Occasionally, she was conscious of a tiny voice sounding in her ear.

"Mary, it's as God made you."

In the strength of her implicit faith, she would stare back at the tabernacle and acknowledge that if God had thus fashioned her, then so she must endure.

Every single night in bed, as she lay beside him, her thoughts raced over the fanciful things she imagined a man would do to her. As she grew older, her thoughts turned to torrid encounters with young men – virile young men in their twenties – what she would want them to do to her and what they would do to her.

It galled her that she had passed up on the only opportunity which had come knocking on her door.

Young Joe Moran came calling one evening. Young Joe, Donal's son, who was now serving his nine-year sentence in Mountjoy Prison. It was the same evening that her husband John got an asthmatic attack and she was waiting for the doctor. John was gasping for breath in the bedroom when Joe dropped by, and he well inebriated. Mary thought he looked extremely handsome, with his tousled head of curls and devil-may-care appearance. As a boy he had spent a great deal of time out on the farm with John and Mary. Mary's love for Joe was of the innocent kind, the natural love for a friend's son. The moment he came into the kitchen, he put his arms around Mary and, facing her, began moving his hands across her back and down her buttocks. Though drunk, he wasn't the type of lad who would get awkward.

"Mary, I've been drinking all day and I'm in a terrible state for the other thing."

It was just typical of Joe, outspoken but not offensive. Mary turned laughingly away from him. He followed after her and grabbed her from behind, his hands around her. He began fondling her breasts, and momentarily Mary laid her head back towards him.

"Mary, you're a fine woman. Did I ever tell you that, Mary? You're a fine woman. Mary, there's a great shape to you."

She pulled his hands away and he made no effort to resist. She told him she was expecting the doctor for John at any moment. He sat up on the corner of the table and regarded her with a broad grin, not being able to fully take in the implications of her words.

"I hope you don't mind me, Mary. I'll tell you something, you're a fine woman. In fact, a very fine woman. Jesus, but you have a great body and legs, Mary. Do you know something, Mary, but you'd bring a longing on a snowman?"

Mary was in a dilemma. Should she tell him to wait until after the doctor had been? Should he get him a drink of whiskey to detain him? Should she tell him to wait a moment and she would run him home? She also told herself sternly that her husband came before anything else in her life, and she would always tend him first. She was shaking a little and at the sound of the doctor's car, her pent-up emotions drained out of her.

A few puffs of the inhaler and John's breath returned to normal. The doctor prescribed Ventolin or Bricanyl, and a Becotide inhaler to be taken.

When Mary returned to the kitchen, Joe had let himself out, and Mary realised she had let the opportunity slip. Or had she? If the opportunity presented itself again, what would she do? Perhaps, she would again find some excuse. However, it concentrated her mind to such a degree over the next few days that she found herself listening for Joe and hoping he might return. Another time, she would be glad he hadn't, and in the next moment she was sorry he didn't.

One evening, when she returned home late from work on the farm, John said, "Young Joe was over here a few moments ago. He's a gas man, is Joe. He had a sup of drink on him, too."

She pretended to show little interest and changed the subject. Her mind was racing and her breath was coming in short gasps. Could she go after him? How could she follow him?

John broke into her thoughts. "As I say, he had a good sup of drink on him. I just hope he'll be alright. I should have held on to him until you got back. We could've given him a bite to eat or something, maybe a bed for a bit. If he returns to his father in that condition, there'll be a terrible row."

Mary said nothing.

John said, "I wonder if he's gone home. Do you think we should check to see if he's still out on the road? Look, I'll get me shoes."

John was in his slippers, the paper in his hand, ready to settle in for the night.

"It's alright," she said at last."You stay where you are. I'll take the car, I won't be a minute."

She drove as far as the Morans' gate, and then, in case she was a little late, drove part of the way up the avenue, her eyes scanning the furthest point of the lights. There was no sign of him.

She had begun driving home when it occurred to her that perhaps he had gone in the opposite direction. So she drove that way, but again there was no sign of Joe. As she drove her breath was coming in short gasps, in anticipation of meeting him, and of what she might let him do to her.

Her stomach twitched as she drove a good two miles along the road, turned round, and returned. She drove past her own gate a second time. She knew deep down that she needed someone like Joe to edge her over the precipice of doubt and frustration to a place of fulfilment as a woman. She didn't doubt that she suffered pain because of her yearning for physical love and, at times, felt devastated because of the void in her life. It alarmed her that she also felt fear welling up inside her. She realised she needed someone like Joe in the worst possible way, to free her body and soul from the pain and torment.

"I couldn't find him any place," she reported on her return. "Maybe I should take another look in half an hour's time or so."

"Dammit, but where did he get to?"

After a while, John looked up from the paper."Did you try the other way?"

"No." For the first time in her life, Mary lied to John. She was immediately filled with remorse and, there and then, she told herself that she would not go out a second time, even though John was anxious. As soon as the half hour was spent, she stood up and announced she was going to give one last look.

She drove the same route as before and though she made a thorough search, somehow she knew she was not going to find him. As she approached a bend, she posed a question to herself. What would she do if she was to encounter him round the corner?

More pertinent, what would she do if he got into the car in the same amorous state as on the previous visit. She realised she had been holding her breath and when she blew it out, momentarily the windscreen clouded over.

What would she do? What would she do if Joe again put his arms about her and needed only the slightest encouragement to reach for the hem of her skirt? Tension and strain built up, and she was holding her breath again.

She shouldn't have waited as long as half an hour. It was too long.

CHAPTER 11

In her dreams and as she lay in bed nights thinking back as she was now doing, sitting at the table on her forty-second birthday, she imagined herself allowing, even encouraging, Joe to reach for the hem of her skirt. When back home later that evening long ago, in the peace and presence of faithful, reliable John in the light of their kitchen, surrounded by all the familiar objects of their domestic life, she had been relieved that she had failed to locate Joe.

On this, her forty-second birthday as she turned towards the electric kettle, a sound at the window startled her in the quietness of her isolated country home. She stood in the centre of the room staring at the drawn curtain. It was a tapping sound, coming from behind the curtain by the window pane. A rat? At this hour of the night, it had to be. A mouse, perhaps? No, the noise was too pronounced for a mouse. It could be a cat. Perhaps even a donkey could be attracted by the light behind the curtain? A person? She searched the crinkles in the curtain and quickly inspected the other curtains in the room for a sign of a chink in the material. She couldn't see out, but the slightest opening would allow someone on the outside a full view within, revealing her like a goldfish in a bowl.

The noise stopped. She went towards the window. The noise started again. Definitely, it was someone or thing tapping on the glass pane outside. She took a careful hold of the curtains without disturbing them and then tugged them back quickly to reveal – blackness.

Suddenly a nose, followed by a mouth and then a full face appeared, pressed against the pane, distorting it grotesquely, saliva from the open mouth began dripping down the window.

It was BoBo Doorley, face pressed against the pane, dripping saliva and laughing. Then she was gone, cackling loudly into the night. Mary stood silently, shocked and paralysed with fright, listening as the whooping and hollering faded into the silence of the night.

Too late, Mary noticed a cowstick resting against the wall.
If only she had had the presence of mind to grab it and chase
the mad bitch. She tried to regain her composure. A few cuts of
a stick might be more beneficial to that girl than a psychiatrist
counselling her on a couch. After all, the hospital rehabilitation
programme hadn't prevented the tinker from assaulting her
poor harmless mother and father many times.

She resolved to be ready another time. She was sure BoBo
would be back. She placed the cowstick near the door. Next
time that girl runs out of the yard cackling she'll have good
reason to, she thought.

Mary turned on the television. There was a late-night film
on. Some distorted head and body on the screen was turning all
colours, and bleeding and growling and frightening everything
in sight. It was enough to have to contend with BoBo Doorley
without having to watch that bloody stupid farce. It seemed
there was never anything else to watch beyond these unreal,
farfetched human monsters. They were of no interest to
Mary.

She switched to another channel. A small, fair-haired
northern European man was posing on a street corner in black
trousers, bare torso, and bare feet readying himself to kickbox
some thirty assorted other races of black, white and yellow
into a cocked hat. Mary took one look at the little perisher and
judged she would be well fit enough to take him on herself. Such
a load of rubbish. She didn't know too much about fighting,
but she had always thought blonde-haired Europeans were no
match for the speed, strength, mental agility and determination
of the black man, and yet, these farfetched films posed these
little gentlemen as supermen.

She turned it off. Were there no real life dramas in the world
any more, that people had to resort to that kind of absurdity for
entertainment? Was this modern age devoid of tales of valour
and romance?

Back home with her parents, BoBo gloated, telling them her
latest escapade.

"Coming home, I seen a light coming on in Mary Boyle's. Must a been about half past two. Light was shining out through a chink in a curtain. I put me tongue out and pressed me face flat agin the window. Then, I made a scraping noise agin the window. Well, didn't Mary pull back the curtain and there was my face and it all out a shape agin the window. I'm not joking you but she leapt with the fright. I let a scream out a' me and off up the road with me."

Never would Mary forget the embarrassment, the mental torture, the charade of John's hospital stay to investigate his problem. To this day, she still felt shame at the memory, for what he was put through. In truth, for what they both endured.

They had had no trouble in finding Dr Morley's residence. His wife met them at the doorway. She was a tall, attractive woman, pleasant, and unassuming. She brought them down to her kitchen, gave them a cup of tea, and put them at their ease. Her husband would not be long, she said.

When Dr Morley entered, Mary saw a small, corpulent, dapper man in his mid-thirties. He fussed a good deal and his movements were in sudden jerks. He didn't so much shake their hands as grab at them, shooting out his hand. Although he welcomed them, it was in a cold, formal voice. From that very moment, Mary took and instant dislike to him and felt unwelcome.

"Come this way, please," he ordered, almost snapping his fingers. "Tea can wait till another time."

They followed him into his surgery where he motioned them towards a leather bench seat along the wall.

"The purpose of this visit," he began coldly, "is to establish where we go from here."

Suddenly, he jumped out of his chair and stood confronting Mary.

"Does your husband have an erection?"

Mary was nonplussed.

"Come on, come on, Mrs Boyle. It's a simple question. Does your husband have an erection?"

The silence seemed interminable until Mary shook her lowered head.

"How can you be sure? How can you be sure he doesn't have an erection, Mrs Boyle?" he bounced the question back at her.

Mary searched about in her mind for the words to describe how she had put her hand over and across whilst John was lying on his back beside her, and the result of her investigation.

"I put my hand ..." Mary began disconsolately, finding it difficult to say the word.

He interrupted her with a bark.

"On his penis? Was it on his penis you put your hand, Mrs Boyle, or was it around his penis you put your hand?"

He lowered his head and glowered at Mary. Tears were forming in the deep recesses of her soul and making their way out through her eyes. She tried to suppress them, but the more she tried the more they spilled over her lashes and coursed down her cheeks, causing bright rings and blobs beneath her eyes.

He ignored her plight. "Come, come, Mrs Boyle, I must have an answer to a very simple question."

Mary shook her head despondently.

Next, the little doctor leapt to confront John.

"Let down your trousers."

With Mary's assistance and much pulling of braces and belt, John stood with trousers held thigh high, his pants still in place.

"The lot down."

He swooped down on John and taking his penis in both hands began to turn it this way and that. He pressed John's testicles and after that his groin. Next, he leapt back into the swivel chair, swinging one leg over the other and jerking backwards.

"You can get dressed now. Three days in Mount Carmel Hospital," he announced autocratically.

Always afterwards, Mary's biggest regret was in having put John through the ordeal – of being poked at and peered at by that obnoxious little man, and of his final hop, skip, and jump about the surgery after John's hospital sojourn.

"Hopelessly sterile, Mrs Boyle," he declared. "That's what your husband is, Mrs Boyle. Hopelessly sterile."

It was extraordinary that one so corpulent, ruddy complexioned and small could jump about the place with such vigour and dexterity.

"Hopelessly sterile, Mrs Boyle."

He gave an enormous leap into the swivel chair on the far side of the table and craned his neck, jerking his head as he declared, "That's all I'm sorry I can say to you. Your husband is a hopeless case."

He clapped his hands in rapid succession and laughed and guffawed as he sat across the table from her grinning like a panting, tongue-lolling dog mounting a bitch.

He said something about inserting a permanent pin-like instrument, but it would protrude. Mary wasn't listening. She was no longer interested. Not for her John any artificial gadget which would protrude. No, not for John, for she surmised there was more than physical to John's problem. After all, she had laid beside him now this many years and she knew that apart from the physical impotency, John suffered, too, from an impotency of the mind in matters sexual. Her own hopes were shattered. From that moment on she began to feel the loss of a physical love even more than before. Thoughts of active lovemaking began to occupy her mind to an extraordinary degree. Just like now, as she sat at the table on this her birthday.

Day in and day out and especially at night, she thought of her loss. Would it never end? How could she stop her lurid thoughts? Was there something wrong with her that her thoughts were so often directed towards men and being intimate with a man? Was it a sin to go on thinking like this?

Yet her love for John never abated. Though thirty years her senior, he was young in his ways and she knew he cared a great deal about her. It wasn't so much that he had grown accustomed to her being around but more that she knew he could not live without her. He had been fifty two when they had married, but his age had had nothing to do with his inadequacy. The doctor explained to her that her beautiful John had always

93

been impotent. She never told him of her feverish yearnings, of her need for sexual fulfilment, for physical love, because she did not want to offend or hurt him. At times, she felt an overpowering desire to have a child in her womb, to give birth, to suckle, rear, and fondle it. In fact, she never told him that. She had happiness, possessions and the love of John, yet there was emptiness in that special, delicate part of her life. At times, she felt she suffered unbearably mentally as well as physically for her unrequited passion.

She wondered if this obsessive state was not after all unnatural, if she didn't suffer from some abnormality. There wasn't anyone with whom she could discuss her problem. She believed as she grew older so the desire and the longing would lessen. Now she was forty two and the need was as great as ever. There was no let up, no lessening in her torment. If anything, the obsession increased with the passing of each year. It was a physical pain. It was an unrelenting mental agony, a constant ache.

Was there something wrong with her? Was it some stain or guilt she had inherited from her poor mother? Some inherited foible, some genetic weakness impregnated on her soul at birth? Or did other women, other men suffer the same pangs of passionate and wanton desire?

At times, she worried about confession, and was relieved when that Sacrament no longer played the crucial roll it once did in the affairs of the Catholic Church. No longer did John and she have to go to confession each month as nearly all Catholics once did – and lived in fear of mortal sin or excommunication or other dire penalty, if they absented themselves for twelve months. At least, the priests no longer berated their congregations as they once did on that matter. She was saved from the trauma of having to tell the priest at regular intervals of her thoughts and desires to have physical love with some man, having to promise that she would banish all such thoughts from her mind and, the hard bit, not to repeat them.

How could she explain to the priest that she often fantasised a physical relationship with a man? How she would let her thoughts drift and conjure up the actions of being taken by a man? How could she tell the priest every month how she imagined what it would be like to have a man lie on her, hold her, and that she often concentrated on what it would be like to experience his phallus entering into her vagina and that she was unable to banish the thoughts from her mind?

It was her most constant prayer, especially to the Virgin, to take away the torment. At times, she beseeched the Lord, and for some reason she could never explain she derived more strength when she pleaded her case direct to God, rather than to Mary. She found it easier to pray to Mary, *Muire na nGael*, Mary of the Gael. Perhaps it was because the priest, when she was a schoolgirl, had taught the children not to pray directly to Jesus, but through Mary, that Jesus mightn't hear little children's prayers. After all, he used to say, Jesus is the son of Mary and we all know that a son never refuses a mother's request. Mary often thought that it alienated her from the kind of warm relationship which she wished to have with God. Perhaps it was the Church's teaching through her priests which caused Mary to be awkward, uncomfortable when approaching Jesus with those kinds of problems which, with her strong and implicit faith, she believed could only be shared with Jesus and could only be atoned by Him. In the event, her prayers were nearly always directed to *Muire an nGeal*.

Alas, her supplications and entreaties, so devoutly offered up, went unanswered. She never gave up on her pleadings and believed implicitly that one day she would be rewarded.

Life had been good to her, she knew, and she counted her blessings. She and John had had a wonderful life together. No two people could have been closer, and she had no regrets about marrying him. On the contrary, if she were to start life all over again knowing all she now knew, she would more than ever choose her John. She reasoned that he was innocent of the problem which lay between them. It was a trauma which lay within herself and only she could resolve or endure it with dignity.

At times, she accepted, with a sense of shame, that she had inherited some abnormal sex drive. Not for one moment did she contemplate her state was that of an ordinary human being.

95

Whether through ignorance or upbringing or a combination
of both, she did not accept that the Creator Himself had so
fashioned her, and that she could no more change that state
than she could alter the shape, the beauty or the power which
lay within her breasts. The nuns had taught her and the
Catholic Church had taught the nuns that there was only one
kind of purity and that was purity in sex. Old priests banged
their pulpits in denunciation of over-indulgence in the sin of
sex. The sin of sex! That is what sex was and is, had been and
always will be in the eyes of the Catholic Church. A sin! That's
the way Mary was brought up. She sighed. Sex was a sin. It
followed from there that her thoughts were those of a sinner.
She lit another half corona.

Her ignorance brought about by programmed indoctrination
meant that it never occurred to her that she could have discussed
her problem, or that a counsellor or analyst could have explained
that her desires were perfectly natural instincts granted by the
Almighty One. That it was as normal a part of a woman's make
up as it was for a man to have sexual feelings. Not for the first
time, as she sat there in the early hours, she wished there was
someone she could confide in. There was no other woman with
whom she could reveal what she felt was her dire secret. She
couldn't even share them with her best friend, Donal Moran.
After all, who wants to expose their dark and infamous secrets
even to a best friend, she thought.

The next time Mary looked at the wall clock, it was after
half past four. Oblique shades of light were beginning to appear
across the land from the east and, in two hours or less, it would
be time to milk. No point in going to bed now. She extinguished
the last cigar and regretted having smoked it. They were a
great comfort at times like this, but she then felt more guilt,
for her mouth was left with a sour taste, her body with a mild
hangover, and her clothes were redolent of the acrid smell of
tobacco smoke.

She went upstairs to the bedroom. John was still sleeping
soundly and comfortably on his side. His chest was perfectly

clear. Not a trace of a wheeze. The Becotide was working wonders for him. Mary gathered up soiled socks, underwear, jeans and all the rest of yesterday's clothing for the washing machine, as Sarah had taught her – everyday a change of underwear and outer clothes, and sometimes twice a day.

And now, Mary recalled her again. Sarah would have Mary up at seven in the mornings to ride out the ponies. She could recall her voice as Mary rode around the paddock, Sarah striding around in the centre, wearing headgear and calling out the commands – "Never go near horses without headgear – Hands closer together – Shorter rein – A shorter rein, Mary – Don't bend down over his head – Don't bend down over his head, Mary – Sit up – Sit up straight, Mary – You're not looking at the jump, Mary – Keep your eyes on the centre of the next jump – On the centre of the jump, Mary."

Sarah was herself a fine horsewoman and taught Mary to be kind but to remember that a disciplined horse is a contented horse. John didn't share their enthusiasm for riding but almost every Sunday, he brought them and their ponies to a gymkhana. Though strong and gentle, few people could handle a spirited horse as well as John. He would secretly carry around in his pockets pieces of sugar and apples for the horses, so that when they all three would go out into the fields, the ponies always betrayed him by making a beeline for him.

"I wonder why that is, now," Sarah would ask of Mary pretending to be offended. Mary would look to John who would press his fingers to his pursed lips and shake his head.

After a lengthy pause Mary would say, "I just can't tell why it is."

"No, nor I can't either," Sarah would respond crossly. "Whatever either of you do, never feed sugar lumps or apples to those horses. It spoils them," she would add.

Thinking of those happy, bygone days reminded Mary she had not been exercising the ponies of late, what with one chore and another she had been neglecting them. Perhaps, there would be time to lunge at least three of them before cow time. Streaks of light from the east were beginning to turn night into day.

After levering the milk churns onto the steel platform in readiness for the pickup lorry, Mary returned to the kitchen to find John putting the breakfast of bacon and sausages onto two plates heating on the Aga cooker.

"Good morning, me auld love," he greeted her with a glass of chilled orange juice, "and happy birthday."

"Thank you, darling. You're up early."

"It's after half eight," John replied as though surprised.

"Oh! Is it that late? I've a confession to make. You know but I wasn't in bed at all last night."

He looked concerned as he searched her face.

"Oh, there was nothing wrong," she answered quickly with a laugh."I was just going to bed when who drove into the yard only Donal Moran and he drunk out of his mind."

"Oh, the poor man! You got him a feed and a few cups of coffee. Why didn't you call me and I'd have run him home. You know what I think of that man."

"The divil a run home! I did me living best to get him out of the car and into the house. Not a bit of him would go for me. As soon as I tried to get the keys from him, off out the avenue he drove like the wheels a hell and the driver's door flying open."

"Do you think should we ring the house?"

"No, need to. If anything had happened, they'd have been onto us by now.

"Then I had another visitor. I was sitting up drinking a mug of coffee and smoking when I heard a kind of a knocking or scraping at the window. That window there."

"Knocking? What time was that?"

"It must have been after two o'clock."

"Well?"

"I pulled back the two curtains and there was mad BoBo and she jeering at me through the window and pressing her face against the glass and spitting like a wild cat."

"We could do without that one around the place."

"There's a good cowstick there in the corner, and she's a lucky girl I didn't spot it before she disappeared."

"Don't get involved with that girl at any level, no matter what you do. She'd be highly dangerous. Don't draw that one on us whatever you do."

"She won't bother me too much. If she starts coming around here, I'll do more for her with a few welts of that stick there than all the doctors and tablets have done for her up to now."

John didn't consider mad Bobo's nocturnal prowling about the place as trivial and wasn't at all happy with Mary dismissing the matter so derisively. He was collecting his thoughts to explain to her that mad BoBo was better avoided than confronted when she changed the subject completely.

"You know the piebald, the mare? Well, she's looking to be serviced again. They're the only class of an animal which is fetching anything like a decent price at the present. We should try and cross her with a good strain of a jumper."

"Do you want me to bring her over to Clooncy Stud? They've every class of a stallion there at the moment. I hear nothing but good reports," John said.

"I'd rather you'd take a look at the fencing at the far end of the horse paddock. It looked loose to me this morning, but I didn't inspect it close up. I have her in the stable with Jonnie, one of the geldings, he walked in after us. She'll be quiet with him in the adjoining box. Still, she was trying to chomp at him through the bars. She can snap all she likes at poor old Jonnie. He just stands there looking at her."

"You're a great girl," John said.

Mary loved to hear John say that to her. He had been telling her so since she had been a little girl and it still brought a flush of pride to her when he looked at her and said, "You're a great girl, Mary."

They finished a leisurely breakfast listening to the nine o'clock news. John had a final slice of brown toast thickly coated with honey. Mary stayed with a few slices of Ryvita lightly spread with butter.

After breakfast, she hitched the four-wheeled horsebox to the jeep and set off for Clooney Stud. Driving up the avenue of the stock farm, a stallion kept pace with her galloping just inside the studded fence. She drove slowly past the farmyard on her right and pulled up outside the stables. A farmhand came from the yard beyond.

"Is it a mare you have there, Mrs Boyle?"

"I've a lovely piebald lady here, Tommy."

"Then you'll be looking for a jumper."

"I hear you've a good one."

"The best! The very best! We're getting great results."

"Do you keep many of them?"

"We've eight at the moment. That's the lad you'll be wanting there in the paddock."

He threw an admiring glance over Mary.

"I think that he's already taken a shine to the both of you."

Mary liked being complimented. She looked up at the lad and smiled.

He asked, "Is she quiet?"

"I only have a head collar on her. It's her fourth time."

"Well then, I wouldn't thank that dam to step out and open the gate herself."

"I'll lead her out," Mary said opening the door at the front of the horsebox.

"Whoa pet! Whoa pet!" Mary called soothingly to the mare."Whoa there! Whoa there!"

To her surprise, the mare dragged her towards the gate and fought her grip on the head collar.

"You're always safer with the bit and bridle. There's not the same control with them auld head collars. And at the end of the day, they're only animals, we always say here," the lad said.

He opened the gate and entered the horse paddock, leaving the gate ajar. He kept a wary eye on the stallion, in case it became dangerous with the mare being around.

The mare continue to drag her towards the gate, and just as the lad had suggested, she had little control without the bit and bridle. For a moment, it looked as if the mare would jump the high fence but at the last moment thought better of it and turned about, dragging Mary with her past the gate.

The stallion remained relatively calm, but every time he whinnied the mare waxed more excited as he kept up a constant ululation calling on her to join him in the paddock. The mare began rearing, twisting and turning dangerously close to the strong wooden paling.

"Slip the head collar off her altogether," the lad called out.

Mary struggled to undo the head collar strap and the mare fought against her.

Mary had no fear of animals. She had been thrown off more times than she could count. She had once been cornered by a young stallion in a closed stable and received a nasty bite from him, but she had not panicked . On another occasion a mare, just after giving birth, drove at her with her teeth flashing, but again she hadn't panicked. Each time she blamed herself. She had been brought up to respect animals and never to ill treat them. Right now, she blamed herself again.

"I'll manage." As she said it, the strap came undone, and off came the head collar. Immediately the mare made off in direction of the stallion. Quick as a flash, the lad opened the gate wide and let her in. She raced straight at the stallion snapping at his withers. He was quick to avoid her. She chased after him, again chomping at his withers. The stallion came up behind her. She lashed out at him with her heels.

At that moment, another man appeared.

"That mare seems vicious," he said. "I hope she doesn't damage the horse. Did you get all the particulars before you took her in to be serviced?"

Since the man was a considerable distance back, the lad pretended he didn't hear him.

"That's the boss," he said to Mary. "There'll be trouble."

The stallion galloped majestically down the field, his raised tail floating out behind him, his head held high. The mare chased after him. As he turned to come back, she drove at him again with her teeth stripped. Again, he narrowly avoided her and galloped back up the park. This time she cantered alongside him still chomping at his neck. Then, he dropped behind, so he was now chasing after her. She was slowing down as if she had suddenly lost her way. Suddenly she stopped altogether, but the stallion continued on and plunged at her. Lunging up into the air, he landed on her back and, at the same time, he drove his jack up into her. Mary was taken aback at the manner in which the mare stood quietly and meekly for him, she that had been so contrary minutes before and now merely whinnied.

The lad turned and shouted back at the man behind.

"They'll be all right now, Boss. There'll not be a bother on them. As for them auld papers, sure I've know Mrs Boyle here for years. She has all the particulars."

Turning to Mary he said, "Leave her here for an hour or so. I'll tell you what. I'll phone you when I think she's holding. You're on the phone, I suppose?"

The stallion, not yet detached from the mare, was audibly grunting and the mare was standing quietly for him.

"Could you write it down there with today's date, and the mare's name as well. We'll have the papers ready for you when you come back. It'll be time enough then to talk about the fee."

It was just part of another day's work for the groom, but Mary found her hand was shaking as she began to write out the particulars. She knew that it wasn't the lack of sleep which had given rise to these unexpected, albeit mild, tremors, or her struggles with the intransigent mare for that matter. It had to do with the stallion's leap onto the back of the mare and the way he plunged his jack up into her, which had brought about Mary's uneasiness.

CHAPTER 12

As she neared the house, Mary noticed a fast car in her rear view mirror rapidly catching her up. Instead of trying to overtake, it tucked in behind. When she signalled to turn right into her own entrance, the driver behind did likewise. She couldn't make out who it was. The car followed the horsebox into the yard and pulled up beside her.

It was only then that she recognised Peter McGinty, the local auctioneer.

"Hello Mary, and how is life with yourself and that good man of yours?"

He was laughing and full of the joys of spring. He stepped out of the car and opened the jeep door for her.

He shook her hand warmly and laughed again.

She asked him bluntly, "And what brings you out to see us?"

It seemed to cause him great merriment, for he shook with loud laughter.

"I decided to call on the wealthy of the countryside to see how they live. Sure you know what brings me out."

"Well, I don't," she answered truthfully. She concentrated for a moment.

"I'd say you're going to try and sell us something. Perhaps O'Donoghue is getting tired of growing ragwort in them fields at the back of the farm."

"You're a shrewd woman, Mary Boyle. A shrewd woman. Only this very day, he was in with me."

Too late, Mary realised she had been imprudent in showing an interest in the land. John would be disappointed with her.

"Is the big man himself within?" He put an arm behind Mary and escorted her towards her own kitchen door. John was inside struggling with a small piece of farm machinery on the kitchen table.

The auctioneer greeted him by standing in the middle of the kitchen and laughing heartily. It wasn't an offensive laugh, but one which he had acquired. He had picked it up at one of those business seminars geared to convert every struggling salesman into a multi-millionaire. Sometimes the organisers themselves acquired a modicum of wealth. In any event at one such, Peter McGinty was told that the best way to approach anyone, especially a stranger, with the intention of doing business, is to greet that other with a smile. It costs, so the organiser reminded them, nothing. There was only one asset more valuable than the smile, so Peter learned, and that was a jolly good laugh.

"Mary here tells me I've come out to sell you O'Donoghue's few acres up here at the back of your place. Smart girl she is, for only this very morning the same Xavier O'Donoghue was in with me to place it on the market."

He looked at John and laughed loudly.

Access to O'Donoghue's fields of thirty acres was gained by a laneway which cut through and divided a field of Boyles. O'Donoghue allowed animals to graze the laneway and there were always cattle breaking down fences. Sometimes, they also broke out into Boyle's farm. It was irksome to say the least having cattle driven through part of their land, and animals left to graze on the laneway without fences being broken down as well. Altogether, having to contend with the laneway was an aggravation.

John had often discussed the possibility of buying those thirty acres. Unfortunately, he could never enquire openly, because it wouldn't be healthy to let O'Donoghue know he was keen to acquire them. Better by far to leave him under the impression that John Boyle had no interest whatever in the lands.

John, though, was always careful not to have words with O'Donoghue about the fencing or trespassing stock lest some day he might want to sit down across a table to make a deal. He knew it was easy to shake hands with a friend across a table, but sometimes impossible to get an enemy even to the table. For this reason, John reluctantly courted a friendship which he didn't particularly value.

Strong as these reasons were for acquiring the holding there was another which far outweighed any other or all of them together a hundred fold. It made the purchase of the thirty acres imperative for John Boyle.

John's father had been an alcoholic and, as a young man, had got into serious financial difficulties. He was forced to sell those lands to a grandfather of the present O'Donoghue for a mere pittance, which was how the laneway situation came about. O'Donoghue had had to have a right of way for his animals and carts to pass to and from the holding.

It was all recorded in a Deed of Conveyance, a deed poor Sarah had once referred to as being a document of shame for every member of the Boyle family past or present.

Now, John was being given the opportunity of reclaiming the lands, of cancelling the deed of shame and, more importantly still, of redeeming the family honour.

He would have to stand tall. At the same time, he must not betray his anxiety to purchase to this auctioneer. He must not allow himself to be browbeaten into paying an exorbitant price and have the countryside laughing at how the O'Donoghues had hoovered the Boyles twice over the same parcel of land.

"What do you have to say to me now, John Boyle? What do you have to say to me?"

Peter McGinty clapped his large hands together loudly.

"Well, John Boyle." He clapped his hands again and rubbed them together and laughed merrily."What do you have to say to me now?"

"I s'pose at this hour of me life it's selling land I should be."

McGinty knew the game well. He had played it every day of his life this past twenty five years, and more. He enjoyed these little jousts, especially with farmers who always seemed to underestimate him. Right now, he was at an advantage for he knew the history of the land. He had taken the trouble of finding that out before embarking on its sale. However, he wouldn't mention it yet, not for a while at least!

He had also learned John Boyle was a proud man, and important as land was to a farmer, the other matter was of greater interest still. He further reckoned that John Boyle would be under the glare of local interest. People would be watching to see how strong John Boyle would be, if asked to walk the line.

So Peter McGinty, auctioneer and estate agent, wasn't in the slightest perturbed when John Boyle said his health might prevent him from entering into further farming commitments. Indeed, he might if anything curtail his present undertakings, rather than extend them. He noted dispassionately how Mary, encouraged by what she perceived as John's progress, added, "We were thinking of getting out of the cows altogether."

Dealing with farmers for quarter of a century, Peter acknowledged that, as a class, they were the very toughest of negotiators. But then, they had more practice than any other group except for the professionals such as himself, and they sometimes forgot he was a professional. Besides, he could appreciate a transaction with dispassionate assessment.

Peter could teach a psychologist how to assess a man, how to know what a man was thinking, and what way a man would act or react under pressure. Few were as adapt at applying pressure as Peter. It required subtlety, cunning and a knowledge of human nature.

There was a family called McCarthys living some half-mile or so from Boyle's farm, a father and three sons who had gained a reputation as troublemakers. Peter didn't know them, but they had been in court a few times recently over fencing. They had also been involved in a case where they were charged with assault on a neighbour over trespassing animals.

Peter McGinty looked at John and asked him directly, "How much is it worth, John?"

"Worth? Worth? Sure a man would have to be thinking of buying to be thinking of putting a price on it."

Peter McGinty burst into a paroxysm of loud laughter as though it was the funniest thing he had ever heard.

He turned towards Mary and asked, "What would you say it's worth, m'dear?"

"Well," she ignored his familiarity, "as John said I'd want to be buying it, wouldn't I, if I was going to put a price on it."

Peter McGinty sat into a chair at the end of the end of the table as if settling himself in for a lengthy session of cut and thrust bargaining so beloved by farmers. John moved to a chair opposite him. He was well pleased at the way the deal was progressing. He hadn't given anything away. Mary, too, believed things were moving favourably, and was just about to suggest a drink or a cup of tea, when Peter McGinty, sounding conciliatory, looked straight at John. There was no sound of laughter now in his quiet voice. His eyes were riveted on John.

"What would you say to seventy five thousand pounds, John and Mary?"

"Seventy five thousand pounds," exclaimed John.

"Seventy five thousand pounds," John and Mary echoed in unison and feigned shock.

"That's a ridiculous price." John took up the deal. There's no way I'd give that sort of money for them few acres. Ridiculous. Absolutely ridiculous. You're in the wrong house now, if you're looking for that kind of money."

Mary didn't speak. She approved of the way John was manoeuvring. It was a high price to start with but John would work him down and with any luck a bargain would be struck at a reasonable price before the day was out. Again, she was about to rise and bring in a tray of drinks and tea things, when McGinty passed a remark which she knew, but thought that McGinty would not, cut John Boyle to the quick.

"Money works two ways against farmers and land. Firstly, farmers sell out their holding because they need money and secondly, farmers can't buy when they sometimes might want to because of a shortage of money."

He denied John an opportunity of responding by standing up unexpectedly.

"Well, if you're not interested, there's no point in my staying around. I'm not the kind of auctioneer who tries to put pressure on people. It was just that your neighbours thought you might be interested."

Mary looked to John with considerable alarm. Twice now in as many minutes, the auctioneer had touched on a raw nerve. He would have no reason to offend John, besides he would know nothing about what had happened some sixty or seventy years ago. Yet to Mary, it seemed as though he was implying the neighbours were looking to John Boyle to redeem the family honour and to ensure there wouldn't be a shortage of money in the Boyle household, second time around, as there had been all those years ago.

"Tell me – do you know people as lives somewhere near here called McCarthys? I believe ,they're interested. Doesn't news travel fast? I'm told they live out this way. What sort of people are they, I wonder?"

All this time his eyes were boring into John's, and every now and then, he threw a furtive glance in Mary's direction.

"A man and his three sons I believe. Do you know who I'm talking about, Mary?"

Mary wasn't listening now to half of what was being said. He had left both her and John reeling. Though his voice was subdued, it was compelling and grated unevenly on Mary's nerves. She couldn't think. She knew only that the McCarthys as neighbours would be totally unacceptable. She knew there was something which she should be suggesting or saying but her mind blanked out. Peter McGinty had to repeat the question but he did so in a quiet respectful voice.

"Do you know them, Mary?"

"Mmm … yes. I know them all right. They're not too far from here at all."

"Where would I find them?"

"Go straight up the road here until you come to a four cross road. Take the turn to your left, and it's the second farmhouse on your right."

"I'll give them a try. If we can make a price or anywhere's near to it, I'll let her off. It's all the same to me who buys as long as the old fees are paid at the end of the day. Isn't that what it's all about, John? We'll get no money for talking."

He was off into raucous laughter again and gone through the door without another word.

John Boyle's world fell in around him and, for a moment, he could neither stir a limb nor utter a word. He was thunderstruck.

His first words on regaining some of his composure were, "The McCarthys! The McCarthys! Surely to God, we're not going to have them as neighbours."

"Do you think would he ever sell it to them this evening, without giving us another shot at it," Mary asked. "We should have held onto him longer."

At that moment, Peter McGinty reappeared through the door and ,by the way he pulled up suddenly, it was as though he might have heard some of their conversation, for he stood for a moment beholding them in mild surprise.

"By the way, in case you should change your minds, I'm off on a little holiday in a few days time and I aim to have this place gone before I head off."

He disappeared as quickly as he had returned, calling over his shoulder as he went, "Take care." And he was gone. His loud laughter echoed after him out into the yard.

Mary felt she should pursue him, but her head was addled and her feet leaden and she couldn't think straight. John had got out of his chair on the auctioneer's return, and now collapsed back into it like an empty sack.

"We've got to do something and that mightily quickly," he said. "We can't have those McCarthy's as neighbours."

"I'll tell you what," Mary said. "I'll put a call through to Donal Moran. He'll advise what best to do."

CHAPTER 13

"You have to buy that land. Tell John I said you just have to buy it." Donal Moran was adamant on the phone even before Mary had mentioned anything about the McCarthys. She knew that he would care for the McCarthys as neighbours as little as she and John did. He would not want them that close to his rolling acres, divided only by the River Barrow.

"It's very run down and needs attention," she said, "so it's probably not worth much."

"But it's what it's worth to you," he counselled, "and you'll get it right with a bit of attention."

"Faith, and it needs that, all right! Look at all those ditches spreading out halfways across some of the fields through neglect. Not a drain cleaned these twenty years and more. Not a fence or a gate to call their own. I don't believe there's a gate on it. All that takes money. And who is going to do it? It's not work for a woman, and I won't have John killing himself up there for any land. He's not able for that kind of work anymore."

"You'll get a man will do that. We'll get a man alright. I'll get you a man. That's not important anyway at the minute. What's important is that you buy it."

"What's it worth?"

"What price did he ask you?"

"Seventy five thousand pounds. I'll tell you but it's a big price for a rundown parcel of land."

"It is a big price. What did you bid him?"

She avoided the question. She didn't want to tell him they'd messed it up and the auctioneer was gone to speak to the McCarthys.

"And the car needs changing as well," she hedged.

"Mary Boyle." There was a hint of impatience in his voice. "Do you intend to buy that land or not?"

"What do you think we should pay for it?"

"You pay what you have to pay for it, and that's the value of it as well. The price you have to pay. Has he anyone else for it?"

There was a pause at Mary's end of the line.

"Are you there, Mary? Hello? Hello?"

"Of course I'm here. He mentioned something about McCarthys."

"McCarthys? McCarthys? What McCarthys? Do we know them?"

"Ah, I'd say you'd have heard tell of them all right. They live just up the road from us here."

She knew that he wouldn't be too happy at the prospect of having the McCarthys as neighbours, but she had no conception their reputation would evoke such anger. He erupted on the other end of the phone.

"For hack's sake, Mary! You and John should have handled the auctioneer more astutely."

"There's no point in talking like that," she remonstrated. "We are anxious to buy the land. What do we do now?"

"You need to phone the auctioneer now and look for an appointment in about an hour's time. Ring me back and I'll go along with you."

"I hope you'll be more sober than you were last night."

"Who told you?"

"You called on us sometime after midnight."

"I don't remember a thing."

"You were in no fit condition to be out on the roads. I could do nothing with you. You hit the door of the car a terrible belt off our gate driving out onto the road like a mad lunatic."

"Ah sure, I know. I should never drink. I can't remember one thing where I was last night, or who I was with, or what I did from the time I was in the pub in the village. I was worried about the door. I couldn't remember a thing. I was about to phone the Gardaí and report the damage to them."

"Whatever you do don't phone that creep of a Sergeant. Phone Garda Jim Furlong. That's a decent lad."

"There's no need to phone anyone now that I know what happened. Ring me back as soon as you get through to that auctioneer."

Two days of hard bargaining and much vain posturing followed, until finally a deal for £68,150 was agreed. A condition of the sale was that John and Mary would be given possession of the lands before the closing date so that they could begin reclamation work. The deal resulted in much drinking to one another's health, hand shaking, fuddled compliments and wishes of the very best.

However, on the journey back home, John was struck with an acute asthma attack and the inhaler had been forgotten in the excitement of the bargaining.

Mary helped John out of the car and to the electrically-operated nebuliser in the house, there for just such a severe attack. It gave excellent results but John always suffered headaches after using it. The attacks were becoming more frequent of late and Mary was afraid the medication might not always arrest the symptoms, which would mean hospitalisation. She consulted the doctor again on the following day and he recommended a stronger Becotide to be taken four times a day, each dose comprising two inhalations.

Later that evening Donal Moran phoned to say he had made a deal with a contractor. The man would cut new drains and breast back all the ditches on the newly acquired lands. As promised, he had also found a good man to do the fencing, the son of a farmer friend of his from the far side of Tullamore. The lad was immigrating to the States at Christmas and would be grateful of the job and the few bob before departing. He assured Mary and John that they would find him to be an industrious young man.

Two days later, the contractors began cutting new trenches and reopening old unused drains with a dragline, and set about breasting back the overgrown hedges and ditches with a mechanical hedge cutter.

That night Donal Moran arrived into John and Mary's kitchen accompanied by a man who looked to be in his late twenties or early thirties. Slightly built, he walked with a limp on his right leg. His dark and plentiful hair was parted to the side and brushed firmly down into place with hair oil. He was neatly, even daintily dressed in pink shirt and dark navy tie.

He didn't look strong enough to Mary for digging into heavy soil and through tough scrub with a spade. He wasn't dressed for tackling hard manual work. He didn't look the average navvy and she certainly couldn't imagine him wielding a sledgehammer to drive in fencing posts.

He smelled faintly of aftershave lotion and as he came into the kitchen the aroma of eau de cologne preceded him. Then to her astonishment, she noticed a suitcase dropped behind him in the doorway.

Donal Moran introduced him: "David Stapleton from over beyond Tullamore."

"You're very welcome," John greeted him warmly.

The young man stepped forward and shook hands first with John and then with Mary, who noticed his bright eyes smiling as he momentarily held her gaze. He said nothing.

"He hasn't a car or a motor bike, so I told him to pack a case and you'd surely have a spare room for the few weeks he'll be clearing up that auld job for you. If not, there's plenty of room over in my place and he can come across at night."

"That won't be necessary, Donal. You've done enough for us already. Of course, we have a spare room here," Mary said, turning towards David Stapleton and throwing an eye over him.

She hoped her shock didn't show for, looking at him, she was suddenly afraid that she would have two semi-invalids living under her roof. She turned aside to the dresser and brought out a bottle of whiskey and glasses and, from the refrigerator beside it, she produced bread and began cutting up sandwiches.

The new man stepped forward, and asked, "Where do you keep the butter?"

Amused, Mary silently went to the cupboard and handed the butter dish to him.

He began spreading it on the bread slices she had just cut and, in a few moments, was making sandwiches of ham and tomato. She watched with interest and ill-disguised curiosity as he cut the crusts off the bread and placed them neatly on a plate before withdrawing quietly to a chair at the bottom end of the table.

"You're a dab hand in the kitchen."

Her comment was more in the nature of a mild barb than a compliment. She found it odd that this stranger being introduced as a manual worker wasn't two minutes in her kitchen when he was preparing sandwiches.

"All boys in our family. Eight of us. Mother died when we were little chaps. So we just had to learn to work the kitchen as well as the land. One way or another, it's all the same to us."

Mary almost laughed aloud. The thought struck her that he might be more suited for the domestic chores and that would release her to do the fencing and the cutting of the drains.

"Before I go, and I can't wait too much longer," Donal said, already moving for the back door, "you mentioned awhile back that you had a blocked drain at the head of the road. Let me have a look at it."

Mary walked chatting to him the short distance to the road, with David Stapleton taking up the rear a pace behind them.

A drain which ran parallel to the avenue was full of water. They crossed over the road to the far side but, because of briars and shrubs, they could not get down into it. As they crossed back over the road, BoBo Doorley was walking towards them. Mary spotted her and immediately turned her head in the opposite direction. The two men didn't notice her so intent were they on discussing the drains.

Donal Moran went to climb down to inspect where the blocked drain crossed under the roadway on the avenue side.

"Leave it until the morning," David Stapleton urged him. "I'll take a look at it then. You'll not be able to do anything about it tonight anyway."

"I suppose you're right." Donal agreed climbing back up the bank. "I need to hurry back to the jobs at home anyway."

I just hope, Mary thought to herself as they proceeded back towards the house, that this new man isn't one of those "never do today what you can put off until tomorrow" sort of workmen.

CHAPTER 14

BoBo quickened her pace. She believed those people had deliberately snubbed her. Right now, she was in two minds about confronting them. As she reached the gate, they were just beginning to stroll up the avenue, their backs to her.

Mary Boyle turned and, on seeing BoBo standing at the gate, she again turned her head away without greeting.

"They're some crowd to ignore a neighbour out walking along the road," BoBo thought, her volatile temper rising. "Where the hell do they think they get their airs and graces from? Bastards, the both of them. How dare that one turn her head away? Who does she think she is? I'm every bit as good and better, if it comes to that than the both of them put together."

Her attention was taken up by the slightly built stranger walking along side them. "Or than you either, Hopalong Cassidy." And she laughed scornfully.

Then, she got vexed again. Saliva began to dribble from her mouth as she muttered, "I'll take youse down a peg or two in the not too distant future. I've a plan. It's forming in me mind. It's nearly complete. And be the time I'm finished with youse, yez'll not be so high and mighty."

In her anger, she was walking slowly but with determined steps into the entrance of the avenue and, with each step, she was making a conscious wish of evil intent towards Mary and Donal, as she argued away to herself, her voice rising heard only by herself.

"You weren't so high and mighty last night, Donal Moran, the night of the big wind and you out in your big car blind drunk, not knowing where you were going to or coming from.

"You were that drunk you drove up on a ditch and didn't know how to drive it. You didn't know I got into the car beside you, you were that drunk. I put that big hand of yours up between me two legs and all you could do was pull it away and groan and try to give me a slap in the gob. I gave you a right good belt across the face and I put your hand back again between me legs and you so drunk you didn't know what was happening. Bet you don't know that, you and your airs and graces.

"And you thought to push me out of the car; but I tripped around to your side, whipping me knickers off as I went and leapt in on top of ye and got me legs around ye and I started to jiggy jig on you. Just like when we used with some o' them auld fellahs in the Mental when they'd be snug in the bed and the nurses wouldn't be looking, and bedad, sometimes when they would be looking, get me legs around them and jiggy jig on them.

"That's what I was doing to you, Donal Moran, for all your grand ways, and it was only minutes after I'd had it hard. That's the breed of a woman that's in me. You were fighting me but I was fighting you twice as hard and bobbing up and down. You weren't able to push me off, with me back to the steering wheel and I jammed agin you. I was ready to jiggy jig with you there and then, only that car come and I made off up the road. You'll not get off so lightly next time."

She was now standing just inside of the gate with the speech pouring out aloud in a wild uncouth torrent of words.

"That's all you meant to me. Just an auld drunken fool with me legs wrapped around your hands and knees and makin' me way up towards yer face and head. You were no more to me than an auld patient in the Mental. I had me legs around ye, and ye weren't fit to get me off."

She remained just inside the gate for a moment longer swinging her arms about her wildly and making little darting steps this way and that whilst spitting out the words with vitriolic hatred. The saliva had turned to froth at the corners of her mouth. Then a thought occurred to her.

Donal Moran might shortly be driving out from the Boyles and along the road on his own. Which way would he be going? Back towards his own house, she reckoned. His posh manor house! She determined now to wait up the road for him, present herself as he approached in his car.

She had only gone a few steps when she heard the car swinging down the avenue and turning in her direction. She stepped off the grassy, ill-kept path so she was well out on the narrow road facing him, her hand raised half in salutation but more in expectation of his recognising her and stopping in response to her unconcealed gestures and gesticulations.

The car slowed down momentarily as it neared her and then to her chagrin picked up speed again, narrowly missing her outstretched arm. She ran a few steps after the rapidly disappearing car, shaking her fists and screaming foul-mouthed profanities after him.

"Oh, you look frightened now, do you? I'll give you reason to be. You don't want to be seen with the likes o me, do you? You'll befriend that hoity-toity Mrs Boyle. She'll tell you not to have anys things to do with me. Bet you can't even remember last night ..."

CHAPTER 15

It was the night after the big wind that BoBo walked the road again in search of the big man or, as she liked to call him, the spirit. She waited patiently at the gate where she had first encountered him and where he had made violent love to her. She didn't as yet admit that he had forcibly molested and raped her. She told her parents of the incident as a warm, torrid love affair between two adult people. It was the way she liked to think of the incident. She was after all a willing accomplice, not realising then, or admitting now that he would have taken her whether or not she wanted him to. In any event on this following night, she was disappointed by his failure to show up. She waited patiently at the gate, before deciding he wasn't coming.

Back home, she drank a cup of tea and then, although it was almost three in the morning, she set out a second time in search of him. She was more surprised than disappointed, on that second night when he didn't show up. She tried to understand that he might have had some valid excuse which made it impossible for him to return.

Perhaps, it was that he was afraid to show up in case she might set a trap for him, betray him or report his activities to the Gardaí. Suppose he now considered that he had roughed her up unduly and was afraid to return. If he thought that, then he didn't know her. Surely, he must have felt in her passion that she yearned for him and had a great need for him. She knew he did, too, by the wanton demands which he had made on her in his uncontrollable desires. If they were two of a kind, and she believed they were, then why was he not returning?

She continued her lone vigil, but as night followed night and she came breathless around that same corner anticipating the scent of tobacco smoke or the distant spark of a cigarette, she was again disappointed, sadly disappointed, monstrously disappointed, so much so that her blighted hopes began to turn to anger.

She was facing a serious problem. How was it she always had problems? How was it she seemed to be the only one in the locality who came up against serious problems? This was the most serious she had ever faced. It was a complexity of gigantic proportions and needed careful thought, intense concentration. She found it confusing to try and put the pieces together and it hurt her head when she over concentrated. She had to work this thing out on her own. If she went to the Gardaí, would the big man, on hearing that she had reported the matter, want to contact her, to talk things over with her?

How could she get him to return to her? Suppose he knew she had been to the Gardaí, would that make him want to talk to her? What would the Gardaí say? They would want a description and she couldn't give that. She didn't want any harm to come to this man as he would be in dire trouble for interfering with her, a female of unsound mind or so the Superintendent at the Mental had explained. Her friend at the Mental, Jeannie, had once answered, "Jesus, sir. It's hard enough to get a man to get your knickers off without frightening him with that palaver." She always laughed when she thought of Jeannie and the way she said it with the Superintendent standing there feeling and looking a right charlie.

She would have to give some description. They would be looking for a lead and she would have to tell them something. A thought struck her. What about Donal Moran? After all, hadn't it taken place in his field, and hadn't he had his hand up between her legs that night, whether willingly or not? She laughed loudly and defiantly into the darkened night as she swung along the grassy footpath with renewed vigour. She could feel the excitement well up inside her at the thought of embarrassing or, better still, punishing that shagger for slighting her on the road, and cowshite too to his friend Mary Boyle. She would make sure Mary Boyle showed her more respect next time they met on the road.

How could she get back her big man, her spirit? If he heard the Gardaí were making enquiries, he might want to talk to her again. Donal Moran would get the fright of his life, if she gave his description. Serve him good and proper!

Would there be any chance that this powerful brute of a man might seek her out to exact revenge for informing on him? He was of enormous strength and could snap her neck like a matchstick with those gigantic hands of his. If she was in danger, she would just have to take precautions. A hatpin could be an ugly menacing weapon. Bobo's mother had one of nine inches in length. It had come affixed to a bonnet as a present to Bobo's grandmother many years ago. The hat had been discarded long since, but it was thought the pin might be of some value and had been placed in a drawer. There was also a darning needle onto which BoBo had painstakingly mounted a grip the better and easier to thrust it through material and into someone, and the man at the Mental had owned a long slender blade called a stiletto. Its sides were as sharp as razor blades and its point was as a rapier. It would have been confiscated in the hospital if the staff knew he possessed it. BoBo knew where he kept it hidden and, the morning she was departing, surreptitiously relieved him of it.

Now she placed all three in a part of her clothing which made them easily accessible, but not visible to an observer. They accompanied her on her nocturnal ramblings and she wouldn't hesitate to use them if the occasion arose.

Donal Moran would be in for a shock. The Superintendent would tell him again about it being a heinous crime to interfere with a female of unsound mind. She wouldn't go to the Gardaí just yet. She couldn't exactly remember how long it had been since the night of the big wind and she decided, for the present, to give that man giant some little more time to reappear.

However, she was losing patience and BoBo had very little control over her emotions.

Comhairle Contae
Átha Cliath Theas
South Dublin County Council

CHAPTER 16

Mary was coming out of the milking parlour at about eight o'clock in the morning when there was the new man David Stapleton, jogging round the side of the house bouncing a football. Seeing her, he neatly kicked it towards her.

"That's what was blocking your drain. It got caught between two stones and a load of sticks and rubbish had backed up behind it, so only a trickle of water was getting through. It's clear as a whistle now."

He was wearing blue dungarees and wellington boots.

"That's great. I was afraid it might overflow out onto the avenue. We'll go in and have breakfast. When you get up early any morning, feel at home to get yourself a cup of tea or whatever. Or indeed at any time. We don't stand on ceremony here."

After breakfast, she accompanied him to the thirty acres. They walked along a worn cow path until it ran out where the two holdings were divided by an ill-kept ditch of brambles and barbed wire. At this juncture, Mary turned to her right.

"We'll be able to cross over further on down this way."

Showing surprising agility, the small lame man placed a hand on a fence post and vaulted across the ditch landing neatly in the other field.

"Here," he said, offering her his extended hand across the ditch. "I'll help you over."

"You must be joking. There's no way I'd get across there."

She watched as he went off at a brisk trot across the field, every now and then stopping and kicking at the grass and weeds to evaluate the kind of land they were dealing with. She noticed the determined look as he set his face towards the right-angled ditch where the dragline and hedge cutter were operating. The dragline driver came to a halt and bending down towards him, the two men were exchanging words. Then, he turned back towards where Mary was still standing in the same field. Again, he vaulted across like a man in a hurry.

"Good on ye, Donal Moran," Mary thought as she watched the progress of the small man. "You don't often get it wrong. How erroneous first impressions can be."

"I'll need," he began immediately on rejoining her, "a sledge hammer. Do you have one?"

"We do."

"And a slasher and a good Bushman saw, or better still if you had a chainsaw?"

"We've a brand new chainsaw hardly ever used, and the slashers and a Bushman. I'll tell you what we have as well, a couple of good spades, four grained forks and something you don't see too often nowadays, a drag."

"I'll have use for every one of them. What you won't have now is barbed wire, fencing posts and staples. You'll have a claw hammer. Maybe John would run me into town. I know just the exact fencing posts I'll need. I can nearly make out in me mind the number I'll want. We can return any I don't use."

John dropped all the implements and materials in the field with the jeep. David Stapleton set about his task of supervising the dragline driver in the digging of the new culverts to drain off the surplus water from the low lying areas and the breasting back, and in the cutting of the hedges to let the wind and the air in to dry up the fields. It was agreed he would be paid by the hour, piecework. John and Mary acknowledged that from the moment he began he wasn't a minute idle when the clock was recording.

The dragline and hedge cutter would be finished in a few days, but there was work for David Stapleton for at least four to five weeks.

As the days went gently by, Mary found she looked forward to David coming down from the fields. He was an even-tempered man and fitted easily into the household. Every evening, he took a shower and changed into neat dress and, invariably, there was a hint of after shave and cologne when he came back down to the kitchen.

These evenings passed pleasantly with the three of them chatting and watching TV. On occasional evenings, they ventured as far as the nearby village of Borriscrea for a social drink.

Mary began to notice that David watched her as she moved around the kitchen, and often his smiling eyes caught hers in a holding glance. She felt flattered when she looked up to discover that he did not avert his gaze.

She began to take a little extra care about her dress. Whereas she was never over discerning about the style of jeans and blouses she sported, now she began shopping for jeans which were tighter fitting and polo neck jumpers which gave good account of her well-endowed figure.

She discarded entirely the long loose-fitting dresses which she sometimes wore in the evenings in exchange for skirts which revealed her shape and appearance to better advantage. Fashionable T-shirts, so the sales girl assured her, gave her a more youthful appearance.

A woman of strong emotions and loyalties, she began to experience an association developing between her and the small quiet man who was sharing these few pleasant evenings with herself and John.

She wondered about his age. She reckoned he was about twenty eight, and then she compared it with her own forty two. It was to her advantage she had always cared for her figure, so it compared favourably with a woman many years her junior. As the old bachelor had said to her when she was a very small girl, and she asked him his age – "Sweet sixteen, and never been kissed." At the time, she didn't understand the significance of the remark, but now it was crystal clear, and she, too, like the old bachelor, looked upon herself as being sweet sixteen and never been kissed. Being celibate gave an eagerness and shine to her innocence.

She knew only too well that it was important she should not betray her feelings towards him, at least outwardly, publicly. However, being driven by strong emotions she surprised even herself one night. The three of them had gone to the village one evening for a drink. They were seated in a back area of the lounge well into their second drink when Molly Browne, a local girl, approached their table.

Molly, ample of figure and bosom, painted her full lips a rosy red. She was in her late teens and popular with the boys of the area. Indeed, it was said of Molly she had a way with the men as well as the boys.

"Are you not going to introduce me, Mary?" She emitted a loud, vulgar laugh.

"David this is Molly. Molly Browne. Molly this is David."

"Pleased to meet ye I'm sure," Molly enthused, holding onto David's hand in both hers whilst she leaned towards him.

"Are you going to buy me a drink, David?" She laughed out loud again. This time David and John laughed with her. Mary didn't.

Mary found she couldn't allow the thought that this single girl had a perfect right to approach the table of a married couple and enquire about their male companion. Deep down, she acknowledged that Molly was free to act as she pleased; but she didn't want to see it in that light. Molly's presence at their table made her feel uneasy.

"There's a twenty-first birthday party up the road tonight," Molly continued."I'm allowed to bring a friend along. What do you say buster?"

She leaned up against him and emitted the same jolly raucous laughter. John and David laughed along with her again. Mary was silent as before. She found herself struggling to try and keep her composure. Inside her, she felt this girl was usurping her position. Inside her, she couldn't control the little pangs of jealousy which were welling up.

Trying to remain calm and seem unruffled, her voice nonetheless came over tersely as she stood up.

"We have to be going, Molly."

"Jazus Mary, but I'm only looking for a man for the night. What's gotten into you? I never thought you to be an auld spoil sport."

"We've all three of us here got an early start in the morning and have to go."

She emphasised all three of them, so no one would be under any delusions as to what her intentions were, and walked with determination, head bent, towards the exit, knowing the men would get up and follow after her.

Later that night, as she recalled the incident she decided that she was right to have acted as she did, and had no regrets. Her emotions ran strong and deep. She was a woman of commitment and she was also a beautiful woman. These instincts, when combined with her generous nature and compelling impulses, could lead to an exquisite fulfilment on the one hand – or tragedy on the other.

It was a Friday evening. Mary was tidying up in the kitchen and detected a slight wheeze developing in John's breathing. He was seated at the end of the table reading the daily paper.

David was down in his bedroom, taking a while longer than usual. Then he appeared, but there was something different. It was the way he was dressed. He was wearing a jacket. He wouldn't need a jacket if he was going to sit in for the night. He never wore a jacket in the house.

Mary looked to him with undisguised curiosity as though she was entitled to an explanation.

"I'm here just a month now and I'll have the job finished by Tuesday or Wednesday coming."

She stopped dead in her tracks at mention of those words, and left the dishes back down on the table. There was a vacant expression tinged with sadness on her face as she stood staring at him.

"Will you be leaving us on Tuesday next? A few days time."

Before he could answer, John had looked up from the paper and joined in.

"Well, I wish you luck wherever you go. You deserve to do well. I'll tell you one thing, but we'll miss you here. For certain, we're going to miss you.

He turned towards where Mary was still standing by the table.

"Aren't I saying the truth Mary? We're going to miss you David, the both of us."

Then he began to cough and the more he coughed the more his chest began to wheeze.

"I've a bad catch tonight. . . Didn't it come on me very quickly?"

"Did you take the inhalers, the two of them?" Mary asked.

"I did that. They're no good for this. I'm afraid I'll have to go under that auld nebuliser."

"That auld thing is very hard on you." It disturbed her to see John suffer. "It's the only thing we can do, then. I got new headache tablets for you. They dissolve in water. The chemist told me to give them to you before you go under the nebuliser. They'll work faster that way."

"I could rig up the nebuliser here in the kitchen for you, John," David offered. "It wouldn't take me two seconds. You might be happier sitting up in your own corner at the top of the table here in the kitchen." He headed to get the machine, but John beckoned to him.

"Every cripple has his way of walking." He tried to sound cheerful, but his breathing was difficult.

"I'm happier down in the room on the bed, where I can go for a sleep afterwards ... a cup of tea and a sleep," he wheezed. "If it's not too late when I wake up I'll join yez ... Ye're very good to me."

His breathing was deteriorating rapidly and he was under considerable strain.

One of the rooms off the kitchen had been prepared with a bed. Mary had attached the nebuliser to the wall just over the bed. A heater had been installed, and being beside the kitchen, the room was always comparatively warm. He wouldn't have to climb the stairs and he would feel more comfortable with Mary sitting in the kitchen close by. On a previous occasion, he had slept right through the night and she had kept vigil throughout in case he woke up with another attack. After that night, she put a small camp bed into that downstairs room so she, too, could get her night's sleep.

David had become more adept than Mary at operating the nebuliser. Now, he quickly opened the small bowl and half-filled it with the medication. He eased John back into a sitting position on the bed and, in seconds, had the mouthpiece firmly in place, so that John was breathing in the preparation. Next, he opened the laces on John's shoes, loosened the belt around his waist and helped him take off his jacket, all without interfering with or disturbing in any way the operation of the machine or the taking of the remedy.

He remained beside John for the best part of a quarter of an hour before suggesting that the mouthpiece should come off to see what progress had been made.

A quarter of an hour to twenty minutes was usually adequate use of the machine to clear the congestion. Not this time, it was a particularly intense attack, and the mouthpiece had to go on again.

Mary sat on the other side of John and, taking his hand, began stroking it.

"My poor John! You're going to be worn out after this. Poor John! I'll go down and make a cup of tea. I can see by you it's beginning to clear up now."

John nodded his head in agreement and then, motioned to David that there was no need for him to sit with him any longer. As he did so, his eyes brightened up in a clear expression of thanks as he looked at David over the mouthpiece.

Mary was pouring boiling water into the teapot when David rejoined her in the kitchen.

"You were going out tonight." She didn't turn around as she spoke, just went on pouring the water.

"Yes. I was."

"Any harm in asking you where you were going?"

"Not in the slightest. It's my last weekend here and I felt like heading into town for a few drinks and maybe a chat with the lads."

His voice dropped then as though there was some guilt attached to what he added next.

"And maybe a chat with a lassie, too."

"I'm going to miss you when you leave us, David." She spoke with conviction. "Will you be late returning tonight?"

Tension was creeping into their conversation and David didn't answer her question directly. "Well, I'll certainly not go out tonight until John has settled down."

"We've held you back terribly."

"Not to worry. It's not important." He added, "isn't it taking poor John a hell of a time to get his old chest clear this time?"

"We've messed up your night."

"Don't worry about me. I'm fine. Anytime will do me to head off into town."

"I think I'll take another peep at John." Mary went back to the makeshift bedroom. It was the longest it had ever taken to get the pressure off John's breathing and when it did he was exhausted. Mary helped him into his pyjamas and gathered up the discarded clothes. He drank half a mug of sweet tea, turned over in the bed and was asleep in minutes.

Mary returned to David in the kitchen feeling much brighter.

"I'll tell you what," she said, "I'm going to get you a drink before you head off into town."

She ignored his protestations and headed off smartly for the dining room where the drinks were kept and where a long bevelled mirror stood in a corner. Standing before the mirror, she was glad she had taken that extra care with her makeup. The mirror reflected the sheen in her blonde hair. She touched it with her hand around the edges.

Next, she turned right about and looking over her left shoulder into the mirror, glanced down at her legs and the length of her skirt. It was touching her knees. She pulled it upwards and looked back into the mirror again from the same angle. She was undecided.

"Oh. What the hell!" she exclaimed half aloud and pulled the skirt up a little further.

"I'm going to join you in a drink," she said, putting a bottle of whiskey and two glasses down on the kitchen table. She was herself again, smiling and controlling as she was accustomed to doing.

"It's turning a bit chilly. I think I'll put a match to that fire," she continued.

A fire of kindling and turf sods were set in the grate. A touch of a match and it was soon blazing.

"There are some nice dry logs in the shed just outside the door, maybe you'd bring in an armful before we sit down?"

On his return, she was pouring him a more than generous glass of whiskey.

"Water or lemonade?"

"Lemonade. That's an awfully large glass you've just poured there."

They sat before the fire sipping their drinks looking sideways at the T.V. which was turned down low so they could chat in comfort, and more importantly, so they could keep an ear out for John.

David was speaking in undertones in deference to the slumbering John.

"You don't have to," Mary said. "He'll sleep now for three to four hours if not longer."

In the way of many pint drinkers, David finished his drink with undue haste, whilst Mary was only half-way down in her glass.

"I'll pour you another," she said rising from her seat.

"Steady on," his protest was half-hearted, "that enormous measure's already giving me a warm glow, but I'll drink another."

She began to pour half-way up the tumbler with whiskey.

"God, Mary but you're pouring too much altogether. You'll have me drunk!"

"Get away out a that with you! You're well able for it."

"Aren't you going to top up your own?"

"I've enough for the moment. I'm not able for it really. I'm not accustomed to it.

"You can do better than that, Mary."

She took a fair good mouthful and shook her head wryly as she swallowed. Then, she laughed out loud and merrily.

He took her glass. She protested, again saying she wasn't accustomed to it. She allowed him to take the glass from her hand. Going back to the table, he poured her a large measure.

"Let's drink a toast," he proposed.

"What'll we drink to?"

"Let's drink to us," he said and there was a twinkle in his eyes.

"I'll drink to that." She laughed and held his eyes.

"Here's to us." They echoed in unison and raising their glasses turned facing one another. They touched glasses. She looked straight at him. Stared into his eyes. He took a strong sip of whiskey.

"Bottoms up!" and raising the tumbler to his lips he drank the rest in one gulp.

"Good grief, but I'd never be able for that."

They were becoming noisier now and laughing at trifles.

"Of course, you would," he urged her. "Come on Mary. I'll shout three and you let her off. A one, a two and a three." He clapped his hands.

Mary put the glass to her lips and, staring at him with smiling eyes over the top of the tumbler, took the tiniest of sips. She didn't want to get drunk. She was feeling excited without getting drunk and she was laughing heartily, coquettishly. She wanted to remain in control of herself. She wondered if he liked her, liked her as a woman as opposed to a person. She wondered, too, how she looked to him right now.

"Well, if I may I'm going to pour meself another little drink."

"Help yourself. As much as you like. Here, I'll pour it for you."

But he was already making his way over to the bottle where he again poured a good measure. When he returned he sat on the floor beside her, his legs crossed and the glass of whiskey beside him. He was looking up at her. She felt the stare of his eyes as they explored her legs.

He pulled a small stool towards him.

"You're very high and mighty up there. Sit down here beside me." He pushed the stool towards her. As she lowered herself onto the stool her skirt crept back higher off her knees half-way along her thighs. David Stapleton knelt upright in front of her.

He was leaning against her knees, but her back was supported against the chair behind her, the heavy easy chair she had just vacated. Suddenly, his two hands were under her skirt, beneath her thighs and he began stroking the under parts of her legs.

"Oh David," she said, "if someone should come in."

Immediately, she remembered that time with Joe Moran years before. How she had turned away, how she did not encourage him, and how she regretted it ever afterwards. Was this now to be the same because of her intervention, because she was afraid of what she might do or let him do to her?

He was on his feet in the minute and pulled the bolt on the door which lead out into the back yard. Next, he went as far as John's room. He peeped inside. John was contentedly snoring. He quietly took the key out, closed the door and silently locked it on the outside.

The blinds had earlier been drawn by Mary but none the less he checked them out. Then he switched out the light, leaving the room lit only by the fire.

"Now we can't be disturbed. You said John will sleep for a few more hours. Besides we will be warned of anyone's approach."

He dropped in front of her as before where she was still seated on the low stool. It raised her bare knees. He knelt between them. Again, his hands began exploring beneath her thighs. He stroked her gently from beneath her knees along and under her thighs. Her entire frame tingled with the thrill of his hands. It was the first time a man had ever fondled her.

His hands crept beneath her jumper, boldly and confidently undoing her bra at the back. Then, as his hands took a firm hold of her breasts, she grabbed him around the neck in her rising excitement and drew him to her.

"Easy, easy," he chided her gently. "Easy."

He took hold of her hands to relieve the pressure around his neck and head.

"My God, but you have beautiful breasts."

He placed his mouth over her right breast; she felt the smooth edge of his tongue as it licked back and forth across her nipple and he sucked it sharply so she could barely keep from shouting out loud, so great was her ecstasy. He changed over to her left breast and she felt like screaming. She could hardly contain herself. Her excitement grew as she realised he was pulling down the zip of his trousers. He took her hand and brought it down to where she thrilled to the voluptuous fullness and rhythmic throb and strength which was now within the palm of her hand. He was tugging at the hook at the top of his trousers and, suddenly, they were down around his knees, at the same time as his tongue sought out her breasts.

She felt her pants being pulled firmly and then they were falling down around her ankles and, all the time, his tongue coursed across the nipple of her right breast. Gradually, she was losing control of her senses. He gently removed her hands and raised them so they now rested on his shoulders and he pushed her legs further apart. Now his hands encircled her buttocks and he drew her closer into him, so she came forward to the very edge of the stool and his throbbing penis was suddenly against her vagina.

His lips delicately touched her lips and his tongue licked her lips with short rapid flicks. Her fear now was that by some whispered word or movement she might break the spell and prevent then making a complete act of love.

"Is something wrong with me?" She cried out in anguish. "Don't stop, David! Don't stop! Please don't stop!"

His mouth was firmly over hers and she felt his rising passion … Suddenly with a sharp strong thrust she realised his penis had come upwards deep into her. Overcome with joy, tears flowed down her cheeks for, all in that moment, the years of frustration, agony and suspense were at an end. She was a normal woman, with normal passions and appetites capable of having her will with a man. Her fulfilment knew no bounds. It might just have been her imagination, and in any event, it was possibly nothing more than an old wives tale, but, for an instant, she thought she felt the slightest trickle of blood running down the side of her leg.

He stayed still, leaving his penis deep inside her, and she could feel its throb, before he withdrew slowly; then grasping her firmly he pulled her to him and thrust with sudden impulse and force back up into her. She moaned and sought out his mouth and kissed him passionately. His mouth was strong over hers, and she wrapped her arms around him. He withdrew and as before, suddenly with great force, thrust back up into her again and continued to penetrate her over and over.

She felt the sweet pang within her body and moaned softly in ecstasy. A moment later she felt as though her whole head would explode as the imminent pulsating orgasm welled up inside her.

She closed her eyes and let her head sway back as inexorably the rhythm brought her closer to heaven. He chased after her mouth and her whole body seemed to shudder as the orgasm continued to build, until she gradually lost control completely. She was being transported away from all her senses on threads of silk. Her body shuddered in her climax, it was the most complete sensation she had ever felt.

As she began to regain awareness, she found he was still kneeling before her and still thrusting into her.

"Welcome back," he was grinning.

Quietly she whispered into his ear, "I'm so glad you did this to me. Oh. I'm so glad."

She kissed his lips, his eyes and all over his face, and as he stopped for a brief moment and she began to kiss him all over again.

Then his face hardened, and the strokes began to pulsate into rapid motion and she felt again as if her head would explode as she held him firmly against her, and he continued to drive up into her as if he would never stop.

"Oh, God!" she moaned. "It's so beautiful."

Still the strokes quickened and again she was losing control and being transported into kaleidoscopic transports of uncontrollable rapture and delight, her head swimming, her whole body bursting with ecstasy.

He was holding her now in a vice-like grip around the buttocks and pulling her into him, their mouths pressed hard to one another and, as he reached a climax, she heard him call out in agony. Her joy knew no bounds. She had just experienced the fulfilment of making love with a man who had passionately desired her and she him.

As his grip relaxed about her, tears of joy began to flow down her cheeks. She kissed his mouth, his forehead and his eyelids, and wet his face with her tears.

"My God! It was beautiful, David, beautiful!

"David, you won't believe this, but that is the first time for me. I've never made love to anyone before. I feel wonderful. I was always terribly afraid there was something wrong with me. I've suffered terribly over the years. It haunted me day and night. It's the most beautiful thing that has ever happened to me."

He was still kneeling down before her.

"You're perfect."

She dropped down facing him in an upright position with her arms about him and again began kissing his lips, his face over and over. She pressed him to her in a warm embrace, and repeated, "It was beautiful. Oh, so beautiful!"

He lifted her to her feet and, gently disengaging himself, went to John's room, pulling up his trousers as he went. He unlocked the door and returned the key to its place on the inside lock.

"He's still fast asleep."

He went across to the back door and pulled back the bolt.

Mary returned to him and putting her arms around his neck hugged him tightly and kissed him. Tears of joy appeared in her eyes but she didn't mind or try to wipe them away.

She talked excitedly as she made tea and sandwiches. She poured herself a cup, another tumbler of whiskey for David, and left the plate of sandwiches on the armrest of his chair. There was still whiskey in her glass but she jettisoned it down the sink. A gentle silence momentarily fell on the kitchen and when she turned around, David's glass had been left down beside him and his head was nodding and his eyes half-closed.

She sat on his knees and touching her forehead against his, whispered to him, "It's ok by me if you want to go to bed now, I understand. The last drink has knocked you over. You drank it too fast."

"You knocked me over." He opened one eye. "Can you come to bed with me?"

She paused, unable to decide for the moment, glancing briefly towards the now unlocked door and then back to searching David's face with a hint of anxiety.

"I want to go with you. I'd love to." She turned apprehensively for the second time towards John's door.

"It could be dangerous if he woke up with an asthma attack and wanted something. I'd never forgive myself for not being there to wait on him if he needed me."

She put her arms around David.

"I want to go with you. To lie beside you. I'd love to. To make love to you over and over. I'd be afraid John might get an attack and I wouldn't be there to help him."

David kissed the top of her head in understanding and blew another kiss from the door before disappearing up to his room.

CHAPTER 17

Mary sat for a long time at the table, going through the paper, disinterestedly turning the pages and reading the advertisements and sometimes, too, the news columns, without appreciating what it was she was reading, so taken up was her mind with the earlier events. The radio was turned down low and she half-heartedly turned an ear to it more for company than entertainment value. Her mind was concentrating on all that had happened to her that evening.

It was late when she eventually opened the door to John's room and let herself in quietly. He was sleeping peacefully, not a trace of wheeze in evidence. The duvet had fallen down off his back. She cautiously covered his shoulders without disturbing him, and very lightly touched the top of his head with her lips.

She didn't experience the slightest trace of betrayal as she started to undress and watch him sleep. Maybe she would in the clear light of dawn. She was relieved to have the camp bed for she might feel uncomfortable within herself to lie beside him during what little was left of the night.

Mary was in the habit of rising every morning at six for the milking as the lorry came from the creamery to collect the milk at about a quarter to nine. She could hardly believe her eyes when she awoke and saw it was after eight o'clock. John was still in slumberland, and she let him be.

The instant she arose she heard the unmistakable high-pitched whine of the milking machine and the occasional low mooing of contended cows being milked. So, David Stapleton was astir and working at an early hour. As she showered, she smiled to herself at the stiffness in her lower back and at the almost pleasant soreness around her vagina. Swiftly, she pulled on a pair of fresh jeans and white woollen top and hastily brushed her soft blonde hair.

The moment she opened the back door, she was met with the acrid aroma of silage. The morning air, too, was redolent of the scent of slurry being washed down with a strong hose. The hose could mean only one thing. David Stapleton had already completed the morning's work. As she crossed the yard, the hose stopped and she could hear the sound of moving milk churns. David stopped as she came through the door and eased a churn back down onto its base. She ran to his arms and hugged and kissed him.

"Why did you get up so early?"

"I woke up parched with the drought before six. I got up and drank near a gallon of water. Then I realised that no one was stirring so I decided to get on with the milking. The reason I'm finished so early is I started early."

He began to organise the churns again. Mary, watching him, was leaning against the sacks of beet pulp which were stacked high almost to the roof. Involuntarily, she stepped towards him and taking his hand said, "I'll always remember you for what we did last night. You'll always be special to me. Wherever you go, whatever happens from now on, you can know you'll always have the prayers of at least one woman," she pressed his hand firmly before adding, with a tinge of sadness, "and also her love."

"David ..." she hesitated, "... would you have known by me last night that it was my first time?"

He shook his head."No," he said thoughtfully."I wouldn't."

"I'd say you have a lot of experience. You must have been with a lot of women."

Again, the question surprised him. He considered it for a moment. "No." He paused and looked serious. "I haven't been with many women. In fact, very few."

He leaned back against the sacks. "But I'll tell you something I can do better than you."

"Like what?"

He grinned. "I'll bet you I'll get to the top of those sacks before you do."

Laughing loudly, she scarpered up the sacks before him.

CHAPTER 18

Bobo was weary with tramping the roads at all hours of the
night in search of the fiendish man who had ravished her
on the night of her rapture, the night of the big wind. She
was tired, too, of relating the story of her conqueror to her old
mother and father in her strange gobbledegook speech, talking
now of men, and then of spirits. They were no longer interested,
perhaps they never were. Why, they weren't even concerned
about her welfare as she tramped at night and returned bearing
stories of a great physical man having his way with her against
a gate.

The poor mother's condition, a delicate, gentle little creature,
was referred to by psychiatrists as mildly mentally handicapped.
Her husband was little better.

Even the erotic details much favoured by BoBo in her constant
retelling of the incident were beginning to wear thin and lack
interest even for her. Her head ached. There was some kind of
pressure on it. She was growing impatient with the mother and
father and everything about them. She found they were becoming
offensive and selfish towards her of late. Also, that Mary Boyle
woman and her friend, that Moran man, were passing her by on
the road as if she was some kind of outcaste.

Moran would be sorry yet for ignoring BoBo. What was it
the Superintendent at the Mental had said, something about.
Oh, what in hell was it? Her head had a terrible pressure on it. A
female of unsound mind. Indecently assault a female of unsound
mind. That was it. According to the Superintendent, anyone
found guilty of such an offence would be severely punished.

She would go to the Gardaí on the morrow. There again, why
wait until tomorrow? Why tomorrow? What was wrong with
today? Why not today? There was little likelihood of anything
favourable coming her way on her nocturnal scouting that
would change her mind between now and tomorrow. So why
not go to the Gardaí now this minute? Why not? Maybe the

big man might hear about her going to the Gardaí. The chances were he would want to speak to her again to make sure she didn't accuse him of sexually assaulting her.

Garda Jim Furlong was in the public office of the station. She asked to see the Sergeant and was ushered into his office off to one side. Sergeant Fergal Donnelly had staring eyes which seemed never to blink or which couldn't blink, and his breathing was peculiar, too. It came out as a rough nasal noise and, coupled with the eyes, could be disturbing to a person being interviewed close up by him. To make his personal idiosyncrasies worse, he used the end of a safety pin to extract wax from his ears, even when interrogating a member of the public. Whilst talking to that person, he would delicately explore the inner reaches of his ear with the pin and always came out with a deposit of wax on the end of it, which he would then carefully scrutinise before wiping it away between thumb and index finger. Next, he would rub the same thumb and finger against the underneath part of the desk or whatever other piece of furniture was nearest to him at the time.

Inclined to be overweight, he was always on some new diet or other and looking forward to a considerable weight loss within the following two to three months. His uniforms were fitted with that expected loss in mind but as he never succeeded in obtaining the desired weight with the result that all his tunics fitted too tightly, and so that he could not fasten up the buttons. This meant that, normally, his tunics were worn opened at the front.

At first, BoBo was quite lucid as she recounted how she had been assaulted and raped, very recently was how she put it. She didn't put a date on it, or a day of the week. She derived a certain amount of satisfaction in relating some of the torrid details to the Sergeant. He put several questions to her but she gave away little precise information.

The Sergeant concluded she was bordering on a partial to full-blown mental disorder, possibly the latter. He was well aware of the dire consequence which might attach to anyone who would interfere with such a girl. He therefore listened to her intently and tried to establish an accord with her.

BoBo found that, as she was talking, she was laying too much emphasis on the description of the man she had encountered that night. That wasn't her intention. Her head began to hurt again. She didn't want that man to be accused. She didn't mind hurting anyone else. In fact, she intended implicating Donal Moran. Her only regret was that she couldn't accuse that Mary Boyle woman as well. She had made a mistake in telling the Sergeant where precisely the incident had taken place. What she should have said was that the man had invited her into his car, but she wouldn't be trapped again. As she concentrated on changing course, she felt the buzz in her head was beginning to make her feel quite ill. Her game must be to impress on the Sergeant that she had been interfered with in the first instance and that she was a female of unsound mind in the second analysis. That wouldn't be too difficult to put across – and nail that shagger Donal Moran at the same time. It was the next best thing to taking a belt at that Mary Boyle one.

What BoBo didn't know was that the Sergeant was going to be sympathetic to her cause for he dearly wanted to be promoted to the rank of Inspector. He had recently joined the Knights of Columbanus for the express purpose of advancing his chances in that regard. He believed the Knights, a secretive Christian sect within the Catholic Church, were known to be influential in helping its members gain promotions in the Army, Civil Service, Gardaí and the judiciary, with the support of the clergy and bishops. He had heard they often gained business deals and contracts by virtue of this association of secrecy. He knew that most ordinary God-fearing Catholics looked at them and their motives with a certain degree of contempt and, especially, the occasional but well-publicised dinner for charity. All that the Sergeant needed right now was one good case to draw the attention of his superiors to his claims for promotion, and membership of the Knights might help.

Up to now things hadn't always gone as favourably as he would have wished. His wife was even more ambitious than himself, and also held the view that with one good case properly handled, together with the influence their friends in the Knights could bring to bear on his behalf, he would get that promotion.

Now sitting opposite him was this daft little girl and she making a complaint which could well change his fortunes. He noticed when he questioned her about the assault she derived a degree of satisfaction in relating some of its more lurid details. There was no doubt she suffered from some form of mental stress or other, making it next to impossible to elicit precise information.

Instead of answering, she would discuss some other topic which had no bearing on the question put to her and the longer the interview progressed the more bizarre her story sounded. Yet he felt certain that there had been some kind of sexual interference or other with her and that she knew the date, time, and night of the incident.

He decided to start at the beginning again.

"Tell me then in your own words what exactly took place on that night."

Her eyes darted about the room. BoBo was thinking. She didn't want to emphasise too clearly the description of the man she had encountered. What surprised her was the interest the Sergeant was taking in the matter. The best thing now would be to come across as a demented girl. She could be clever when she wanted. She had good practice in these kinds of situations with the doctors and nurses at the Mental.

"It's because you are unwell that you think that way," the doctor at the hospital had said to her. "When you get better you will not think about sex as being violent."

"But doctor," she'd said to him, "isn't it the way God made me?" That doctor had a reputation for religiosity.

"If He'd wanted me otherwise He'd surely have made me differently, wouldn't He?" She had then said to him, "How is it, Doctor, that your medicine hasn't changed me either?"

Yes. She could be quite clever when she wanted to even to the extent of being able to judge perfectly how far she could go with the authorities at the hospital without jeopardising her comforts or privileges. Now, she would confuse this man without his losing interest in her case.

Besides, she wanted to get her own back on that Boyle woman and her friend Donal Moran, who considered themselves superior to others. Weren't most of those in the locality the same, thinking they were superior to the likes of BoBo? Well, she could be superior too, and she was in the right place now to teach them all a good and lasting lesson. The thought made her smile as she looked up at the Sergeant. There was a cold chill to her smile.

The Sergeant repeated, "Tell me then in your own words what happened on that night?"

He could afford to be patient. He determined he would tease this thing out to the last, even though he was annoyed with her infuriating habit of putting her hand on his arm in a familiar gesture as he was writing. He found the practice not just disconcerting but an affront to his dignity as a police officer.

He lent forwards encouragingly but was assailed by a strong smell of medication. Stronger still was the girl's body odour. He wondered if she ever washed. He as quickly lent back in his seat again.

"Please, we'll start again at the beginning."

He re-opened his notebook and, pencil poised, asked her for a description of the man. She became agitated and went off into a grotesque yarn of gibberish, prattling on incessantly in a manner which only confused the issue.

"I'm not long in the bed really."

Once she started speaking she didn't stop, either to think or draw breath.

"It must have been six o'clock. Um, no," she corrected herself. "Of course, I wasn't long in the bed on that morning was what I meant to say. Is that what I said the first time?"

She looked to him as she posed the question but continued talking without pause.

"It must have been about six o'clock when I was getting in from the town. I think I was in the town that night. Sure, I had to be close to it anyway. I must have got a lift. 'Cos I left Kilderry at two or three and how could I've got back so quickly unless I got a lift? I was talking to a dead man. I must have been given the power to talk to him. I wasn't a bit afraid of him. He was tall and dark and dressed in black. They say nothing good comes dressed in black. He gave me the name of the man who killed him. He killed his brother, too, and he knocked his eye out. He warned me against him. I wasn't afraid of him. His weaknesses were light and water. He couldn't stand light or water, he told me. 'The running river is the death of a man,' is what he told me, and it must be the truth. While I was talking, a man passed on a bike. And the spirit turned his head away. The man saw me ,but he didn't see the spirit."

The Sergeant had to shout at her to stop her flow of twaddle, not once but several times, and when he put the question to her, he found he was still shouting.

"Are you not afraid?" He had to make a conscious effort to speak in a more relaxed tone.

"Are you not afraid?" His voice was more subdued. "Are you not afraid to be out on the roads at those unseemly hours of the night? Are you not afraid of being attacked by some drunk or maniac?"

She poured forth again, but he wasn't listening, he was concentrating on a more pressing aspect of the case. There was something turning about in his mind about corroborative evidence in cases of this nature, or was it in the case of an infant? Someone else to corroborate or strengthen the evidence of the infant or insane girl in case she might be telling lies. One weakness in this case was that she had left it very late to report the incident. He would get over that one, though, by referring to her unsound state of mind. The important issue was that she was of unsound mind and that turned the case into a far more iniquitous crime than assault or indecent assault, or even rape simpliciter. It made it harder for the accused to defend such a female's assertions that she had been interfered with and easier to obtain a conviction on that account.

He wondered if at this stage she might have the outline or trace of marks on her. Not that the Sergeant was too concerned about her, or how many marks might have been inflicted on her, or how many belts she might have to endure in the future. What concerned him was getting from her some indication of whom the man was. Then, and by God!, he would swing for him. He would frighten the living day lights out of him to such an extent that the extraction of a confession would be as easy as pissing in bed. Get a signature onto a sheet of paper. Once there was a signature, why then little bits and pieces could always be added afterwards. Once there was a signed voluntary statement from the perpetrator, a conviction was certain to follow. He would have done the whole lot on his own without referring to the special crime force at Divisional Headquarters. He would be complimented, for he would make sure that there would be the best presentation of his investigative procedures.

A worrying thought suddenly frightened him. What if he failed in the case? He would be in serious trouble on two counts. First and foremost, for not immediately reporting the incident to Divisional Headquarters as he was obliged to, and secondly, for not calling in the assistance of a woman detective. There was at least one in every division specially trained to deal with these kinds of situation.

He quickly dispelled the thought. There must be no negative attitudes. He could always overcome the delay aspect simply by reporting it in the next twelve hours or so, if he was not coming up with answers. He felt she knew more than she was saying. Take her easy and she might yet come up with a name, a culprit. What does it matter whether he's guilty or not, let him be an innocent victim if needs be so long as a charge sticks. Results count in this business, the same as in any other. It was the prospect of promotion which was important to him. If the case could be wrapped up quickly, neatly packaged and laid on the Chief's desk, he, the Sergeant, would be on his way to Inspector.

As BoBo prattled on incessantly, it occurred to him that such a girl would have encountered more than one man on her nocturnal ramblings who would have grasped the opportunity of burying it to the hilt in the simpleton. Some of the lads were innocent, some not so innocent. What did it matter, so long as he got one name from her? For certain, but he would get a name and once he had it, well, by Jesus! he would frighten the living day lights out of him, whoever it was. After all, she was a female of unsound mind. That was the exact terminology and he liked the sound of it. He repeated it in his mind – a female of unsound mind.

There would be more than one chap, that was for certain, and he was sure she would give one name. Lads would be watching her, waiting for an opportunity to get her down. It's hard to blame any full-blooded young lad, he thought to himself, with the urge a few pints can bring on, and knowing that she was out there on the road in the pitch black of night.

Sure, it had even happened to himself, out at a remote house in the country in his first station. He had been sent to a home shared by a mother and daughter. The daughter not only had a speech impediment, but was also unbalanced. The mother used to have to send for the Gardaí from time to time when the daughter, an irascible girl, would become physically violent.

She ran at him, the moment he entered the kitchen with her hands raised as if to strike him. Thinking back on it now, there wasn't much bother in fending her off, but in doing so, he had got excited. He couldn't have been more than nineteen or twenty at the time.

It had happened simply enough when getting behind her to pin her two hands in front, she stooped down, and whatever way she bent forward, it damn well near transported his full weight onto her back so that, there and then, in those few seconds of struggle, her actions and heaving had aroused him uncontrollably. With his free hand he had pulled up her jumper at the back to reveal her naked white skin – and that had set him tearing at his trousers in a frenzy. Jesus, but he couldn't stop himself. He held her in a vice-like grip as he engaged her naked back with besotted vigour, the while she stuttered at him.

"You're a bad man! A bad man!" The more he lost control the more she shouted, "You're a bad man! A bad man!"

When he released her, she ran at him with a raised accusatory finger pointing at him.

"You're a bad man! A bad man!"

With her speech impediment, the words sounded inept. She stretched her hand up under her jumper at the back and when she withdrew it, she held it out towards him.

"Look! Look!" She accused him holding the semen-covered hand at length from her. She grimaced and made an ugly face.

"Look what you did to me. All wet and slime from you." She stuttered and began to cry. It was quite amusing really.

He recalled, though, how kind and considerate he had been to her in getting a tea towel from the back of the range. He had wiped her back and then returned to the barracks and forgotten all about it. Not today, you wouldn't! Jesus, no way! Nobody thought anything about that sort of thing in those days. Wouldn't the lads in the station have had a good laugh if she had come in to report the incident? She would have got absolutely nowhere whatever, with her serious staring eyes and vacant-sounding, hollow-echoing voice.

In those days, girls didn't run off to the Gardaí every time a lad got her measure. In those days, a girl took her medicine. It's all these do-gooders who have brought about the changes and the present attitudes. All these auld social workers and their ilk! Since they took over certain areas from the clergy, a man has to be very careful. Very careful indeed! Look at the situation even in the home nowadays, since them social workers took over the role of family counsellors from the clergy. Any time a woman gets a deserved click in the rear, nowadays she's off into the Garda barracks and the courts.

Still BoBo was prattling on incessantly the while his thoughts were drifting. How to get a written statement from her was going to be a major problem. It was vital to the proper presentation of the evidence for him to obtain written information from her. A few words on a sheet of foolscap and her signature well down at the bottom was all that was needed. He would fill in the rest himself. Clever like, so it would stick to some bucko out there. It was with great difficulty that he was able to disrupt her interminable monologue.

"Are you not afraid to be out on the roads during the late hours of the night? Are you not surprised that you were attacked on this night?"

Again, she put her hand across the table and left it to rest on his shoulder, then craning her neck towards him her foul-smelling breath enveloped him to the extent where he almost became ill.

"What can a girl do only put up so much of a fight and what's to stop him overpowering her? I was bet by that man all right. He had a terrible belt. He hit me there on the side of the head and I had no chance."

Definitely, she had spent a night recently engaged in some kind of sexual psychotic activity with the man she referred to as the spirit. At some time during the night, they were on the roadside and the man did not want to be seen with this demented girl. That would be because of some business association or because of his marriage locally in the area. In any event, he did not want to be seen with this girl and hid his face from the passing cyclist. A tall man dressed in black. A priest? A lay brother? Not a priest again! He had one already under investigation, and was keeping the file under wraps. He would meet the bishop soon and he would mention the upcoming promotions. The bishop was friendly with the Taoiseach, and that little man would do anything to ingratiate himself with the hierarchy.

"You'll want to point out to me on the roadway as near as you can the precise spot where you were attacked. I've my car outside and I want to have the spot searched as soon as possible for any clues which, even at this late stage, might be still lying around."

He stood up. He had one good friend at the station, one he could depend on, Garda White, and it would be prudent to bring him along. Not a word would he impart to any of the others, especially that Garda Jim Furlong! That shagging alcoholic!

No one was going to say afterwards that he didn't do the job properly. It was going to be a tedious investigation and she could prove troublesome all the way. He would not be diverted from following through a complete investigation so he could hand over to the Serious Crimes division a well-conducted inquiry.

CHAPTER 19

oBo sat into the passenger seat, though he had intended her to sit in at the back. Whilst Garda White was opening the door for himself, she jumped in past him to the front seat. Each time she turned towards the Sergeant, which was often, he was enveloped in the heavy aroma of her medication. It seemed as if she wanted to blow her foul-smelling breath all over him. Even with the windows open, it was as much as he could do to keep his composure.

"Tell me when we are getting close to the place. We can't be too far from the spot now from what you told me back in the station."

They were proceeding slowly towards her house and when they were about a quarter mile from it, she said, "Slow down now. Do you see that gate down there on your left? Pull up at that."

As soon as the car stopped, she jumped out and rushed over to the gate in a terrible hurry, followed by the two Gardaí.

"It took place right here at this gate. Look inside the gate. Do you see that bar there? That's the one he made me hold onto. Gave me a terrible blow so as I had to hold onto it. It was late and dark and he said he was a spirit and if I did not help him, if I did not hold the gate and stay steady for him, he would strike me again. Right there he hit me! There, Garda, on the side of the head! I can still feel the belt from his hand."

No sooner had she pointed out the spot and identified the bar than she realised she was making the same mistake as before in directing the enquiry to the scene of her moment of rapture with the big man instead of to the car, Donal Moran's car. Now, she would have to come up with something quickly to get this Sergeant man concentrating on Donal Moran and away from the big man.

"Can you get a clue from the field?"

The Sergeant clung to the statement and stared hard at her to see if he could illicit some further information. He looked out across the fields as if they were about to reveal some hidden clue as in detective stories, but found he was just looking at hedges and green grass. He mustn't let go now. He could feel excitement building up inside him.

"What do you mean? What has the field got to do with it?"

"Donal Moran owns that field, doesn't he?"

For a moment, he couldn't speak. The blood began to pump furiously through his veins. Donal Moran? Donal Moran! Why, he was one of the wealthiest men in the district, the area, the county. He was a household name known throughout the county. This was exactly what the Sergeant needed, had been waiting for. It was for this very reason he hadn't contacted Divisional Headquarters, lest it was one of those cases which required exceptional investigative talents – one of a high profile but simply solved. It would attract massive media attention. Donal Moran and this half-demented girl! He couldn't believe his good fortune.

She, the simpleton, would bask in the publicity, whilst Moran would wither as a fallen flower in the desert heat. As for himself, why he would soon step up to take a bow, and receive the epaulettes of promotion to the rank of Inspector of An Garda Siochána.

If it was Moran, then the bigger they come the heavier they fall. If Moran had been fingering this dirty little runt or been anywhere near her skirts, he vowed he would get his signature onto a sheet of paper – and the promotion into the bargain, come hell or high water. He could always embellish the statement, titilate and alter it, and all the rest afterwards. This was an incredible, unbelievable stroke of luck. At last, at last, his goal was in sight!

"I want to be run home," she said.

A look of disappointment crossed his face.

"I want to be run home now."

"Hold on a minute like a good girl. What, may I enquire, has Donal Moran got to do with it?"

"I'm not feeling well. I want to be run home." She was an old hand at feigning an indisposition, even a seizure if needs be.

"You'll have to run me home now. I'm beginning to feel unwell. I think I might be going to faint."

She went directly to the car, opened the door and sat in. The Sergeant and his colleague followed. He started up the engine and slowly pulled out onto the road, but he was taking his time. He was thinking hard. He had been taken aback at mention of the name Donal Moran. Now was the time to be careful, vigilant. He mustn't get it wrong now.

"Was Donal Moran at the gate with you?"

"Would I get him into trouble?"

The Sergeant turned around towards the Garda behind him to ensure he was listening. It was important that he put the right question to her now, but BoBo interrupted.

"Why are you driving so slowly? You know I'm not well. I want to be brought home. Why won't you bring me home?"

"But I am bringing you home. I'd just like to know more about Donal Moran."

"His wife had to leave him, didn't she? So did his son. He often comes up here, especially late at night, especially if he's drunk. Oh, here's my house now."

Even before they had got to the entrance, she was opening the door, putting her legs out whilst the car was still in motion in a manner which precluded further conversation. The instant they stopped she ran off into the house, calling over her shoulder as she went, "It's up to you now, Sergeant."

They debated for a moment whether they should follow her, but then the Sergeant turned the car around on the road and they headed back in the direction of town. He realised she had implicated Donal Moran, in fact more than that, she had informed on him.

"Well, what do you think now?" The Sergeant addressed the question to his assistant.

"I think you'll never get the smell out of the car. That's what I think," he said. "I thought I'd throw up on the way. Open up all the windows for God's sake and slide the fecking roof back as far as it'll go. That bloody stink would rot yea. When did she last wash her ass? We'll never get it out of the patrol car. Jesus, but you'd want the stomach of a horse to take on that one!"

"But what do you think of her story?"

"It's hard to tell. She's mad as a hatter. I'd definitely say she was attacked in some way or other. Maybe a half-attack with her consent. Whoever he was, if she only knew it he was doing her a favour. I couldn't get over her mentioning Donal Moran. Jesus, but you wouldn't get a finer man than Mr Moran!"

"When it comes to the sex urge and the few pints under the belt, you'll never know what way any man or woman will act. There's no accounting for niceties when it comes to the bit of sex, appearances have nothing to do with it. Look at your own sister, the finest of men after her, and saving your presence a fair few of them laid her. Then, she turns around and a marries a little runt of near seventy years of age. What is she? Twenty two or three at most?"

"He had the money. That's where the real shortage is. There's no shortage of the other thing."

"Oh, definitely, you can say there's a fork in every trousers," the Sergeant said, "and some of them bucks I know are doing so much damage I wonder maybe they've two or three outlets." They both guffawed loudly and lewdly.

"I'll have to question Moran anyhow."

"That's not going to be easy. How do you think we should approach it?"

The Sergeant fell silent for an instant as he contemplated the question.

"I think the best way to do the job is simply call straight out to the house to him and confront him with her story. I've learned over the years that there's neither a good nor a bad time to confront someone with bad news or a terrifying issue such as the mission we're on. We'll just go straight to him and see if we can't bowl him over with the fright."

"You wouldn't have expected a man like that to be implicated with a girl like BoBo Doorley, would you now?"

"Either way we have to question him, and accuse him too. Don't we? You know something but a man like that would be terribly vulnerable to an accusation by the likes of BoBo Doorley. I'll tell you something for nothing, but I'll put some pressure on the bastard. Sure, hasn't she as good as accused him? It's not important how far he went or if he got anything off her or not, so long as she says he tried to sexually assault her. By Jazus, but I'll put it up to that gent, Garda White! With any luck we might get ourselves a nice little capture before very long. I feel it in me bones."

"Well then, why not invite him into the station?"

"That could be interpreted as a kind of a half-arrest, couldn't it? Suppose he was the guilty party at the end of the day, then we'd be in trouble with his legal team. They'd make out we arrested him, brought him to the station but failed to charge him. It's a complicated field. You'd get away with that sort of thing in England. The judges there would back you up. I was over there at a case. They backup the police every time, auld toffs every one of them. No. Its better we call on him at the house, interview him, and put pressure on him."

"Now that you're talking, his place is just at us, here around the corner. So why not call on him right away?"

"Why not? Like I said there's neither a good nor a bad time to bring a party bad news. Let's go then. Wouldn't it be great for us if this thing worked?"

CHAPTER 20

Donal Moran was in high good spirits. Sharon, Joe's girl, had just phoned to say she was being allowed to take Julie out from the convent with the consent of the court for a few days. Her problem was fear that Tommy Gavin might interfere with her, or worse, take the child on the grounds that he was the child's legally registered father, and there was not in existence any court order against him depriving him of his rights to the child.

Immediately after receiving the call, he phoned Mary Boyle.

"You know the girl I was telling you about, Joe's girl? The one who married Tommy Gavin."

"Yes. Yes. Of course, I do! Sharon."

"Well, she's coming down here with her little girl. Joe's daughter. My ... My ..."

"Your granddaughter. I hope you made them welcome."

"Yes. My granddaughter. I'll tell you something Mary, but I'm thrilled. Of course, I made them welcome."

"I'm delighted for you, Donal. It's no more than you deserve. How is she able to have the child? I thought there was an order against her?"

"There is too. It appears Julie, the little girl, has been transferred by some kind of judicial or administrative order to the temporary care of Sister Carmel in Blackrock pending Tommy Gavin's application for sole custody at the court in Drogheda. That's his home place.

"I wouldn't mind but both Joe and Sharon are prepared to swear he has no call whatever to the child. He's doing it out of spite. I can't understand it. Imagine, Joe, the fool, saved that bastard's neck. Apparently, Gavin is doing a double-cross. Joe it was who asked him to give the child a name in exchange for his not naming him at the trial as his accomplice. It was the most stupid thing imaginable. How in the hell does he now expect a judge to believe his story, with Gavin's name on the child's birth certificate and on its mother's marriage certificate. How would anyone believe the word of a bank robber, a criminal?"

"Cool down! Cool down! You still haven't explained how the mother is going to have the little girl for a few days. After all, I thought the custody order was directed against her?"

"The courts in Ireland, where the parties now live, are prepared to review the application of the mother for regular access to Julie, and also because the probation authorities were pleased with Sharon's rehabilitative progress, they are prepared to review the entire case. Sister Carmel that thinks it would be a good idea for the child and mother to have a few days together.

"But, here is where the snag is. There is no order against Tommy Gavin, principally because he wasn't around and he was never named in the proceedings in Liverpool. Now he maintains that Julie is his legitimate offspring and he alone has the right to have her in his sole custody. Sharon is afraid if he becomes aware she has the child, he will come and physically take Julie.

"He knows of the rift between Joe and me, so this is the last place he'll think of looking for them. He has issued a summons, a subpoena or something they call it, on me. It was served on me the other day. He is going to have it put to me that I ordered Joe out of the house, out of the family, disowned him. He has the lot of us up a gumtree."

"I think it sounds good, to me at any rate, that the authorities are beginning to accept Sharon as being a reliable person to look after Julie, even if only for a few days. I think it improves her position," Mary said.

"You never know. You never know. That Tommy Gavin must be a bad lad."

"When are they coming? I can't wait to see her. I wonder who she's like?"

"She's phoning me later on tonight to tell me."

"Don't you hesitate to tell her you'll go up to Dublin straight away and pick the two of them up. In fact, I'll go along with you, to keep you company on the journey and to break the ice so to speak when you meet the two of them."

"I know you would, Mary. It's kind of you. However, this is something I have to do on my own. I have a lot of ground to make up. Joe, she tells me, is still as antagonistic as ever and not likely to change. I never thought right about it at any stage, did I, only now when it's too late. I'm a lot to blame for what happened. I know that."

"That's water under the bridge. Time heals all wounds. I know Joe. Joe will come around in time. Besides you're getting a good break now."

"Mary, I'll have to go. Priscilla's beckoning to me. She's just after letting a few people into the drawing room, I think. I'll ring you as soon as I hear tonight."

Priscilla showed the Sergeant and the Garda into the drawing room. She liked people calling and showing them into that room. Everyone admired it. It was of gracious proportions and appearance, with high ceilings and ornate cornices. People's reactions intrigued her as they first entered and took in the fine mahogany tables, cut glass artefacts and the off-pink wallpaper which she herself had chosen.

The carpet was the most expensive item in the room, but Priscilla, who was not brought up to gracious living, sometimes had difficulty in appreciating some of the valuable possessions around the house, and to impress on a stranger the true worth of this particular article often alluded to its cash price. To Priscilla, one carpet was much the same as another so it would be a pity if people didn't realise that handsome as the furnishings and drapes were, the carpet was the most expensive. Overhead was a delicate eight-piece cut glass Waterford chandelier. The view through the heavily draped windows was of the tree-lined lawns. She knew the two policemen were impressed.

Donal Moran entered a few minutes later. He crossed the room and shook hands with both of them.

"You're most welcome, Sergeant. Would you care for a drink, tea, coffee?"

"Oh no, thank you very much. We're on duty."

"Then what can I do for you, Sergeant?"

"I regret to say I'm not on very pleasant business."

"I'm sorry to hear that. How can I help you?"

"You might be able to help me. A complaint of a serious crime has been made to us. It's to do with a girl. She alleges she was attacked one night recently."

The Sergeant took out his notebook and leafed through it in silence as if he was checking up on some specifics. Then, as if he was satisfied on the issue, he looked accusingly at Donal Moran.

"Were you out late any night recently?"

"Why?"

"Because she mentioned your name." He looked under his eyes at his accomplice. He wasn't sure yet where this line of questioning might lead. If there was an immediate and compelling denial, an outright rejection, it might be difficult to make progress. Everything would depend on his answers to the next few questions.

"May I enquire who this girl is?"

In a loud clear voice, the Sergeant bellowed out her name.

"BoBo Doorley."

At mention of her name, Donal Moran sank into an easy chair and the Sergeant noted the reaction.

"I'll have to put the question to you again, Mr Moran. Were you out late any night in recent times along the back road, late at night?"

"I was."

"And what night might that have been?"

"Tuesday night, some weeks ago. I can give you the date." He inclined his head in thought for a moment. "It would have been Tuesday, the 16th of last month."

The Sergeant again referred to the notebook. After consulting a blank page, he looked up at Donal Moran.

"That's the night she alleges she was attacked," the Sergeant lied.

"And where does she say she was attacked?"

"On the back road to here. On your own lands. At a place known around here as – the field gate."

"The field gate."

"Yes. The field gate."

"Were you in the vicinity of the field gate at any time on that Tuesday night at about midnight to sometime in the early hours of the morning?"

Donal Moran was conscious of the implications and their dangers, but he was brought up to tell the truth and he would not now even in this dire situation allow himself to act in a devious manner.

"I can't remember."

"You can't remember."

"That's right. I can't remember. You see I was drunk on that night. I was paralytic drunk. Maybe I shouldn't say that, but I was blind drunk and I don't remember the first thing where I was or who I met. Oh, come to think of it now I did meet a girl earlier in the day at the field gate. That girl was the same BoBo Doorley."

"The girl who made the complaint to me. Do you realise, Mr Moran, you could be in trouble with a girl like that?"

"Oh my God, but I was warned against her. That she was dangerous. That, however, was after."

"You were warned. That was after what?"

"Well, a friend of mine told me I shouldn't have anything to do with that girl. That she was dangerous. My friend Mary Boyle. You can ask her yourself. When I told her I had encountered BoBo Doorley, and given her a lift in my car."

"Tell me about that."

"I don't know how to put this now. She was coming back from the hospital. As a matter of fact she … found me … she came across me in a … she came across me in a compromising position. As a matter of fact, Sergeant, I was having a slash at the gateway when she came up on me unawares."

"That's not now how she described the incident to me." The Sergeant was lying again. "I want to be fair to you. What she said to me was that you exposed yourself to her."

It was the first the Sergeant had heard of the incident. BoBo had not mentioned it to him. He was pleased with himself for the manner in which he handled it and the way he reacted to it. Then, he looked knowingly at his companion who surreptitiously nodded his approval.

"In any event, you gave her a lift in your car. Have you often given her lifts in your car?"

"No. I have not."

"Why did your friend warn you against her?"

"Well, I don't know if you could call it a warning."

"That's the word you used," the Sergeant interjected sharply. Like a bloodhound scenting a quarry just up ahead, so the Sergeant's instinct told him he could be in for a kill. It could be promotion.

"You said your friend warned you against BoBo Doorley. What I want to know is why it was necessary for you to be warned. Like no one ever found it necessary to warn me against her. No one ever warned Garda White against her. Why was it necessary to warn you against her? There must have been some reason. Had something happened between you and BoBo Doorley, that you were being warned by your friend not to repeat?"

"It wasn't serious like that, Sergeant."

"But it is serious, Mr Moran! It's very serious! She alleges an assault and, Mr Moran, she alleges more, much more. If you know what I mean. You can't get much more serious than that, now can you? All I'm asking you is why you had to be warned off that girl of unsound mind."

Donal Moran felt enveloped in a cloud of shame and recrimination. A terrible fear took hold of him. He wondered if he would be able to look in a logical manner at the charges being levelled against him, so terrified was he by the accusations.

He had been drunk, terribly drunk, that night. Maybe he did encounter BoBo Doorley at the field gate. He had been that drunk, he wouldn't remember anyway. Drink did that to him. She would have been willing to engage him in any activity, improper or otherwise. He knew that from her attitude and promptings earlier on that day. He couldn't lay any blame at her feet. After all, she was nothing more than a very sick girl. Surely, he didn't make an ass of himself with her when he was drunk? Was the Sergeant now saying that he had made some kind of sexual suggestions to that terrible girl or worse still assaulted her? That's the word the Sergeant had used, assault. He had used it because that was what the girl had said. The Sergeant, after all, was only doing his duty, investigating a complaint which had been voluntarily made to him.

"Mr Moran, she accuses you further. She says you raped or tried to rape her."

Holy divine God! Rape! Had she gone and reported that he had raped her? His whole world was collapsing around him. A terrible fear seized hold of his being and paralysed his senses and powers of reasoning.

He was at a loss to explain to the Sergeant why Mary Boyle had warned him against BoBo. In his present state of agitation, he could not think straight.

The Sergeant felt he was making progress and decided to stick with the same line of questioning. He would repeat them and dog this man for the sole purpose of frightening him into making a statement.

"Why did you invite her into your car earlier that day?"

"I think she might have asked me if I was going in her direction and I said I was."

"You're not very certain. If I told you that she maintains it was you who suggested to her that she should come for a drive in your car what would you say?"

The Sergeant was making it up as he went along, but he could tell it was having the desired effect on Moran who now spread his hands out before him in a gesture of total disbelief and bewilderment.

"You were aware she had only just that morning been released from the psychiatric hospital in Portlaoise?"

"Yes. I was aware she'd been a patient there recently."

"She says the attack took place at your gate. It would be the same gate at which you'd encountered her earlier in the day, and you told her then you would meet her there late that night. Yes?"

Donal said nothing.

The Sergeant continued, "It's about half a mile from her house. That's where she alleges the attack took place. Are you sure it was the Tuesday night you were out late?"

"Yes. I'm certain."

"Tuesday night did you say?"

"Yes. It was Tuesday night."

"That's the same night, alright. I wrote it down here when she gave it to me."

Again, the Sergeant took out the notebook and began to leaf laboriously through it, a deliberate delaying ploy. Leafing slowly through the book – giving credence to the lie, as he turned a blank page inwardly towards himself.

"It was late in the night," he continued."What time were you out till on that night?"

"I don't remember. Honestly, Sergeant, I just don't remember. I was at a pub in Borriscrea on the same night and after that I called to John and Mary Boyle."

"And after that?"

"I don't remember."

"And how do you remember calling to Boyles?"

"I don't, but I've talked to them since and they told me I was with them on that night."

"You must have been very drunk."

Donal didn't reply. His mind was racing onto other matters.

"Am I in trouble, Sergeant?"

The Sergeant gave no response. He kept him waiting. He took out the note book again and pored over it, as if he was checking on some important data. Incredibly, the case was falling into the palm of his hand like an over ripe plum.

"She mentioned your name and your name only. No one else's. You tell me you don't remember what took place on that night. What you're really saying is you cannot deny the charges she's making out against you. Would you be prepared to make a statement to that effect?"

"Why should I want to make a statement? I can hardly make one when I don't recollect that night."

"It's just that assault, as I'm sure you can realise, on a female of unsound mind is serious, but to sexually assault her and worse is something you would want to consider in the light of a statement."

Donal Moran rose up out of the easy chair he had been occupying, gripped in a dread fear.

"Did she really say those things about me?"

"I'm sorry, Mr Moran." It was Garda White, and he spoke with what sounded like genuine concern.

The mounting sickening fear increased in its intensity as Donal's mind raced out of control. The suddenness of the bewildering rush of fear overwhelmed him, and he found himself struggling to hide his terror from the Sergeant and his assistant. They were staring hard at him, expecting him to say or act in a certain way, maybe anticipating him to admit. His stomach began to churn and his head to ache.

Suddenly, he remembered that morning years before when he awoke after a terrible night's drinking, the bedroom was disturbed with clothes all over the place and then his wife had come in and accused him of having attacked her. That morning, he could remember nothing untoward occurring during the night except that, at some stage, he had passed out from over consumption. On the other hand, Mary Boyle always maintained his wife was not only devious but was also a pathological liar.

Was this not the same thing happening all over again?

"Divine God," he whispered in his mind, "but I'm in terrible trouble! The worst possible kind of trouble a man can make for himself. Jesus, but I'll be ruined!"

He felt incapable of acting in any rational manner which might be to his advantage. He went over to the window and looked out onto the lawns, the avenue and the trees but without seeing any of them. His heart was thumping out of control. Sheer naked fright obliterated any possibility of his exerting even a modicum of influence into the interview. Nauseated, even his arms and legs, as well as his mind, all seemed overcome by inertia.

"What can I do?"

The Sergeant wasn't finished yet. This man could be ready to sign a statement. There was need for caution, perhaps a slight change of tactics. Besides he hadn't thought out yet how precisely the statement should be phrased. He would need an hour or two to ensure its contents would stand up to scrutiny.

"She said you beat her. She also said you assaulted her, and I'm sorry but I have to add, sexually."

Returning from the window, Donal threw himself helplessly into the chair. The Sergeant had peculiar eyes and they were now fixed, riveted on his victim.

"I know myself what it's like to be drunk," the Sergeant continued, and the eyes and the voice softened as if he sympathised and wanted to help.

"Don't we all get drunk from time to time. We're all capable of doing wrong things in drink. It's just unfortuante if a girl like BoBo Doorley crosses our path when we're under the weather. Couldn't any one of us try something on with her and not know what we're doing."

The Sergeant got out of the chair and walked to the window; the impressive vista stretched before him. Much depended on the next few minutes and Donal Moran's reactions to his questions. He must get them right; his promotion could be decided by them. The sergteant let his mind drift for a moment to his wife, and her glee which would follow if he successfully prosecuted this very important man. Of course, a man of his calibre would be defended by a battery of lawyers ... but a carefully taken statement which had subsequently been astutely doctored prior to the accused consulting with his solicitor, would defeat the best of legal brains.

The only thing standing between him and his ambition was the man sitting behind him. If only he could obtain a statement, he would be back in the station typing out a holding charge and arranging for a special sitting ot the local court, and then phoning the Superintendent and the Chief to relate, casually, the complexities of his capture. He must now repeat the allegations to Moran with unequivocal composure to test him again. He turned round and, for just an instant, froze Moran with the same cold stare, before again adopting a conciliatory attitude.

"I'll tell you exactly what she said. She said that you, Donal Moran, assaulted her a number of times. She said you hurt her. And she said you sexually assaulted her."

"Good God, but I'm ruined!"

"Could I take it, Mr Moran, that if she says it was you, then it was? And God knows I'm very sorry for you and I'll help you in every way I can. If she says it was you, are you telling me you cannot deny her allegations, because you were too drunk to remember?"

He waited for a response. At the same time, he didn't want to break the spell his own voice was creating, nor did he want Moran to offer some submission which might sidetrack the positive direction in which the conversation was developing. It would be unwise, now, to let Moran offset the advantage being created and whilst pausing momentarily, he nontheless decided to continue without giving the other an opportunity of answering.

Moran had not denied the positive allegation he had made against him.

"What we'd want to say ..." he was now within an ace of his goal, he was winning. "What we'd want to say is that you were very drunk on the night and don't have too clear a recollection of what happened between yourself and that girl."

What he was now telling Moran was that he had encountered the girl on that night and still there was no response, let alone a denial. He was placing Moran at the scene of the crime. It was easier than he had anticipated.

"Now, I might be able to help you insofar as I might get her to reduce the seriousness of the complaint. None of us wants you in criminal trouble. We all respect you around here, Mr Moran. Like you had no intention of doing any harm to anyone. How about if I could manage to have her allegations reduced?"

"Glory be to God! I don't know, Sergeant. I don't know, I don't know. All this thing has come on me so suddenly. I just don't know. I'll be ruined!"

"Ah, no you wouldn't. It would all depend on how I'd manage to reduce the serious charge. Then I'd go into the witness box meself and testify to your good character and you'd be surprised how influential I would be when the time came."

When the time came. What was the man talking about? The witness box. The witness box. The words seared through Donal's mind. The witness box. Was he already in court charged with the rape of a young girl just released from a Mental institution? What would his sons think, and Mary and John Boyle, the neighbours, all his workers, his employees? What about the papers, the local papers? His hands began to shake visibly.

"It would all depend on the nature of the charges. If I had your written word that you didn't mean to do her any harm."

He was making progress so he repeated the salient words, "If I had your written ... " that was the important bit. So again he said, "If I had your written word that you have no recollection of what happened then I might be ablt to get her to drop the serious charge or you know, she might agree to say she more or less consented to the carry on. I'm only trying to help you, Mr Moran."

It could be Moran didn't know that intercourse with a female of unsound mind, even with her consent, is still statutory rape. Once he could get Moran to put pen to paper, he would have him nailed to the Cross of Calvary. And he, Sergeant Donnelly, would be writing out his own promotion, with what those boys in the Knights could then do for him.

His voice became soothing, helpful, inticing again.

"If we could confine it to say some kind of an assault when you were under the influence of drink and with her consent. I could work so she wouldn't have to give evidence. Maybe she wouldn't even have to come to court."

He paused only for a split second to gauge how Moran was reacting.

"All you have to do is put your signature to a piece of paper and I'll do the rest. I think I could maybe get her to say in her statement that it was somehow with her consent."

He almost smiled openly, as he thought of the alterations which he would be able to insert afterwards. Men in Moran's position seldom argued the toss, they were too vulnerable and easily compromised. He had seen it umpteen times, men of his ilk handcuffed in mind and tongue by shame and the attendant publicity.

"And if I didn't?"

It was the first note of dissent, but Sergeant Donnelly determined not to weaken. He musn't show anger, even though the remark had irked him exceedingly. He must continue in the same easy, placatory manner. However, he did feel rebuffed. Perhaps a tougher aproach was required again

"Well, then, I'd have to come out here and arrest you formally. I'd have to charge you with the full facts as complained. There'd be maybe a three- or four-day hearing in court. She'd formally give her evidence alleging that you beat and raped her. Then, you'd have to go into the witness box and deny all that. The counsel for the State would cross-examine you and, to be honest with you Mr Moran, you wouldn't be able to deny the charge. Like, if you have no recollection of the incident then how could you deny her evidence of assault and rape? They'd make bits of you.

"Of course, you'd be found guilty. I'd still give as good a character reference as ever you've heard. You know with rape, especially on a girl of infirm mind ... At the same time, I must write down your response now to her allegations. Really, I should be much more officious."

He took from his pocket the same notebook, a biro and a safety pin. With the pin he began to explore the deep recesses of his left ear, whilst he balanced the notebook on his lap and, writing slowly, called out, "I was too drunk to remember."

He extracted a considerable deposit of wax on the end of the safety pin, turned it about the better to scrutinise it. He cleaned it off the pin with thumb and index finger which he then drew down along the side of the armchair.

Donal said, "And if I signed the bit of paper, then what?"

"Then the statement, I needn't tell you, would be drawn totally in your favour. I'd soften the part about the indecent exposure and the rape. I'm sure I'll obtain a statement from her along similar lines – then what's there to worry about? I don't want this any more than you do. I don't benefit one iota if you get a stretch of ten to fifteen years, nor do I want any gossip in the area. I just want to clear up this terrible allegation as simply as I can with as little damage as possible."

He glanced furtively towards his assistant and received a barely visible nod of approval and congratulations. Garda White well knew that such a statement would be a plea of guilty to assault and sexual assault while drunk, which was not a defence to the charge. Rather, it was a clear plea of guilty.

"And if I do sign the statement? Tell me again."

"Well, one thing for sure, I wouldn't have come out here and formally arrest you and charge you with assault, indecent assault, buggery and rape of a female of unsound mind. I wouldn't have to arrest you and take you in custody to the local court and arrange a special hearing, get a District Judge to remand you, possibly in custody to Mountjoy."

He stared hard at Donal Moran, fixing him with an evil eye. "I wouldn't have to formally read out those charges to you and caution you as follows". He barked out the words – as if he was actually putting the charges that very moment, to further unnerve Donal Moran – "you don't have to say anything in answer to the charges but anything you do say will be taken down in writing and maybe used in evidence."

Again, his voice softened."But if you signed the statement, why, I've no doubt I'd get the Super and the Chief to agree to serve one, at most two, summonses on you. There'd be no need for an arrest if I can possibly help it."

"Whatever you do," his voice hardened, "I'd advise you not to put me to the undesirable job of having to come out here and arrest you, and lead you down to the local court like a common criminal, charged with the worst possible offences against a female of unsound mind. What sort of an eegit – oh, I'm sorry, I didn't mean that. What sort of a man are you that you can't see what you should do, and that as quickly as possible."

"There's just a friend I'd like to talk to first." It was the second time Moran had disappointed the Sergeant. Delay was not a good thing when it came to securing a signature to a statement. A glint of wariness, suspicion, even doubt, flickered in the Sergeant's eyes. He was faced with making another challenging decision. He moved back towards the window and, looking out, told himself to ignore the trees, shrubs, lawns and gardens, and to see instead the light blue uniform and epaulettes of an Inspector of An Garda Siochána, and to steel his resolve.

Yes, in the light blue uniform, being congratulated by his colleagues and friends, especially those at the golf club, of his wife going down the town being congratulated. He thought, too, of that drunk Garda Jim Furlong back at the station; he who was reported as having said loudly one night in the hotel bar, "not whilst his ass is turned towards the ground will the shaggin' Sergeant ever see promotion." He could imagine the guffaws and leers that had brought ringing around the hotel lounge. He would make Jim Furlong eat his words.

"Is it a solicitor, by any chance?" He put on an unconcerned face.

"No, not a solicitor."

"I wouldn't advise a solicitor." The Sergeant walked around the room in a more self-assured manner. His confidence had been restored. If a solicitor were introduced prior to the statement being signed, the Sergeant would be faced with a major problem. Once signed, it didn't matter two figs who Moran consulted.

"I had a case some years ago. Not very different from this one. I gave the man the same option as I'm giving you now, but he went to his solicitor who, of course, had to justify his fee. Well, the solicitor advised him not to make a statement on any account so the poor man arrived into the station to say that. The station Sergeant simply walked around the desk, put his hand on the man's arm, arrested him and charged him with rape."

He paused, to ascertain the amount of fear he was putting into Moran, and then continued, "He was charged before a specially convened court that same evening and his solicitor was in Dublin and couldn't be contacted. So the unfortunate man was remanded in custody to Mountjoy Prison for a week. By the time the first day's hearing was over, after the girl's evidence, it didn't matter two figs whether he was found guilty or not, because when a woman starts to talk about being raped, a man is ruined whether he's guilty or not.

"He came to us in the court and pleaded with us to take some kind of a plea from him. All the officer in charge could say was, "It's too late now."

The Sergeant got sharply out of his seat.

"We'll be off, Mr Moran. I can't give you any two days or anything that long to discuss the matter with your friend. I'll be out here tomorrow at noon, and I'll have two documents with me. The one a statement for you to sign yourself. I'll make it so it's as harmless as can be. If you sign it, I'll try and get permission to serve summonses on you instead of having to arrest you. After you sign it I'll put the utmost pressure on her to drop the serious charge, try and leave a charge only of assault and of sexual assault inso far as you accidently laid a hand on her, try and make it as innocuous as possible. We'll try and put the emphasis on ordinary assault. You can be certain I'll make a good job of it. I'm not in the force to persecute people."

He drew breath. "The second document, should you not sign the first, will be a full charge of rape, indecent assault, buggery, and unlawful carnal knowledge of a female of unsound mind. In that event I'll charge you, arrest you and take you into custody. An application for a remand in custody always follows in cases of that nature.

"I'm sorry I can't be of any further help to you," he said abruptly and walked smartly through the drawing room door and let himself out of the front door without further ado. His assistant followed after him. They got into the car without once looking back. In the mirror they could see that Donal Moran had followed them out.

Without moving his lips, the assistant said, "You were brilliant."

"It's in the bag," the Sergeant murmured. "Don't let the suggestion of a smile cross your face. He could be watching us. In fact, don't glance back at him, but keep looking deadly serious."

He swung the car around on the wide drive and drove down the tree-lined avenue.

Only then, did the Sergeant let out a triumphant, "Yipee!"

His assistant said, "My God! I'll hand it to you. You did a great job. Do you know, but you'll get your promotion after this one, and Jim Furlong will have to eat his words."

"Just what I was thinking myself, in there in the middle of the fray. Garda Jim Furlong, drunkard and good for nothing, will have to eat his words. Keep him in the dark about all this. He's dangerous. You wouldn't know what that man might do."

"Inspector Donnelly," Garda White pronounced the words with special emphasis. "Do you know, but it has a natural ring to it. As for Donal Moran, he'd be a fair capture. At the same time, I'm wondering if we didn't make a mistake."

"A mistake! How?" The car swerved as he spun round to face him. "What mistake?"

"I wonder if we'd put more pressure on him there and then if he wouldn't have signed a statement, not given him any tomorrow."

"No, he wouldn't have signed. Besides, I didn't have the statement thought out. We'll have to word it in a way that it looks innocent enough but that at the same time nails him to the cross. With all his wealth and success, you wouldn't expect him to be so kind of innocent, now would you? How was I to know he was going to plead literally guilty there and then.

"But he'll sign. I tell you, I'll make sure of it."

CHAPTER 21

The moment the two Garda officers left, Donal Moran drove straight to the Boyles. Mary was in the yard.

"Jesus, Mary, a terrible thing has happened to me."

The whole story tumbled out, he omitted nothing. He emphasised that he had been unable to tell the Sergeant where he was that night, or if he had indeed met BoBo Doorley.

"And what sort of an eegit are you to say you couldn't remember!"

"I was brought up to tell the truth, and that's what I did."

Never before had Mary been so vehement in the words she spat out next. "And if you didn't remember doing it, why in hell's name didn't you, like any right-minded person, simply say, 'No, I didn't meet, see, or have anything to do with that girl whatever.' And that, too, would have been the truth as far as you were concerned if you couldn't remember."

She paused, and studied the shocked and frightened face of her lifelong friend. She was upset to see him so distressed. Her thoughts were racing.

"We'll fight," she said at last.

Donal knew that when Mary said that, she would be no pushover. She would go to any lengths, expense or toughness to defend a friend. No man could wish for a more loyal or generous friend.

They were still standing in the yard.

"Let's go in," she said. "John and David are inside, but they'll have to know sooner or later."

Donal hesitated, "What about the new man?"

"He's alright, you won't have to worry about him."

They went into the kitchen.

"Of course, the girl is telling lies," Mary said. "There's no doubt in my mind, and we'll prove it. You were in here that night, Donal, and you were incapable of doing anything like that. And what about that, Sergeant?"

"Well, like I explained, I found him helpful."

"Watch him," she said sharply. "You know the Garda who works in the station there with him, Jim Furlong, he told me that man would prosecute his own mother if he thought it would advance his promotion. Watch him, I say. He's dangerous. And don't be in a hurry to sign anything. Especially without seeing a solicitor."

"But the Sergeant said…"

"Don't mind what that man said," she interrupted. "You'd want to hear what Jim Furlong says about him. Isn't that right, John?"

John stood up, crossed the room, and took Donal's two hands in his.

"Listen to what that woman has to say to you. Jim Furlong comes out here regularly, sits in with us often at night. You wouldn't believe what that Sergeant is capable of. Anything, it seems. Donal," he looked him straight in the eye, "we're your friends and aren't likely to lead you astray. I have no doubt but that girl is telling lies. I would also have no doubt whatever that the Sergeant could be telling lies as well."

"Maybe we should phone Jim Furlong," David Stapleton suggested. The others agreed and he tried phoning him at his digs. His landlady answered and she promised to convey the message as soon as he returned.

"I'll tell him its urgent and, if I've gone to bed, I'll leave a message."

David thanked her and returned to the kitchen.

"I was thinking," Mary said. "Surely BoBo Dorley would have to give evidence, isn't that right?"

"What's the point you're trying to make?" John asked.

"Well, what if she doesn't. What then? Surely, it means There's no case."

"You're right," David said. "There was such a case recently, I read it in the papers. No evidence, no case. That was what the judge said and he dismissed it. The judge said the case should not have been brought."

"Mmm … I think I'll have a little chat with that BoBo." Mary's mind was racing. "She was around here recently and I had it in mind anyway to have a word with her about that. Besides, remember, it was I who called the ambulance the last time she beat up the old pair. She was packed off to the Mental. If you'd seen that old pair and their condition after the beating she gave them you'd like to address her on the subject. I've a few words to say to her."

David at once cautioned her to be careful, stressing that she should not do anything she might later regret. Her mind was made up and not even David was going to change it. She turned to Donal.

"I'll speak with her tonight." She paused, then added, "I doubt if she'll give evidence against you."

A dark shadow fell across Mary's determined face. She had seen Donal out and was rummaging in the old clothes cupboard.

David Stapleton joined her.

"You're going up to that girl now." He sounded concerned.

"Yes."

"I'll come with you."

"No."

She got up off her knees and held out an old leather jacket and a thick winter coat which had once been John's. She put on the jacket and studied the coat which was several sizes too big. She slipped it over the jacket and buttoned it right up, covering much of her face. She tried an old slouch hat but, unhappy with that, she searched around again and came up with a beret. David watched as she rammed that down over her ears and forehead and then placed the slouch hat on top. A further diligent search produced what she was looking for – a pair of old-fashioned driving gloves made of thick leather which came up above her wrists almost to her elbows.

"Now, David, like a good man, fetch me the cowstick."

"Do you mean the one in the corner?"

"There's only one cowstick in this house. Do you mind getting it for me?"

He handed her the gnarled stick. It had knots down the length of it.

"That's it, thanks. I'm off now, I'll be back shortly."

She pulled on a pair of wellington boots and, with John and David staring at her bizarre garb with incredulity, she was gone.

John called out after her. "Mary! Where're you going?"

"Back soon." She slammed the door, muttering, and headed off determinedly towards the Doorley's by foot. She didn't want a car engine to alert them of her visit. Neither did she knock on their door or call out.

She lifted the latch and walked directly into the kitchen. The old woman, as BoBo's mother was known, was seated in a high chair at one side of the open fire, and her husband on the other. On the rare occasions on which the couple went out, they seldom spoke to anyone.

BoBo was in the centre of the room, in one of her tantrums. Mary marched directly towards her, menacingly.

"What talk are you going on about?" she demanded. "About people in this locality. What stories are you telling about them to the Gardaí?"

Mary noticed the girl's eyes dart sideways towards the kitchen table. On it lay a short, thin, tapering two-sided knife, more a stiletto than a knife. It certainly wasn't designed for cutting bread.

Its presence goaded Mary into being even more belligerent. She challenged BoBo again. "We don't want any more of your lies. And for that matter, we don't want any more of you attacking your mother and father, and then running off to the shelter of that hospital.

"You're a bad bitch, that's what you are. And I'm going to put an end to your ways. Mad is it, they say you are. You're not mad ..." her voice was rising."You're just plain bad. A bad and a lazy bitch of a girl."

Angry she might be, but Mary was also watching BoBo as she sidled towards the stiletto. Suddenly BoBo lunged forward and snatched it but Mary was ready. She raised the cowstick and brought it down hard, full force on the back of BoBo's hand. The knife dropped with a clatter as BoBo shrieked in pain. She clutched her hand to her breast, and covered it with her other hand. Mary struck that one with a cutting side lash from the cowstick.

All the while the old couple remained motionless in their fireside seats, their glazed eyes staring vacantly in the direction of the fighting women.

BoBo flung herself to the floor, screaming hysterically, at the same time as wriggling her way on her stomach towards the knife. Mary raised the cowstick again and brought it down hard against the girl's bare legs. With her foot, she pinned BoBo's clutched injured hands to the ground. Satisfied that she wouldn't reach the knife, Mary kicked it further out of the way. She remained standing over BoBo, stick raised.

"Now, don't you ever go to the Gardaí again and tell lies about Donal Moran, you bad bitch! Let that be an end to your tantrums in this area. Decent men have more to do in this locality than compete with your idle tongue, you lazy bitch. I want to hear no more of your going into any Garda Sergeant."

BoBo cried pitifully on the floor, cowering.

"Stop! Leave me alone!"

"Let that be an end to your trouble-making." Mary lowered her voice, "and no more talk about Donal Moran."

Mary was shaking. It was the first time she had ever struck another human being. She knew she had hurt the girl, but that had been her intention. She had done it for her friend, Donal.

BoBo's shrieks lessened to sobs. Mary put down the cowstick and knelt beside the girl, drew her towards her and cradled her in her arms. BoBo began rocking to and fro. Mary glanced towards the fire. Both the old man and woman were rocking back and forth in their chairs.

The back door flung open, and John and David strode into the kitchen.

"Are you all right?"

" 'Course I am," she said, hoping they wouldn't notice how much she was shaking. "But it would be as well to call the doctor. Just in case her hand is damaged. I don't think it is, though."

She glanced down at BoBo. "And she's going to be a good girl from now on."

The first thing the doctor asked on his arrival was how she had been injured. Mary nodded towards the tapered stiletto, still on the floor.

"She tried to attack me with that and I fended her off with a cowstick. I'm not going to report her to the Gardaí. We're all friends now, aren't we, BoBo?" She looked down at BoBo still rocking in her arms. "Aren't we?"

The doctor examined and treated her hands, gave her a note for an X-ray the next day, and a pain-killing injection. He recommended bed and left two painkillers for her to take in the morning.

Mary supported her down to the bedroom and helped her undress. She was almost overcome by the stench in the bedroom and the fetid whiff which came from her body as she was undressing her. BoBo was hardly in bed when she was sleeping peacefully.

Mary herself still felt highly agitated and tried to compose herself as she walked out of the house and across the small front garden. John and David were waiting for her under a silver birch tree by the gate.

"Are you all right?" they asked in unison.

"Shaking, but I'm OK."

John Boyle put his arms around her and held her to him in silence for a few moments. Then he murmured, "Mary, you were a great girl to do that for Donal."

CHAPTER 22

Sleep was impossible for Donal Moran. He had gone to bed just after midnight but his head was still spinning from that Sergeant's visit, and his stomach was churning. He wondered how Mary had got on. Had she really been to see BoBo? Might she have persuaded her not to give evidence against him? He tried reading. He watched TV. At one stage, he even got out his accounts book.

It was no good. Sleep was out of the question. It was late but perhaps his neighbours were still up. It was worth a try. He dressed and drove over. He pulled into their yard and was relieved to see the kitchen lights on. David Stapleton greeted him at the back door.

"Well?" Donal asked.

"Come on in and get the story from herself."

Mary and John were at the kitchen table, drinking tea.

"Well?" Donal asked again.

"She'll not be giving evidence against you."

Donal sank into the nearest easy chair and was silent for a minute. He felt as if he had been reprieved from a death sentence. At last, he spoke.

"Dear Mary Boyle, I'll never forget you for this, never as long as I live. What happened? How did she change her mind?"

The cowstick lay not a yard from where he sat, resting against the table edge. Mary nodded in its direction. The joy on his face faded and his features darkened.

"Oh, no, Mary, not that. Was anybody hurt?"

"She went for a knife and I gave her a few well-aimed and deserved strokes of the stick. Yes, she bawled, don't you know. You'd expect that from her even if she wasn't hurt. Just in case, however, I called the doctor, to be on the safe side. He said she'd be all right and confirmed nothing was broken."

She brought the teapot from the range and poured him a cup.

"The main thing is that I'm confident she'll not now give evidence, I'm sure of it."

"But you could have brought all sorts of trouble on yourself."

Mary laughed. "I couldn't care less, I can handle that kind of trouble – why do you think I wore so many layers of outer protective clothing. No, I'll face any kind of trouble of like nature that comes my way.

"But the other, where she has implicated you on a charge of sexual assault, is a different kettle of fish entirely. There's no way you could handle that in court."

The phone rang.

"That'll be Garda Jim Furlong." Mary made off down the hall to answer it. Donal and David followed. John stayed in his chair.

Mary outlined to the Garda the details of the Sergeant's visit to Donal Moran.

"I knew it, I knew he was up to something," Jim told her. "It explains a lot of his antics and secrecy of the last few days, him and my colleague, Garda White. What have you done, or have you done anything yet?"

Mary told him of her own intervention with BoBo. There was an ominous silence on the other end of the phone.

"Hello, Jim? Jim?"

"Well, that's about the worst thing you could have done. Of all the stupid things! Jesus! I didn't think, Mary Boyle, you could be such a stupid woman!"

"I bet her because she went for a knife, and because I was the one who had to call the ambulance for her poor mother six months ago after the merciless beating that bitch gave the poor creature, and then ran off to hide in the Mental hospital."

Mary straightened up and with a mix of defiance and confidence she added, "Finally, I did it out of loyalty for a friend, and I regret nothing, Jim Furlong. I'd do it all over again this minute if I had to. So there!"

Furlong hesitated, then said resignedly, "Ah, sure, I know you would."

"So where do we go from here?" Mary asked. David and Donal hovered nearby. "Donal has to make a statement tomorrow, I think before noon."

"A statement. A statement? What kind of statement?"

"I don't know. Just that the Sergeant told him it would be ready for him tomorrow by twelve. I don't really know too much about that part. Here, hold on, he's here beside me. I'll put him on, hold on."

She turned back from the small table and handed the phone to Donal, stepping back behind him, beside David. David reached out and touched her shoulders with his fingertips and then her neck. She grabbed his hand. She was still shaky.

Donal was in deep conversation, explaining to the Garda exactly how the Sergeant had tried to procure a statement from him.

David lent into Mary's ear and whispered, "You're the most beautiful woman in the world. I'm madly in love with ..."

The phone was let back onto its hook.

"He's coming out," Donal said, turning to the pair. There was unconcealed relief in his voice. "Do you know what he said? Well, he said he personally believed there was no case against me whatever. I wonder how he knows that."

"Come on, David," Mary urged. "Sandwiches. We'll make a plate of sandwiches, tea and coffee."

John, still seated by the fire, looked up. "Jim Furlong won't thank you for that. You may do a bit better than that, my love, and I think I'll have a little drop to keep him company."

"I'll have it for you in two seconds, love."

"No, not now Mary, I won't have it until Jim comes. I don't like drinking on me own."

She and David set to with the sandwiches.

"Do you know, it's as if I knew that we were in for a late night. I brought home a cake and apple tart from town this morning."

It was gone 1a.m. when Jim Furlong arrived.

"Right," he said, addressing them all together, "we"ve work to do before morning. I've been thinking coming out in the car."

"Well, a little drop of whiskey won't dim the brains," Mary said, picking up the bottle.

"Keep it on hold, Mary. There's work to be done first. Just everyone listen to me for a minute."

He stood by the table and spoke quickly. "The Sergeant has made a mistake." He paused to let the importance of that assertion sink in. "A monumental mistake, let me add."

He glanced towards Mary. "According to you, the Sergeant alleges a rape took place at the field gate. Maybe it did. However, not with Donal, here," he nodded slightly towards Donal. "You see, two men were on that road that night coming from Tullamore. They saw the lights of a car in the ditch and pulled up to help. It was you, Donal. You were paralytic drunk and had dropped the keys of the car on to the floor and couldn't find them. You were stuck in the ditch. Miraculously, you did no damage, except minor to the driver's door. The car might well have gone over the top. There was a considerable drop into the field on the far side. Anyway, these two men towed you home, you in the passenger seat of their car and the other steering your own car. They left you seated in an easy chair in your own kitchen. You were hardly able to walk, that's what they informed me next day in case something should arise out of the incident. And now bedad it has.

"They told me in confidence. They were not reporting it officially in case that bleddy auld daft Sergeant would charge you with being drunk in charge and summons them as witnesses."

"Besides, there was more to it than that, and they didn't want the story to get around in fairness to you.

"You see, the bold BoBo was in on top of you when they pulled up. Both of them know and recognised her. You know she's mad, and no one should ever have anything to do with her."

He threw Mary a short sharp look of disapproval before continuing.

"As I say, she's bonkers. What they had to say wasn't very nice and I'll spare your blushes, but they saw her and she was sexually assaulting you. The driver's door was wide open. It wasn't very nice what she was doing. You weren't able to fend her off. As soon as they stepped out of the car, she bolted and ran off down the road. It was about a half-mile from the field gate."

He paused and looked from one to another of his listeners around the table.

"Mother of God!" John announced with incomprehension breaking the silence."What's the world coming to?"

Jim Furlong continued, "About a year ago, just after the Sergeant came here, a valuable racing saddle was stolen. A newly-married itinerant lad undoubtedly took it. We didn't have any evidence to prove the case against him. The Sergeant and I went out to the camp and the lad, as you'd expect, denied all knowledge of the theft, but, he says, I'll keep an eye out and if I find it I'll let yez know.

"The saddle was left back that evening. Now, we hadn't cautioned the chap and, of course, he'd denied the matter, so there was no case whatever against him. As far as we were all concerned in the station the matter ended there. We never saw the saddle in his possession. It was left back."

Jim paused, looking at the others. "But the bleddy Sergeant put a summons on the itinerant. In court he lied outright. Of course, he was believed rather than the lad. I couldn't believe he'd tell a deliberate lie. Back at the station one night I got out the file to see if I could learn some reason why the Superintendent hadn't called me to give evidence and, damn it, if the Sergeant hadn't said he'd been on his own. The lad got three months.

"There's another case too, but I'm saying nothing about that at the moment. I'll trap him with your case and then I'll bring up the other two. The one concerning the young itinerant and the other which relates to a priest, and I believe there's a further matter still.

He looked at Donal."In your case, he has obviously made out a statement for you to sign. That's highly irregular. I'm going into the station tonight and getting hold of that file. Tell me," he looked to Donal, "have you a photo copying machine at home?"

"I have."

"Then I'll copy the file before morning and return it before anyone comes into the station in the morning. I want to know what the Doorley one said in her statement of complaint. That'll be an interesting one. We'll copy that as well. We'll copy the whole file.

"You do the driving, Donal. I don't want my car to be seen near the station. You come too, David, and keep watch while I raid my own barracks."

The town was deserted as the three men drove up the main street. They turned into a side road, which brought the back door of the station into view.

"I have the key to that door." Jim Furlong held it up. "It's a door which's seldom used, in fact never. I hope the damn thing isn't stuck."

He held up a second key. "That, gentlemen, is the key to the Sergeant's desk."

Then he explained to the other two that one of the most fascinating aids in the detection of crime is the number of unsuspecting witnesses who make themselves available to the investigators, those people who, even at night, watch and note the goings on of everyone who is abroad.

"That's why I don't want to go to the front door. I want us to avoid those prying eyes if at all possible. I don't want some busybody accosting the Sergeant early in the morning and smarmily greeting him with something like, "Oh, Sergeant, I see ye're busy these nights at the station. I want to move against the Sergeant before he's got time to cover up."

He got out of the car and walked up the laneway towards the door which looked out across an empty space of fields, gardens and allotments. There were no houses, doors or windows overlooking it. The key turned in the door. The handle also turned but there was no movement of the door itself. Donal, seated in his car, and David up at the far end of the lane, watched and waited in silence.

Jim Furlong put his shoulder to the door. It wouldn't budge. He gave it a light jostle and that had no effect either. Then, he put his right knee to the timber and threw his right shoulder against the door. The silence of the night was shattered by the jammed door giving way. It was like a gun shot in the night air.

Jim Furlong pressed on regardless of the disturbance, there was little else he could do but hope that the noise had not been heard and that his movements were not being watched by some late-night observer. He moved swiftly through the darkened outer office and into the Sergeant's room where he groped down along the desk until he reached the bottom drawer. It was locked as always. Immediately that anyone entered the room, the Sergeant would shutter and lock the drawer which led Jim Furlong to suspect there was something amiss or even shocking in there. The key fitted and the lock turned. The drawer contained three files. One was about BoBo and one concerned the priest. Curious about the third file, he held it under the pool of light that shone through the window from a street lamp. From the brief precursory glance this dim light afforded him, he decided it should be photocopied as well.

He closed the drawer but didn't lock it and letting himself out onto the back lane drew the door to, but without fully shutting it.

Under the car map-light, he went hurriedly through the file. It contained an official foolscap sheet with some incoherent notes scribbled on it – a tall man dressed in black – a peaked cloth cap – field gate of Donal Moran's – Got a lift from him in morning – pissed at gate – indecent exposure. This was followed by a question mark and the comment – maybe I can establish.

The statement which it was expected Donal Moran should sign before midday was on file. It referred to his exposing himself to BoBo that morning. It was at the end of the first paragraph. There was no full stop and there was a considerable space before the next sentence began. Further down it read, "I may have assaulted her. I was drunk and didn't know what I was doing. I have been told by Sergeant Donnelly that she is accusing me of having assaulted ..." There was a blank space again before more typing – "If I interfered with her I am sorry. I didn't realise because of the drink."

"Jesus!" exclaimed Jim Furlong. "That's dynamite! You're being set up. If you put your hand to that, you'd swing. Christ, but he's a danger to society! This time, though, he's gone too far. As soon as we have these three files copied, we'll leave them back."

As he was speaking, he was turning the two sheets of paper back and forth and looking behind them, before adding excitedly, "Do you know, but there's no statement from BoBo on this file. There's no information accusing you of any wrong against her. Yet in your partially completed statement, you acknowledged she has accused you of rape. Don't you see – either she has refused to sign a statement or else she did not nominate you as her attacker. Or finally she's playing some crazy game which would need investigating by one of the girls in the force who have been specially trained to establish the truth in these kinds of cases. I know the way that man's mind works, but this time it's worked against himself."

Jim Furlong continued, "The complaint against the priest was made four weeks ago. There are two statements in it, both by women who allege to have been attacked by him in a most vicious manner. As far as I can see, the Sergeant is trying to placate the two women to ingratiate himself with the powers that be in the Church. He's a bigger fool than I thought. He hasn't yet reported that file to Divisional Headquarters."

Then he glanced hurriedly through the third file.

"Holy divine God!" he exclaimed. "But the feckin' Sergeant has gone bonkers. I always knew there was a bent in the bastard. But Jesus, this is ridiculous!" As he turned over the few pages, he was laughing nervously at what he was reading.

It was a dossier on the movements and activities, along with personal descriptions such as appearances and vulnerabilities, of any woman who had alleged acts of violence against their husbands before the Family Law courts in recent times.

Though neatly catalogued, scripted and painstakingly collated, it had nothing whatever to do with his work as a police officer. In fact, no senior Garda officer or authority would tolerate the keeping of such a file on record in a Garda Station let alone counsel or cooperate in its preparation.

Some of the entries were accompanied by a pencilled-in synoptic note such as: Young woman – poor background – husband barred from home for twelve months – told her I might call to house some night. She said, "Yes, Sergeant".

After entering the name and address of another woman, his comments began as in the previous portrait: Young woman – age 22 or 23 years – poor background – weak – frightened – outside the court put hand innocently on her shoulder – no objections – rubbed thumb along bare neck – no objection – told her I'd call some night to ensure she was alright.

Another entry, having described the woman as about forty years of age, the pencilled note read: body ageing – but lips beautiful – could make her use lips? – call some night.

The Sergeant did not have a reputation for womanising, but he wouldn't be the first administrative officer since time began to develop in midlife a fetishism towards women who are easily dominated or compromised.

"Jesus, but the bastard has gone bonkers! I just can't believe what's in here. He has no right, no right whatever to keep those kind of records in the station. I'll be with the Superintendent first thing tomorrow morning."

At eight thirty the next morning, Garda Jim Furlong rang the doorbell of Superintendent Joe Murphy's house on the Dublin Road, Portlaoise. He was nervous about meeting the Super, even though he had the reputation of being a friendly man, a plain talker and strictly honest. Nonetheless, Jim was apprehensive. The Super was well acquainted with Jim's drink record, and that put him at a disadvantage in respect of the mission he had embarked on.

The Super's wife, a pleasant cheerful woman who taught at the local secondary school, opened the door. Jim Furlong apologised for his presence on her doorstep so early in the morning. She made him welcome and insisted on his coming down the hallway into the kitchen where the children were being got ready for school.

Jim Furlong was greeted coolly in the kitchen by Superintendent Murphy. He was formal and the Garda felt decidedly uneasy in his superior's kitchen. For a moment, he wished he hadn't bothered taking on the task. Beads of sweat appeared on his forehead in the heat of the kitchen. The look the Superintendent gave him seemed to say, "So you're over here now looking for some favour because of trouble you're in over drink."

Jim Furlong only ever acknowledged his weaknesses. He never recognised his attributes.

"What brings you over to see me here at this . . ." the Super hesitated for a brief moment; he looked out of sorts. "At this awkward hour of the day. Could it not wait until later on?"

For a moment, Jim White was tongue-tied.

"No, sir. It could not. As you know I've never bothered you before and only that it's very serious in my opinion, I wouldn't be here now either."

The Superintendant led Jim into a side room, away from the chattering children.

"Go on."

"There are odd things happening over there in that station of ours that I thought you should know about."

"Like what?"

"Well, for a start, sir, two women complained about a priest interfering with them."

"Do you mean sexually? And do you mean, they complained he used force?"

"Yes, to both counts."

"Go on."

"He's a diocesan priest. Well, what the Sergeant is trying to do is to get the two women to withdraw their statements. One of them came to me last week and complained bitterly. Said it's because she is a poor woman. The Sergeant has been in discussion with the local parish priest about the incident and I believe he's had a number of meetings with the bishop. Maybe I'm wrong now. Correct me, if I am. I believe it hasn't been reported to you as yet in the normal way as laid down."

"It certainly has not. Are you sure about this?"

"I'm telling you one of the women complained to me of a cover-up."

"How long is it since the women first reported the matters?"

"About a month ago."

"A month," the Super emphasised in disbelief. "Are you sure? Are you certain of this?"

"There's a file on it in the Sergeant's office."

"What's in it?"

"I've a photocopy of it."

"You know you're not supposed to do that."

"I do, sir."

"Have you got it there in that envelope?"

"I have, sir. And sir, there are two more I think you ought to see."

"Let me see it. What else have you got?

Jim Furlong now began to feel a little more confident that he had done the right thing and that he could be more resolute in explaining the details of the Donal Moran file. The third file spoke for itself.

"Do you know Donal Moran?"

"Of course I do. Doesn't everyone? A very fine man."

Garda Furlong related the whole story of Donal Moran's drunken lapse, of Bubo's nocturnal wanderings, and of her allegations.

"The Sergeant is trying to get Moran to put pen to paper and acknowledge he fingered BoBo. What the Sergeant doesn't know is the part about the two men who saw him from their car. Of course, Mr Moran is terrified and, at this stage, he'd sign anything. I've had a word with him. When the Sergeant calls on him today with the prepared statement, he is going to have a solicitor concealed in the room."

"Have you got the statement?"

"Here it is."

After glancing at it for a few seconds, he looked up in horror.

"God almighty! This man is a lunatic! Incidentally, that should have been reported to us immediately and it hasn't either. You've another file."

"Here, sir."

After reading the first statement on it, he closed it. Jim Furlong couldn't resist the temptation.

"Who would have ordered him to investigate those women and record it in the station?" he asked in his most innocent voice.

The Superintendent looked as if he was being mildly ridiculed and threw a derisive look in Jim Furlong's direction. Ignoring the question, he went to a phone in the corner of the room.

"Hello, Chief. We've got a problem. Yes, it's serious alright. You know that new Sergeant?" There was a pause."Well, Garda Furlong is with me and he's brought me evidence that's serious enough to put the lot of us on the front pages of the English Sunday papers."

After further discussion he said, "O.K. I'll go to the station immediately and take over all files. I'll see you there as soon as you've fully alerted the Commissioner's officer of the possible scandal."

He left down the phone and turned to Jim. "What time does the Sergeant get into the station in the morning?"

"On the dot of nine forty five."

"We'll be in time."

"This is serious stuff. You could be saying goodbye to your Sergeant before this day is out. How did you travel over here this morning?"

"By car."

"Your own car?"

"Yes."

"What breed of a car is it?"

Before Jim Furlong had time to reply the Super said, "Come on, we'll take mine. We have to move fast to get to the station before the Sergeant does. I want to be seated behind his desk when he arrives."

"If we park behind the station, your car won't be seen. I've left the back door unlocked."

The Super glanced sideways at him."If you could only stay off the drink, Jim Furlong, you'd have my job."

Jim phoned Donal Moran as soon as he arrived at the station.

"I've got good news for you. I don't think there'll be anyone looking to you for a statement today. In fact, I don't think you need to worry about this matter anymore. I'm here with the Superintendent and he has allowed me to make this phone call."

There was a pause. Finally, Donal replied. "I don't know how to thank you. I'll never be able to thank you enough." There was a break in his voice. "To think I'd have signed that statement believing the man was doing me a favour. Do you know something? I was terrified out of my life. I never understood before how people sign statements to things they didn't do. Now I know."

As Garda Furlong put down the phone, Sergeant Donnelly walked into the station and looked at Furlong.

"Sergeant, Superintendent Murphy is in your office and would like to have a word with you."

CHAPTER 23

Donal Moran couldn't believe his eyes when the small girl, Julie, was presented to him. He stood speechless for a few seconds taking in every aspect of her appearance.

She was the picture of his mother, slimly built with the same straight hair parted down the middle of her head, and the slightly pointed nose. She was only a little girl but the similarity was uncanny, even the eyes, especially the eyes, were those of her great-grandmother.

He bent down and lifting her slowly in his arms pressed her to him, their faces touching.

"Are you my granddad?"

"I am."

"Why didn't you come to see me before now?"

Donal remembered the book Mary had given him, a short treatise by a child psychologist to help people such as Donal in the kind of situation he now found himself. The chief lesson he had learned from it was to tell the child the truth. No fairy tales or excuses. So, he was careful now to tell the little girl the true situation.

"I never knew," his kind voice was tinged with regret, "that I had a granddaughter. I only heard about you the other day. Same as you only heard about me the other day."

She seemed perfectly happy with the explanation. They were now jointly responsible for the enigmatic position in which they found themselves. It was a good start, better than their journey down. Sharon was driving and Julie repeatedly stood up out of the back and positioned herself between the two front seats, ignoring her mother's protests and regarding her newfound grandfather with great interest. She had refused to be drawn into any further conversation with him. When they arrived at the house, he carried their bags inside and upstairs.

"I have the two of you here together in the one large room. I hope you'll both stay with us a long time."

As he came down the stairs, he heard the little girl's steps following him. He waited for her and, to his astonishment, she took his hand in hers and they went down together to the drawing room.

"Have you any toys?"

"I don't think so. Isn't that a shame?"

"But haven't you got a nursery?"

"A nursery? Oh, there's an old nursery," he said. "Who told you about that?"

"Joe. Joe told me."

"Your Dad used to ...." Then, he realised what he was saying and stopped. She hadn't noticed.

"My two sons used to play in the nursery when they were children. I don't know if there are any toys up there now. It's been years since anyone's been into it."

"Will you show it to me?"

He had been sitting in the easy chair appraising her, still struck by the noticeable resemblance she had to his own mother. He felt odd sitting alone in the room with a child who was his beloved mother's great-grandchild and a replica of her. He had never looked at either of his two sons in that light. Whilst there was a similarity between Joe and his grandmother, it was nothing like as noticeable as that of the child. Besides, Joe had much of his own bulk about the shoulders and chest. Being a girl emphasised Julie's likeness with his mother.

He sank back into a reverie. He wondered, if he were able to go back in time, would he find in some rural cottage of bygone days a boy, a man who was his own exact replica? On the other hand, could some man now, this very minute, in some other far-flung corner of the world, look like his twin? Maybe a man driving across Brooklyn Bridge with his eyes in the sun and his thoughts on some business matter in the city could have a double in some far away foreign place. Or would a well-tailored girl striding down Oxford Street, with long gait and stunning looks attracting the attention of the other shoppers, have a distant-unacquainted cousin pulling pints in a pub overlooking Bantry Bay, and possessing her every single look and characteristic?

What if those of all the generations, past and present, could be gathered up from Bantry to Brooklyn, from Dublin to Durban, from Liverpool to Limerick and from Boston to Botany Bay, from over the entire globe, would there be hundreds or thousands who would match perfectly one with another, and would the girl in Oxford Street and the man driving across Brooklyn Bridge find scores of twins not just in appearance but having the like voice intonation, mannerisms, fears, and hopes?

His daydreaming was interrupted by Julie, just as his mother would have done, to ask the same question as before.

"Are you really my granddad?"

"I am."

"And you didn't come to see me before now."

"I couldn't," was all he could manage.

"Why," she persisted, "didn't you ever come to see me? Never at all?"

"I suppose ... I was waiting."

She considered the answer for a moment, her bright eyes sparkling.

"What were you waiting for?"

In total disregard for the expert on child psychology, he lifted her into the air and swung her about.

"I was waiting to give you all the kisses and hugs of six years at the one time."

They went hand in hand up the stairs to the old nursery and there searched amongst the drawers which contained faded and battered toys. She was delighted with the trip. They lifted out teddies, trucks, games, and balls, and she laughed and cooed for the first time.

He brought her over to see Mary Boyle who hugged her over and over and cried copious tears as she held the little mite.

"The poor little pet," she called out again and again, as she squeezed and hugged Julie to her bosom.

To his amazement on the following day, Julie accompanied him everywhere he went and she was beginning to be less solemn. She even managed an occasional smile.

He had no doubt she was his granddaughter. They were tied together and he became determined that Joe would gain custody of his child.

She went everywhere with him and began to grow on him and he became attached to her in a way he would never have thought possible, and there was no doubting Julie's affection for her granddad.

The little girl would never have taken to him as she did had there not been this blood affinity between them, of that he was totally convinced. He loved her innocence and she loved him simply because he was her granddad.

The peace was shaken by a telephone call. It was from the Registrar of the court in Drogheda where the custody case had been listed. The judge, Judge Evan Suleman, would like to see the parties in court the following afternoon to set a date for hearing. The Registrar stressed with clinical firmness there would not be a hearing or indeed any evidence taken on the morrow. The purpose was to agree between the parties the number of witnesses they intended calling for the forthcoming case, and for the judge himself to nominate any witnesses whom he considered necessary.

That evening the prison authorities phoned to say, because of the seriousness of the parental suit and the exceptional circumstances, that they were releasing Joe under powers vested in the Minister for Justice.

Sharon, Donal and Julie travelled to Drogheda in good time to meet with Joe and the solicitor, a Mr Georgie Ryan, a lawyer with an exceptional reputation. They soon discovered why. He was from the Dundalk area but he did not speak with a northern accent. If anything, his voice was harsher. However, it could also be full of charm, compassion and coaxing when he chose, especially when on his feet in court. His clothes were so dreary and unkempt that a stranger might be forgiven for assuming he had slept in them. The jacket was of a dull green with nondescript pattern and always shabby, even when it was comparatively new. The trousers were so big and baggy that he could have fitted both his legs into one trouser leg. They were of a military green which clashed with the jacket. The shirt could be any shade of brown and his dull brown shoes were unpolished.

It was said that he once arrived in court still wearing his bedroom slippers, to the embarrassment of his colleagues, but not to himself. He had a head of thick, wiry, tangled auburn hair which never saw a comb or a brush. It looked as if it would be impossible to pull the teeth of a comb through it.

Though when he spoke of legal import, his mind was crystal clear. Gifted on his feet, he possessed a devastating tongue, and he could also be extremely witty. His presence and manner were compelling. Whenever he rose in court, those present hung onto every word he spoke.

The judge smiled when he walked out onto the bench. A young man with a mane of dark black hair, he wore an expensive navy suit with a rich red handkerchief pouring out of his breast pocket, and a large red bow tie to match. The hearing lasted but a few minutes.

The solicitor on the other side, Mr Jack Browne read out an agreed list of the witnesses who would be called by both sides, with a brief synopsis of the kind of evidence each was expected to give. The judge seemed satisfied with the number. Two doctors were being called to give evidence on behalf of Sharon. These doctors had been assigned to her rehabilitation programme and were going to say that she was now fully capable of looking after her child.

The hearing date was set for that day week. Then the bombshell came. The judge said he would like the little girl to go back into the care of Sister Carmel until the day of the hearing.

Sharon made a move from her seat.

"Judge," she addressed him, "she's very happy just now getting accustomed to being away from the institution. She's already spent too much of her time in institutions. Through my fault. She'll be broken-hearted."

At this, Donal Moran expected an eruption from the bench. He was reasonably familiar with judges seemingly incapable of acting in a patient, dignified manner when so addressed by a concerned member of the public.

In a pleasant, affable voice, the judge replied that he appreciated her concern and assured her that it was being done for a very special reason. He then further ordered that he would prefer if none of those interested had access to her until after the hearing.

He looked about the court. "Is there anything else?"

"Nothing else, sir," the Registrar replied.

Donal felt he should also protest. He felt he had failed the little girl. How often already in her young life had she been disappointed? How long, he wondered, would it take next time to put a childish smile back on her cheeks? So many institutions, convents and orphanages had left her solemn, feeling rejected. Now even the granddad to whom she was clinging had disappointed her and was allowing her to be taken back to the orphanage. He moved to contribute something but Georgie Ryan, with a firm cautionary finger, bade him return to his seat.

The judge's decision saddened him greatly. Worse, because of the judge's order, he couldn't now say goodbye or give Julie any explanation. It set a terrible train of thought buzzing about his head. What if the decision next week were to go against them? The judge stood up and bowed. Everyone in the courtroom stood as he left the bench.

Donal, deep in thought, was almost the last to leave the courtroom when he became aware of an altercation developing between Tommy Gavin and his solicitor.

Donal pretended to read the paper. He strained his ears. The solicitor was vexed.

"I told you to have your father here today so that I could have a word with him. After all, the little girl spent nearly three months with him. You've got to have him here the next day. He's on the list of witnesses. If you are reluctant to call him, then you should have said so, and let me decide whether to call him or not. I don't know what we can do now since it might look bad for us, if the other side questions why he is not available.

"What's more, you were to have an agreed sum of money with you today. Where is it?"

"Honestly, Mr Browne, I'll definitely have it next ..."

The solicitor turned on his heel and stormed out of the courtroom saying, "You had better have it here the next day – and your father as well."

Donal Moran hastened to Georgie Ryan and related to him what he had heard.

"Interesting! Very interesting! Then we'd better serve that man with a witness summons and viaticum. He's on the list of witnesses, but as things now stand his evidence is at the option of the other side, and maybe, just maybe, he might be helpful to us and they might decide to leave him at home. So we'll serve him with a witness summons, get him up here early on the morning of the hearing so as to learn what he has to say before calling him to the witness stand."

CHAPTER 24

These were happy days for Mary Boyle. There appeared not a cloud on her horizon. She was in love with a commitment which was absolute. She made love high up on the beet sacks above the milking parlour, in the reek of straw, amongst the bales of hay. In the mornings, she sought out David where he was now engaged on a new project and would sometimes drag him into a dry drain. There was one never-to-be-forgotten, wonderful day with the rain pelting down when they rolled in sport and play in the wet green rushes of the lower pasture. She loved every moment of every balmy day and, above all, she adored the physical pleasure of lovemaking.

She guessed David must be at least ten years younger than she was, but it didn't seem to matter. For one so slight of build, he had incredible strength. She had noticed it first when he was driving fence posts into the hard ground, but nowadays more especially when he was holding her and shaping her to his physical needs in moments of passion. Her own John, for all his height and strength, was as effete in the requirements of nature as a eunuch in a Sultan's palace. This man of slight stature and lame leg was as bold as a stallion at stud. She asked him once what had caused his limp and he brushed it aside with, "Oh, a mishap in my youth."

Though naive in the matter of men's physical prowess, she perceived there was something special about David. As some men can run faster, others lift heavier weights, play better football, and others still are endowed with exceptional brains, then there are men like David who are surely more virile than their peers.

She knew that the evening she stood facing him, their arms about each other sheltered from view in the small birch grove at the bottom of the farm. He had lifted her skirts and whilst still standing had entered up into her with powerful thrusts, and enormous bursts of strength so that she had cried out with the ecstasy and the sweet pain.

At the weekend, John went with Donal Moran to the Doncaster sales. All that weekend, it seemed there was no night or day. They engaged one another from the bed to the kitchen floor, the hay reek to the fields, in daylight and in the darkness.

She now enjoyed more shopping for clothes – tight jeans, stylish jumpers, clothes which flattered her figure, and were soft and feminine. Her natural blonde hair had always been an attractive feature. She discovered a hairdresser who shaped it so it fell in thick clusters of gold and yellow and had streaks running through it.

Occasionally, she wore silk stockings and, on that weekend, rushed down one night to the bedroom before David, and presented herself to him in black lace. He knocked her playfully to the floor in a mock attack and tore at her undergarments as she held her head back and laughed coquettishly.

She had no feelings of remorse for much as she loved her husband, they had never been lovers. The only tinge of guilt which she experienced was in buying the clothes for herself because always before she would buy for John first, or share with him some domestic purchase. To make amends, she began to read up all the literature available on asthma and purchased every conceivable gadget which might bring relief to him.

She felt no adulterous regrets for her behaviour. John was a friend. She loved him as a brother, a father, but not as a lover. There would never be anyone in her life to compare with him but she had not betrayed him. A lover is betrayed only when his love leaves his arms for the arms of another. Mary had never lain in John's arms.

Sunday posed a problem. On every Sunday of her married life, Mary had received the host in Holy Communion with John at her side. The Church had become ambivalent towards many of its sacraments and sacred traditions. It was now uncertain on whether Holy Communion could be received by one in sin. It used to be necessary to go to confession almost every week in order to receive Communion, but all that had changed. Nevertheless, Mary was brought up to believe that you cannot receive the host if the stain of sin is on one's soul. Mary did not feel as if she was committing any sin, either mortal or venial. She did accept the teaching of the Church and acknowledged there was technically a mortal sin to contend with. As such, she believed she could not receive at the altar without having her confession heard first. To be absolved so she could receive the host, she would have to say in confession that she was truly sorry for her sins and, the hardest part, would be to give a firm resolve to abstain from committing the sin in future. This Mary knew she could not do. Therefore, she could not accompany John in future to Communion in public, which could be embarrassing. She prayed that John would not ask her why. It grieved and pained her greatly that in the eyes of the Church that she was living in a state of mortal sin though she felt no pain of sin. It grieved her she could would not be able to accompany John, her beloved John, to the altar and worse still, worse than all else, might cause him hurt or scandal.

Mary had been brought up with a dread fear as well as respect for the Church and in particular, for the Blessed Sacrament. When it came to that Sacrament, she was no different from any other Catholic motivated by fear in the obeisance to the Church. She had grown up hearing stories, such as the one about the young girl. It had to be a girl – it would never do for the Church to tell improper stories about a man, priest or bishop – who in a state of sin went to receive Holy Communion. No one ever doubted but it was the sin of sex, for in the Catholic Church sex was and is a sin and, once upon a time, was the only sin in that Church. There, before the entire congregation including her father and brothers, the host floated up above the girl's head and remained in midair. It would not go onto her tongue. Since Mary was a little girl, bullyboy clerics had shouted out that story as they beat their fists off the pulpits. She reckoned that they were men who knew nothing of the compassion, love and humility of the One called Jesus, the Nazarene.

David helped to resolve the problem by suggesting she could go to early Mass, and he and John to the later one. The need for change could be attributed to some domestic necessity or matter of husbandry. It still made her unhappy, principally because acting out the full spirit of Catholicism was important to her.

Mary had been influenced by other childhood stories, such as the one of the careful squirrel and the impecunious grasshopper, of the colourful, carefree but careless butterfly plucked from the sky for flying too high by a greedy bird, or drowned in a summer rainstorm when most other creatures sought out the shelter of trees and bushes before the storm broke.

Now, Mary didn't stop to ask herself if there would be a consequence, some event or happening which might alter utterly her idyll, turn her world upside down. Life had never been so euphoric. Until now, she had always walked the straight line and worked each day to the full. For her, to pause now and ask herself where she was going would be like stopping the merry-go-round at the fun fair and stepping off, swopping the excitement of the whirly-gig for the more mundane tedium of terra firma.

She was too full of joy and excitement to consider the possibility of taking care, or ensuring that nature would not hand her a poisoned chalice. She was a beautiful woman in love.

One day a fear did strike her. Maybe it had been worming away inside her head for a time. Mary stared at the calendar. She turned back the page to the previous month. She couldn't quite remember when, and then for one awful moment, she folded the calendar back two pages. Divine God! What day last month? Oh my God! My God! Could it be the previous month still? Two months? On no, surely not!

Gone in that moment were the days of tumbling excitedly amongst the flowers and soft brown leaves strewn like petals on her bed of enchantments, to be replaced by the harsh days and nights of bitter reckoning and purgatorial worry.

Her thoughts immediately went out to John Boyle. He was her problem. It didn't matter except for John. The shame she would bring on that good man. Would she ever be able to face him? Would she ever be able to lift her humiliation to meet his eyes? Would he be hurt? Disappointed? Would he suffer?

Would that poor man cry softly in the sadness and loneliness of his heart? Would he ever forgive her? Would her future baby ever be a reminder to him of her infidelity and of his debility instead of being a thing of beauty bringing hope and joy into the world?

David was coming back through the fields when she ran breathlessly towards him. He stopped to rest the implements he was carrying.

"David! Oh, David! You'll be vexed with me. Oh God, I'm sorry, David! But I think I'm pregnant."

At first, he said nothing. Then, a little smile brightened his features.

"I suppose it's the least we could expect from what we've been at these past weeks and months." He smiled again, bigger this time, through his evenly shaped white teeth. "Have you been to the doctor?"

"No. I just know. I've had delays before, but then it didn't matter. I never took much notice and it always sorted itself out. This time, it's different. You see I never keep a check on the dates or time. There was no need to. Now, I don't know when the last time was. Six weeks past, two months, more. I just can't remember. What a stupid woman I've been!"

She walked over beside him and taking his hand squeezed it firmly.

"David, you know I love you, but I'm not a fool. I realise that you're due to leave here shortly. It's my problem and I don't expect you to wait around to share it. I would prefer if you were not here when it breaks. I have to make my own mind up about this. John is my problem and I alone can decide when and how I will tell him."

Again, David Stapleton was slow in responding. He looked towards the ground, stubbed at a weed with the toe of his boot before looking up.

"I wouldn't like to add to your concerns, Mary. But don't forget it's my baby too."

"It's very nice of you to put it that way. Certain facts have to be faced. Certain things cannot be changed. What cannot be changed is my marriage to John Boyle, plus the fact that you're a young man and you have your life before you yet to live."

David bent down and picked up the tools which he had been carrying earlier and slung them across his shoulder. He took her arm and they walked back towards the house hand in hand.

The thought of breaking the story to John appalled her. She felt she owed it to him to tell him in good time before the birth, or before any busybody broke the news to him. She would have to tell him herself. The prospect concentrated her mind to a frightening degree both night and day, and throughout the day, and first thing on wakening in the morning; sometimes, too, it woke her with a start at any hour of the night. Always, the one thought was uppermost in her mind – the shame she would bring on her husband.

Another week came and went without bringing the relief she had hoped might yet come as a benediction. She found herself visiting the church and kneeling before the statue of the Virgin. She beseeched the Mother of God to take away her torment. She asked that the wish be granted for her husband's sake, not for herself, but solely for him. She moved as near as she could to the altar and stared straight at the tabernacle where the host was kept – the host which she believed to be the body and blood, soul and divinity of Christ, Son of the living God.

She reached out with her mind and soul to the presence that she knew was in the tabernacle behind the curtain, protected by the door of gold. She asked, begged, for confirmation that it was not true, that she was not pregnant.

In these moments of utter concentration, she never questioned the responses her supplication might bring. She would accept it as being the will of God, in the divine design of things and in the best interests of herself, however painful or shameful her own personal position or loss might be at the end of the day.

She heard a voice. It couldn't be the voice of her conscience or yet the promptings of her own will. She never doubted – how could there be doubt – when she was prostrate before Jesus. Jesus, the truth and the life, the way and the life. It could be none other than the voice of the humble one, of Jesus, of the truth speaking through her thoughts. She had listened to it even as a little child and prayed so Sarah would not be cross when she forgot to bring home her copy books from school. In that time long ago, the voice answered firmly, but truthfully, "But she will be cross."

Now, as then, Mary heard the voice and accepted its truth implicitly. It sounded somewhere in the back of her mind and it was saying, "But you are pregnant, Mary. You should not regret the greatest gift that can be granted in My name." She struggled with her thoughts and, concentrating with all her being on the divine Presence, she pleaded, "But it isn't so, yet." The response was immediate and convincing."Mary, you know it is so."

She looked back down the church because she thought she had heard footsteps, but the church was empty. Again, she turned her concentration back to the tabernacle and asked, "Is that the way it is?" The voice answered, "That's the way it is, Mary."

So be it.

She walked down the aisle with a heavy heart, wondering as she went about all the women like herself who, over all the centuries and in all the other parts of the world, had been thus struck down. She thought of all those who on the one hand had leapt for joy on learning that a child had been conceived in their womb. Again, she thought of all those who had beseeched heaven that they might conceive a child and on all those who, before contraception, had beseeched that they might not. "Glory be to God," she whispered sorrowfully as she dipped her finger in the holy water font at the back of the church.

David knew as she came towards him that her worst fears had been confirmed. Before she spoke, he climbed out of the drain and going toward her, put his finger over her mouth and smiled to assure her of his support. Placing an arm around her back, he guided her towards the gate which led out onto the main road. They walked the small piece along the road to the entrance to the wood and followed the path until they came to a place where the River Barrow flows gently between banks of evergreens, and where the long grasses bend down into the passing waters to drink. They lay down on their bellies side by side staring into the river.

Neither spoke for a while. David pulled a daisy from the grass and began slowly plucking out its petals with thumb and index finger. Mary placed her hand over his.

"Don't, David," she said softly. "I feel a pain inside me every time you pull out one of its little petals."

He rolled the flower into a ball and flicked it far out into the passing waters. There was silence again, barely broken by the sound of another daisy being plucked from its bed. Mary took the small flower from him and began twirling it around between her thumb and finger by its stem.

"Isn't it beautiful?"

"Mary, I love you." He hesitated for a moment. "I'll always love you. My love for you doesn't falter just because of what has happened. My love for you hasn't grown cold just because you are now pregnant with my child." He took her hand in his. "Mary, I'm crazy about you."

CHAPTER 25

The pit of Donal Moran's stomach churned uneasily as the hours dragged by on the eve of the custody hearing. It was a fear brought on in anticipation of the hearing taking place in one of those large awesome buildings with their draughty corridors and ill-kept rooms. It was a fear of waiting in one of those long corridors with people in wigs and gowns rushing this way and that. It was a fear of the power of the court to make decisions affecting the very lives of those who were before it. It was a fear of the finality of those decisions.

As soon as the clocks in the hall proclaimed the midnight hour, he knelt down to pray as his mother had taught him so many years before. He used to hold her hand in front of the open kitchen fire in the cottage where they had lived. She had taught him, but it was no good now, for his mind was in such turmoil that he couldn't recite any of her prayers. He was neither in the humour for praying – nor for sleep. The events of the following day had become an obsession, especially with the other side summoning him as a witness to give evidence against his own son.

If only we had the opportunity of living some parts of our lives over again, he thought for an idle moment. What changes we'd bring about!

He had turned his back on his son Joe when he stood trial for armed robbery. He knew, now, that he should have been four-square behind Joe, as his father. Was he now being expected to tell this court that he had spurned his son, refused to visit him in gaol, cast him out as a good for nothing drunkard?

The hour of one a.m. came and went. He doubted he would get any sleep now.

In his helplessness and sorrow, his mind turned to the judge, about whom he knew practically nothing apart from the brief appearance of the previous week. Would he be a caring person, a man of compassion capable of differentiating between the truth, on the one hand, and the abundance of lies on the other with which he would have to contend in this case?

Such an important decision required the wisdom of a Solomon.

Donal Moran had no doubt about the child's paternity. Would the court accept Joe's story? Would it be looked on as nothing more than fabrication? Would the judge avoid the truth, opt for the easy way out, by declaring the father of the child to be the one registered on the birth certificate, Tommy Gavin, and rule accordingly? Would he find Joe's story preposterous, and decide Joe, rejected even by his own father, was nothing more than a common criminal and an impostor? Would the judge ignore the little girl's wishes, ignore her needs, ignore her best interests and decide that, this being a family matter, then as a judge he must decide in favour for Tommy Gavin? Would the rule of the family come first and justice and truth for the little girl go out of the window?

He knew that Irish judges have long been known for their impartiality and independence but, of late, it was being darkly whispered some had joined a secret society of a quasi-Christian influence. Would it be possible for some member of one of these semi-clandestine societies to influence a judge within the organisation, like whisper a word in his ear at one of their *séances*?

Would he be a judge with the integrity to put justice, tempered with humanitarian virtues, before other considerations to ensure that justice would be done, and not be influenced by any bias or representation outside the courtroom? Would he kneel unobtrusively in his chambers before coming out onto the bench and ask the Judge of judges to assist him in coming to a just decision? In other words, he wondered, apart from being a judge would he also be a man, a man of honour and strength?

The solicitor had expressed a wish that all should meet in the courthouse a good half hour before the case was listed for hearing. Therefore, he would want to leave at about 7 a.m. or earlier to be in Drogheda in time. At that hour, the roads leading into and out of Dublin city would be chock-a-block with traffic, and he would have it both ways, entering the city from the south and exiting on the north for Drogheda. That meant getting up at around 5.30 a.m. to have time to shave, shower and take some breakfast – if it was possible to eat on such a morning. It was now moving on for 2 a.m.

A thought suddenly struck him. He went to the phone and dialled the Gresham Hotel number. It was answered by one of the night staff whom he immediately recognised as Paddy, the Head Porter. He decided it might be easier to snatch a few hours sleep in the hotel, and then the town of Drogheda would be only twenty miles away in the morning.

Hastily he threw together few items, toothbrush, white shirt, socks, cufflinks, razor, and a dark suit with shoes, into a small overnight case and he was on his way.

As could be expected in the early hours, traffic was light, except for the quays where there were the usual few late-night revellers. There were a few drunks lurching across the roadway and a number of those girls who plied their trade in that area. Mostly, they were a slovenly looking collection, he noted, with many of them well advanced in years and no doubt suffering from or carrying one kind of illness or another.

He turned left at the bridge onto the broad expanse of O'Connell Street, cluttered with what he considered incongruous stone and concrete statuary. At the top of the street, a green arrow indicated a U-turn back down the other side to the front approaches of the Gresham.

Paddy was coming down the steps with his hand out in greeting. They were old friends, and he handed Paddy the keys to have the car parked. He then accompanied him across the deep piled carpet of the gold and pink vestibule to the lift, stopping at the third floor. They walked along the broad corridor for some distance, before Paddy stopped and opened the bedroom door of a magnificently appointed room of large proportions. Its heavy drapes and dark mahogany furniture gave it the impression of grandeur. Besides the large double bed was the remote control for the television and radio as well as an assortment of daily and evening papers.

Outside, he could hear the nightly shouts and cries of more drunks, hooligans, and late-night partygoers filling the area from the Mater Hospital to the Gresham and beyond. As the capital city of rural Ireland and once the second city of the empire, he couldn't help reflecting what a violent and shabby city Georgian Dublin could be.

Between occasional glances at the television and papers, he slept fitfully in catnaps for the few remaining hours of the night. He got up early, showered in barely lukewarm water just long enough to be refreshed, and then shaved.

At 7 a.m., he headed out for a walk. He didn't want to sit and worry in the bedroom or lobby of the hotel. Breakfast was out of the question. Better by far to walk in the fresh air than sit in the car outside the court waiting for everyone else to arrive.

He went out through the rear exit of the hotel, through a narrow passage which led onto the dingy street at the rear of the building, and walked past the kitchens giving off breakfast aromas from their inner depths. Lorries were pulled up outside the doors at the back, delivering vegetables, milk, meat, and other food, all the necessities for the daily needs of a hotel. Barrels and iron lungs were being unloaded off a drinks lorry. They were being expertly eased down onto a ground pillow and then wheeled away to the basement in small hand trolleys. Some of the hotel staff stood out in the roadway checking the deliveries against the order sheets. The two men in the parking bay were bright and cheerful, stirring mugs of steaming tea and chewing on thick rasher and sausage sandwiches.

Donal walked past the lorries, the parking bay, empty drink cans, and a discarded condom, doubtless thrown from a passing car during the night.

A shaft of sunshine shot slantwise through an aperture in the narrow alleyway and for an instant blinded his eyes with its brilliance.

He continued walking until he came to the church of Adam and Eve on the other side of the river, supposedly named after a medieval alehouse. It reminded him of his history lessons as a schoolboy. Under the Penal Laws, when people were forbidden

Mass attendance. They covertly celebrated the Sacrament in such places as public houses under the unsuspecting noses of the militia who believed the penitent was heading for a drink in the well-known licensed liquor establishment of Adam and Eve.

He walked into the church but found it difficult to concentrate on the face of Christ, and, as on the previous evening, he was unable to offer up any prayers. To his surprise, when he came outside again into the sunlight, he felt more relaxed.

Having retrieved the car back at the hotel, he drove past the airport north to the old port town of Drogheda with its dark, dismal, unkempt courthouse. It hardly looked conducive to the administration of justice.

The timing of his arrival was perfect and he didn't have to wait on the others. They were all there before him and were being ushered into the courtroom as he came along the corridor.

After a short while, the judge came out onto the bench, the same Evan Suleman, similarly attired as on the previous occasion, except now in a suit of a lighter shade with navy-blue bow tie and handkerchief.

He bade those present good morning in a friendly voice.

The Registrar got to his feet.

"This case, judge, – Gavin and Gavin – though a custody application is also, I understand, in the nature of a paternity suit. The application is being brought in this jurisdiction because the applicant Tommy Gavin resides in Drogheda. The parties were married six years ago and the subject of these proceedings is the only child of that union, Julie."

He continued, "You will remember last week you made an order that Julie should spend the week away from the parties or their families. That has been done and she is here today with Sister Carmel. She has not been in contact since the making of the order, or today, with any of the parties. Presently, she is in my office with Sister Carmel should you wish to speak with her."

Judge Suleman thanked the Registrar and then addressed the parties and their solicitors.

"Before we embark on this case, there are the usual few comments which I believe are necessary in dealing with this type of case. Since both legal teams are familiar with my views, I address my comments to the witnesses and expert witnesses.

"During my early years on the bench, I spent some considerable time attending courses in universities outside Ireland mainly on child psychology. From the several courses, I attended I came to the conclusion that any decision made by a judge in respect of a child should be made solely in the best interests of the child and not ...."

He looked around the court and stressed the word, "not", a second time.

"... and not with any social or religious bias, such as that oft-repeated old chestnut, the family comes first. It does not. The child comes first. I am not going to decide this matter by what a mother or father want me to do. I will decide it, in so far as I can, to the best of my ability by what I believe the child wants me to do, on what is in the best interests of the child. After all, it's the child's future, the child's life, which we are deciding on today.

"Secondly, I do not want an over exuberant cross-examination of the witnesses especially of the mother or father. Points which the solicitors wish to emphasise can be done, even in our antiquated, inappropriate and adversarial system, by discussion and enquiry.

"Finally, as you both know ...", he was now addressing the two legal teams. "if there are any points of agreement then I want to hear about them before we begin, and of course, if either side has made discovery which might greatly influence my decision, and by revealing it, contributes more to our establishing the truth early on, I will want to be informed of every single detail and phenomenon. Remember that we are dealing with a child's life.

"If everyone is now satisfied with the court, that it is a properly constituted court within the meaning of the statutes, we can begin."

The legal teams turned their heads to look about the courtroom and pronounced they were satisfied.

The solicitor for Tommy Gavin, Mr Browne, rose to his feet.

"Judge, the applicant, my client Tommy Gavin will be saying that he married Sharon Gavin on the fifth day of January 1986. The Certificate of Marriage is available in court. He will say that he had intimate relations with his wife before marriage and as a result, the wife became pregnant, they were married and Julie, the little girl the subject of these proceedings, was born.

"He will further say he loved his wife and child, but regrettably, he will be saying the wife was and is unfit to look after Julie in so far as she became and is an alcoholic. He will also have to admit, though it pains him, his wife practiced the trade of prostitution."

Here Georgie Ryan was on his feet protesting loudly and reminding the court there was a recognised way of proving such allegations, and to his knowledge none such was available and that it should never have been mentioned. He described it as a preposterous lie levelled at his client to blacken her character before the court without there being a scintilla of evidence to establish the charge.

Heated argument on the point followed before the judge asked Mr Browne to continue.

"Well, in any event Julie was taken from the mother and placed in care. What more evidence do we require of the mother's unsuitability, due to her behaviour?"

He threw a triumphant look at Georgie Ryan who shook his head in disapproval, but made no comment.

"Mr Ryan, judge, will be making the preposterous assertion that one Joe Moran, a man who has just been released from serving six years imprisonment for armed bank robbery, is the father of the girl. We have no idea why the mother is going along with this deception except she plans to marry Mr Moran and deprive my client of his parental right to Julie."

He paused for a moment and glanced sideways again towards Georgie Ryan.

Georgie Ryan got to his feet.

"As the evidence unfolds, judge, I hope it will become clear that neither of my clients will indulge in any deception before this court."

Mr Browne then called Tommy Gavin to the witness stand and in answer to a general question talked quietly, in a reserved tone of voice as if portraying the role of a concerned parent.

"I am twenty eight years of age and was born in a place called Quinnclooney just outside the town here. I was twenty one years of age when I met Sharon Diplock in Liverpool. She is English. We fell in love almost immediately and had intimate relations on a regular basis until she got pregnant and then we got married and we have a child called Julie. I have here with me, judge, the marriage certificate and Julie's birth certificate."

He looked towards the judge and there was compassion in his voice.

"Judge, I'm crazy about that child. I should explain here, judge, that my wife is an alcoholic. I don't like to have to say it, but she's also a prostitute.

"Well, judge, fearing for the child's safety, the Corporation officials in Liverpool took Julie into care, fearing she might be damaged or interfered with by one of the men clients Sharon would be entertaining. Sharon, my wife, has no morals whatever and since she came to Ireland has been visiting Mountjoy Prison on a regular basis and often has affairs with prisoners on their release. She's now friendly with Joe Moran, that man seated there at the back of the court beside her. They're going to live together and are bent on claiming my little girl."

He stood up in the witness box and, turning towards the judge, he dramatically simulated a knife making an incision to open his heart by drawing his finger across his breast.

"Look, judge. Look." He pointed to his heart by tapping his breast with his index finger. "Look, Judge. In there, my little girl is engraved."

Sharon could not endure what he was saying any longer. She stood up in the courtroom and pointed an accusatory finger at him.

"May God forgive you, Tommy Gavin. But you're a liar, and a damned liar!"

Donal Moran, sitting near the back, expected the judge would immediately intervene, but he didn't. Instead, he looked at Tommy Gavin to assess his reactions. Clearly, Tommy Gavin was taken aback by the interruption and looked to the judge to take his part. The judge ignored the appeal and merely stared back in silence, scrutinising Tommy Gavin.

Tommy Gavin threw Sharon a dark and threatening look that was not in keeping with his earlier demeanour.

"You can't frighten me now," she said. "You can't hit me now, Tommy Gavin, in front of all these people here. Can you? We're not on our own now."

She moved into the aisle and took a step forward towards him.

"You couldn't try to rape me here either, could you?"

Tommy Gavin turned red in the witness box.

"If you loved Julie like you said you do, then where were you when I was neglecting her?" Then she looked up at the judge. "I regret to have to say, judge, that I did neglect her through drink but through no other reason. But where were you Tommy Gavin?" She turned back towards him.

Her manner now was brave and defiant. Here in the protection of the courtroom, she could face him with conviction and impunity, as many a poor broken woman had before when coming for the first time under the aegis of the Matrimonial Court. Here, she couldn't be dominated, bullied or threatened.

His eyes blazed with rage as he looked down menacingly towards her.

Beside her Joe Moran began to get to his feet, his eyes fixed on the man in the witness box. Georgie Ryan cautioned Joe with a raised finger of admonishment. Joe relaxed back into his seat.

Tommy Gavin knew the girl had trapped him. He could not answer her. He had always hated her self-righteous honesty. As he sat there, staring silently, he recalled the many time he had felled her with a blow when she had adopted that same attitude towards him. Of course, she knew he had never been a father to that awful child nor had he ever intended being one. He grimaced behind his hand. He had never thought he would be trapped so easily and by her. He was furious. Since he couldn't answer the question the next best thing was to adopt a devious attitude, so, acting as if he was the injured party, he turned towards the judge.

"It looks as though I have no rights, judge. Is she allowed to say what she likes in your court?" He emphasised the words "*your court.*"

The judge smiled as if the most perfectly normal question had been put to him. Unperturbed by the insinuation, his voice when he replied was tempered. In fact, there was the slightest trace of amusement in it.

"You are quite right, Mr Gavin ..."

Tommy Gavin smirked openly.

"... the only persons who may examine or cross-examine witnesses are solicitors or barristers. The judge, at a trial, may himself ask a question in order to come closer to the truth, and that precisely is what I intend doing now."

He shuffled some papers in front of him on the bench and fixing the witness with his judicial eyes, he asked, "I would like to know why you didn't take care of Julie, whom you profess to love in the extreme, when her mother neglected her as she has so very candidly admitted."

Tommy Gavin was unhappy with the unexpected turn of events. He glowered at Sharon, trying to intimidate her. She remained standing defiantly in the aisle.

"Come, come, Mr Gavin. It is something which could have a vital bearing on the outcome of this case."

Sharon spoke out again.

"He was in trouble with the police in Liverpool for forging a number of cheques, and for assaulting and wounding his common-law wife with a knife, and two other girls he had working the streets for him."

"Please! Please! Mrs Gavin, don't you interrupt anymore or I shall have to ask you to leave the courtroom and wait outside until your own evidence is required."

"I will not interrupt anymore, judge. But I'm not Mrs Gavin. I divorced him in Liverpool and cited violence as the main grounds for the divorce. He did not defend the proceedings and I have the decree here with me."

"Please, Ms ..? Ms ..?"

"Diplock."

"Ms Diplock, will you please sit down and don't interrupt again."

Now Mr Browne, Tommy Gavin's solicitor, was on his feet.

"Judge, lest there be any misunderstanding, I have repeatedly referred to her as Mrs Gavin, insofar as we even entered the title of Gavin and Gavin, please accept that at no stage have I tried to mislead the court. I was not aware that the parties had been divorced."

"You mean, Mr Browne, your client didn't bother to tell you of such an important matter? Of course, I accept you didn't know."

The judge turned back to Tommy Gavin.

"It is of the utmost importance to the court to establish why you did not take Julie when she was neglected by her mother. After all, you now want to have full and total custody of the girl."

"Her mother was supposed to be looking after her. I was away at the time. This is the first opportunity I've had to get custody of my child and she is my child."

The judge remained calm and in control as he returned to the same subject.

"Mr Gavin. Don't try to avoid the question I've put to you repeatedly. I would be obliged if you would answer it."

Tommy Gavin was still furious with himself that he had been trapped so simply by that bitch standing there provocatively in front of him. He could even appreciate the reason the judge was trying to establish why he should now be given control, if he hadn't looked after or cared for the child in the past. He searched furiously around in his mind for some answer, some inspiration. It was no use He just couldn't come up with an answer, so he decided his best ploy would be to go on the offensive again – his goddamn solicitor was no help either. He just sat there gaping at him, he noticed.

"If she's going to decide what course the case takes, there's not much point telling my story."

He made a conscious effort to sound as if he was the injured party and that, even in this court of justice, he was not getting fair play and that it was all one sided.

At that moment, Mr. Browne got to his feet angrily. There was a bark to his voice as he addressed his client, Tommy Gavin.

"If you cannot keep a civil tongue in your cheek and answer the questions then I agree with you, there's no point in your continuing any further. Are you going to answer the simple, but extremely important, question put to you by the judge?"

Tommy Gavin hesitated and a mischievous smirk crossed his face.

"Of course, you're not going to work for me seeing as I wasn't able to fully pay the exorbitant fee you asked." He was still determined to brazen this thing out.

"Fully pay?" Mr Browne echoed with emphasis. "Fully pay? Why you haven't paid anything whatever of the very reasonable fee I asked. You kept none of your promises."

He turned to the judge.

"Under normal circumstances, judge, I would withdraw from this case right now. But because of all the circumstances attending this bizarre matter, I will remain to assist the court until such time as a decision has been reached."

He addressed his witness again.

"Mr Gavin, you may now leave the witness stand. If you are required later I shall recall you."

Georgie Ryan got to his feet and began addressing the judge.

"A matter has come to our attention, judge. That is, to the attention of Mr Browne and to me. We believe it may influence you in your final deliberations. It concerns a grandfather with whom Julie, the little girl, spent some while."

Donal Moran's heart missed a beat. He had been standing at the back of the court and now walked quietly so as not to disturb the proceedings, to a nearby rail and leaned his arms on it for support. His heart began to beat quickly and he felt a nauseating ache in the pit of his stomach.

"I would suggest to Mr Browne, in the interests of good justice, that witness, the child's grandfather, should be called at this stage of the proceedings."

Beads of sweat began to form on Donal's forehead and taking a handkerchief from his pocket, he dried his face and hands. He could feel dampness forming under his armpits. This was it then. He was being called to say he had disowned his own son, had found him a good for nothing, ungrateful boy, unworthy to be a member of his family, and his girlfriend, Sharon, about whom so many unsavoury things had already been said, was an alcoholic and proposing to set up house with this ex-convict rejected by his father, and now proposing to live together and expecting the court to give them custody of the little girl. Just as the case seemed to be turning in their favour – and Tommy Gavin had been a terrible witness – now his evidence might swing the scales back to Tommy Gavin's advantage.

He mopped his brow. The solicitor looked past him and called on Mr Cornelius Gavin, Tommy Gavin's father, to the witness stand.

After Mr Gavin had been sworn in, Georgie Ryan turned to the other solicitor and said, "This witness, though summoned by me to attend here, was originally on Mr Browne's list of witnesses. Accordingly, I have no objection whatever to Mr Browne taking him through his evidence. Your witness, Mr Browne." He sat down and Mr Browne rose again to address the court.

"Whilst this witness, judge, is the father of my client, the applicant Tommy Gavin, it was Mr Ryan who insisted on his being served with a subpoena and viaticum to appear rather than at the behest of my client, his son, as might be expected. Because of the extraordinary evidence he is about to give, I have agreed with Mr Ryan that the witness be called early in the proceedings. I will lead him, your Honour, over the introductory part of his story, after which I shall sit down and allow him to give the evidence in his own words."

"You, Mr Gavin, are the father of the applicant, my client Mr Tommy Gavin."

"Yes, I am."

"And I believe you are also acquainted with his wife Sharon, sorry, ex-wife, notice party in these proceedings."

"Yes, I am."

"I believe you also know their daughter Julie, who is the subject of these proceedings today."

"Yes, I do." He added, "Julie spent almost three months in my house outside Drogheda here last summer."

"Finally, Mr Gavin, I believe you know Joe Moran who has just completed a sentence of six years for armed robbery and you are familiar with his claim to be the biological father of the girl."

"I am."

"Will you now tell us in your own words anything which you think might be helpful in bringing this matter to a just conclusion?"

Cornelius Gavin was a man of such enormous bulk he had difficulty in settling into the witness box. At first, he rested his elbows on the rail surround. Finding this position not to his liking, he shifted his weight so his large bronzed hands were now resting on the rail in front of him. He seemed ill at ease in the witness stand, cleared his throat and tried to settle into a more comfortable position. He found it difficult to express himself. Eventually settling his hands on top of the rail again, he began hesitantly, as if naive.

"Judge?" He looked up and across to where Judge Suleman was sitting. "Is that what I call you?"

"Yes. Judge will do fine, Mr Gavin, or if you prefer, sir."

"Well, judge, I haven't an easy story to tell."

He paused for a considerable time as he inspected his strong hands resting on the rail surround.

"That's my son there, Tommy Gavin." He indicated by pointing him out with his right hand.

"Well, last summer he arrived in my home with a girl, not his wife, and Julie. He was living with this girl. Well now, that's his business. It's none of mine. He remained with me for some three months or more. During that time he didn't speak two civil words to the little girl."

He took his hands down off the rail and put them on his lap and turned his head downwards so he could inspect the hands. He kept in that position for a long time with his head turned downwards except when he raised it to look at his son sitting on the edge of a bench seat at the back of the court.

"During that time, I brought Julie once every week at the request of her mother to see Joe Moran in the prison at Mountjoy. I have a fair bit of respect for that chap. He may be a criminal, but he's now served out his time and paid his debt to society. It was for armed robbery. But I'd have to say he's not as bad a chap as he's made out to be."

He paused and looked towards Tommy. "As for my own son, I don't know where he went wrong, but he has gone wrong. He's turned out to be a right bad lad."

He looked up and along the bench to where the judge was seated.

"Judge, every man must stand four-square behind his own children. I've always done that, but if there comes a time when your own are hell-bent on damaging another, in this instance an innocent little girl, then you cannot stand idly by."

He looked down the courtroom and fixed his son with an icy stare.

"Like I said, he was never civil to little Julie and mostly ignored the child during the time she was in my house. He was always ..."

It seemed he couldn't conjure up the word he needed to describe the thoughts floating around in his mind.

"He was always nasty to her. So, I asked him one day, "Why are you always nasty and why do you always ignore that little girl, after all she is your own daughter."

"She's not my daughter," he answered me.

"Then whose child is she, I asked him."

He was telling his story quietly the while he continued to look down at his hands where they now rested on his lap.

"She's Joe Moran's child. That's what he told me."

"So I told him, 'Then you've no right to her, and I have no right to have her in my house.' I was vexed with him. Well, he left us that night with this girl he was living with to go to town for a drink. I didn't see them again for surely two weeks. They came back early one morning and took Julie with them."

Here he stopped and shifted his position in the witness box. He picked up the Bible in his right hand and looking over towards the judge continued, "There are few things we can ever be absolutely sure of in this world, judge," and as if guaranteeing the sacredness of what he was uttering, he held the Bible in a raised demonstrative manner over the guardrail, and continued with conviction.

"If there was one thing that I could swear to it's this. My son is not the father of that little girl. Her father is Joe Moran." He identified Joe by pointing him out with the Bible in his right hand.

"I suppose I should have done something about it, like gone to the Gardaí or a solicitor. In any event, I didn't. As soon as I heard what he was about today, I made myself available to tell the true story. I also told him I intended coming here to give my evidence against him. Last night, he called to the house where the missus and I live alone in the heart of the country. He threatened both of us and he struck me with his fist."

He now looked around the court and satisfied there was nothing further to add he ended by saying, "There you have it, judge. That's the truth as I know it."

The judge sat in silence for a few minutes staring at the bench in front of him. Those present were all silently looking to him to contribute something appropriate. After a notable delay, he turned towards Cornelius Gavin.

"You are a very honourable man. All of us here learned something from you today, including me. We have all been privileged to have sat and listened to your evidence and your comments. I am most thankful to you. Apart from my position as a judge, I am grateful to you. As a judge, I have to acknowledge that your evidence will be most helpful in ascertaining the truth in this complex issue. I am obliged to you, sir."

The judge looked down to the bottom of the courtroom to where Sister Carmel was now standing beside the court Garda. The judge nodded in her direction, and immediately she made for the door. The Garda opened it for her and held it open after she had gone out. In seconds, she returned holding Julie by the hand.

Conscious that all eyes were upon her Julie looked coyly about the room. The sister released her hand. Julie took a few hesitant steps forward. Nearly everyone present smiled towards and at her. Tommy Gavin was the nearest to her and he beckoned her towards him. She went in his direction. As she got to him, she suddenly ran forward and past him towards where Joe was seated on one of the bench seats. She leapt into his arms. He lifted her up and embraced her. Tears were coursing down his cheeks.

"My baby! My baby!" He hugged her to him, his voice charged with emotion, and kissed her, crying audibly, and moved towards the bench. He looked up at the judge through tear-stained eyes.

"Thank you, judge. Thank you, judge." He was ahead of himself, anticipating the judge's decision. Joe proceeded along through the bench where the solicitors were seated, shaking them by the hand and thanking them. Joe was a big man and Julie was as a doll in his arms. A female law clerk was also wiping tears from her eyes and Sharon was shedding tears uncontrollably. Then Joe came face to face with Cornelius Gavin and found himself staring at him in silent disbelief.

"What can I say? I don't know what to say. What you've done for me is so gigantic that I can't put the right words together."

"I only told the truth, son. I'm glad you have your baby. After all she is your baby, and there's no doubt about that."

Sharon was called but her evidence was brief. She spoke of her intimacy with Joe Moran and of his prison sentence and of the pact he made with Tommy Gavin. She didn't say what promise, precisely, was made to Tommy Gavin for allowing their child take his name instead of that of a convicted criminal. Now, both Joe and she realised how stupid they had been, she told the judge.

It was quite clear the proceedings were coming to a successful conclusion for Sharon and Joe. They could not have hoped for a better ending. It was beyond their wildest dreams. The nightmare was at an end. Tommy Gavin had been found out.

Even though Joe didn't come near him, Donal, still leaning on the guardrail at the back of the benches, was overjoyed. It was as though all the bells of Dublin city were peeling out in triumph and all the choirs of angels were shouting out in unison "Alleluia, alleluia!".

It all came to an abrupt end. The solicitors were on their feet and the judge was making the order in Joe's favour. No one seemed to be listening. Joe nodded towards the judge and walked to the back of the court, still clutching his child and followed by Sharon. Everyone was shaking hands and offering congratulations. The solicitors and court Gardaí dispersed. Donal also left the court, leaving only Cornelius Gavin still in the witness box and his son Tommy seated in one of the benches.

Joe stood in a little knot of happy well-wishers. Donal approached him and tried to speak.

"Maybe you should come down..." He paused for there was a hollow ring to the word but he nonetheless pronounced it hesitantly. "Maybe you should come down home for a few days." Joe just stared at the ground in silence but uttered not a word.

"Well, Sharon and Julie would be most welcome."

Sharon nudged Joe to say something.

"We're all going to Liverpool," Joe said at last. "I've got a job there as a lorry driver and I want to get the licence organised."

Then they were gone and Donal stood alone and lonely looking after them as they went hand in hand, Julie swinging happily between her mother and father. A few steps later, they stopped and Julie ran back towards him.

She kissed him hurriedly. "Joe says I can come and see you in the summer. Bye." She then tore herself away and raced after them lest she might be left behind once more.

CHAPTER 26

To Mary, lying asleep in bed, it was as though someone had called out to her, shouted into her ear or as if some hand had stretched out and shaken her by the shoulder, so suddenly did she awake and sit up in the bed. In that instant, she remembered she was pregnant and she was going to bring a terrible shame down on the head of her unfortunate husband. This sudden alarm at all hours of the night, and finding herself sitting up in bed with the fright of her pregnancy, was becoming a constant pattern to the extent she was becoming a nervous wreck. Now on this night, she could not remain in bed any longer. She had to get up, but at least she had slept until almost four thirty a.m.

BoBo was out on one of her nocturnal rambles and was approaching Boyles when she saw Mary's light come on. She ran up the short avenue and found a chink in a curtain at the back of the house through which she could view Mary Boyle putting the kettle on the stove. An evil rage took hold of BoBo. The sight of that woman reminded her of the whipping and injury to her hand which she had received from her.

Aye, and on her own kitchen floor at that! In her own house! Did that bitch Mary Boyle expect to get away with that sort of behaviour? Not on her life! Not on her sacred life!

She watched Mary Boyle put down a cup of tea on the table by the window, oblivious to BoBo barely three feet away, on the other side of the glass. As BoBo watched her, she began planning her revenge. Involuntarily she tapped the large inside pocket of the loose coat she was wearing to assure herself that she had, as usual, the dagger-like darning needle, the hatpin and the stiletto.

Excitement built up inside her as she assessed the situation. This time there would be a fairer fight. This time she would choose the moment and the place of attack. She reckoned Mary Boyle would go to the milking parlour as soon as that cup of tea was finished. The thing to do was to get there before her and lie in wait for her, set herself in position to launch an attack and let every person in the district know BoBo was nobody's fool. No matter what happened she could plead the pains in her head as the cause of her attack on Mary Boyle.

She hurried to the milking parlour and secreted herself amongst the sacks of meal piled high above where Mary Boyle would soon enter. She hid herself from view and tested the balance of the loose sacks beneath her feet. She made sure they would not give way beneath her when making her jump. It was important she should land full square on Mary Boyle's back. Whilst she sat there waiting, a cruel twisted smile crossed her face and every now and then, she bared her teeth in the manner of a vixen or a frightened hound, except there was no fear in BoBo, only a determination to be avenged.

This morning Mary Boyle remembered it was the day of the custody court hearing, the application about Julie. There was nothing, at this stage, that she could do to help. She whispered a prayer that all would go well for Joe and Donal. Donal might be helpful to her. He was about the only one with whom she could discuss her terrible predicament. If anyone would come up with a resolution, it would be Donal.

She sipped her cup of tea and, even though it was early, she decided it would be as well to head on out to the milking parlour. Maybe physical work might relieve the tension. The tea was no help.

Out in the milking parlour, she began forking hay into the mangers and, resting for a moment, she stood facing the cows contentedly pulling sweet-smelling hay from the racks. Her back was to the sacks piled high behind her. For a moment, she thought she detected a sound or movement behind her, more like a shadow, a fluttering sound as if something was being launched from behind and in that moment, she was struck heavily on the back, neck and shoulders by a flying weight and knocked headlong to the ground.

At the same time, there was an exultant, triumphant shout and, in that instant, the stiletto blade sank deep into her back between her shoulder blades. It was repeated frenziedly over and over again.

Mary cried out in agony and called on God to forgive her attacker, for Mary knew by the intensity of the pain that her heart had been pierced and that her last moments were at hand. She was going to die. The pain was unbearable and she was shrieking from the excruciating agony. The repeated penetration from the blade caused a searing throb. There were blood-curdling yells. She didn't know if they came from her or her assailant. She only knew she was going to die. Only death now could relieve the intensity of the pain. Death alone could transport her tortured body to a place of ease where there would be no more torment. In that instant of dying, nothing other than pain occupied her brain. There was no concept or memory of her beloved husband, John, of her best friend, Donal. She didn't even think of her one and only lover David, not even of Sarah. Pain alone wracked her.

Suddenly, there was an explosion of light and an incredible incandescent illumination enfolded her. In her agony, she recognised the figure of white light. She stretched out her hand and called to Him.

"Jesus! Jesus!"

Comhairle Contae
Átha Cliath Theas
South Dublin County Council